THE STALKER

THE
STALKER

A NOVEL

Theodore Taylor

DONALD I. FINE, INC.
New York

Library of Congress Catalogue Card Number: 86-46403

ISBN: 1-55611-022-7

Manufactured in the United States of America

10 9 8 7 6 5 4 3 2 1

*The book is printed on acid free paper. The paper in this book
meets the guidelines for permanence and durability of the
Committee on Production Guidelines for Book Longevity
of the Council on Library Resources*

FOR WENDY

Who was never supposed to say four letter words

with love

This night, methinks, is
but the daylight sick.

A Midsummer Night's Dream
W. SHAKESPEARE

1

EVEN AFTER THE HAIRLESS MAN with the peach-colored skin seemed to have departed, Ellen Trenholm Hickel felt she was being watched from somewhere behind the books. Several times she interrupted work to squint and sweep along the stacks but saw nothing at all. There were just too many shadows to pick out anyone standing or kneeling and looking over the spines. And aside from an Asian boy way down at the other end, she was alone up there, so far as she knew.

At 8:20, a brittle voice announced that the library was closing in ten minutes, causing Ellen to flex her shoulders and wipe her eyes and pack up research, look around to see that she'd gotten everything put away into the canvas tote bag, one that her mother said was big enough to hold a small kangaroo.

Then she arose, tiredly, taking the elevator down to the second floor where lights were already going off. Faces of the computer screens over in Reference, appearing as ghostly green rectangles, side-by-side, each saying "Melvyl," were left to their electronic thoughts for the night.

She crossed wearily toward the exit where a scanner would alert the desk if any of her books hadn't already been checked out. The clerk behind the desk, a curly-haired male student in a gray Coors sweatshirt, said, "A nuthin' night, huh?"

Ellen grinned at him. She'd seen him before, same time, same place. "Half a nothing night."

On through the exit arm and out into stillness, illumination around the boxy concrete building dim rather than bright to satisfy the aesthetics of the architect. There'd been complaints from plenty of females that there were "too damn many shadows" all over campus. Boogeyman places.

Ellen kept going, wearing a thin white golf jacket, yellow cotton blouse and denim skirt. Her daddy swore that she'd look good in a scorched flour sack and he was right. Streamlined, she was lean without being spare. Tallish, like her daddy and mother, her breasts were full and deep; legs and arms long and well-formed. They displayed nicely on the California beaches or on the tennis court or on any avenue. Sensuality without exaggeration, a flowing thoroughbred walk. Men usually looked twice or more at the colonel's daughter, as the library clerk had just done, seeing the promise of something special merely in that walk.

Having just spent twenty mostly satisfying years on earth, Ellen was a natural blonde and centerfold sexy without trying to be sexy at all. Swedish blood attributes of mother Katta were all there, and she was daddy's own special jewel, a child to brag about. Three point eight average at UCI, sure to be Phi Beta Kappa. So many unique things about this beautiful "brat" of his.

Two more flights of concrete steps down from the library before she got to ground level, then the considerable walk down North Circle Drive, where rows of new-leafed trees stood guard, until she would reach P-4, partially metered for visitors; also serving stickered students such as Ellen T. Hickel. She was a sophomore, bound and determined to become another Jane Goodall, to startle the whole world with some exotic finding. Write books, make TV documentaries: be an anthropologist. *Do* things.

The University of California, at booming Irvine, in mostly booming Orange County, was unexpectedly quiet this chill Spring Break. Even squirrels moved stealthily. There were a few lights still on over in the Commons building; Women's Resource Center active, talking and planning going on; several cars going around on

Campus Drive on the eastern edge, having come out of ten or fifteen parking lots arranged strategically around the perimeter.

Trees and shrubbery thrived all over the green acres. Modern, glassy non-ivied buildings jumped up as rectangular spokes in a giant wheel. UCI was about five miles from the Pacific Ocean, set back in low, rolling hills between dying Santa Ana, which had been Chicanoized and graffitiized by illegals, and Newport Beach with all its investment money, million-dollar yachts and cocaine sniffers. UCI was an extra fine centerpiece for Yuppie dwellings, hi-tech research complexes and spiffy towns called Woodbridge and Northwood.

Four heavy assault helicopters, flashing lights, beating wind, thundered low over Ellen on their way to the Marine base at Tustin after having finished night exercises at Camp Pendleton. Daddy's "whopper" choppers. Having grown up with their drumming sound, in a half dozen places, chopper bases, she paid no attention to them. In fact, the sky over Orange County was owned by the Marines. Choppers thudded away night and day; jet fighters whined in over angry Leisure World retirees to slick down at nearby El Toro base.

Ellen went on past the lighted kiosk—plastered with notices of everything from having your baby underwater to saving the Arctic skuas to an old "Fuck Old Ronnie" sign. Never before had she felt uneasy making this walk. Campus police continually toured the parking lots, often ducking into them. Usually, twenty or thirty other book-wearied night owls trod along the pathways to their cars. Now, during Break, there were none. Not a soul. Most of the Asians, the most tenacious studiers of all, were resident students and walked back to their lamps and beds via a different route.

Ellen increased pace, hoping to see the campus cops come by. Just the sweep of their headlights would be reassuring. For no good reason she could think of, her heart began to pound. Silly, she thought. God's sakes, only the squirrels were hopping around. Looking behind her, seeing nothing, she still tightened her grip on the heavy tote bag.

On the right of the path by North Circle Drive was a line of trees, one about every thirty feet, umbrellaed, showing new life; on the other side of the paved pathway were giant eucalyptus towering up in the night sky. Soon, in hot weather, they'd smell like incense. On windy nights they thrashed high up and were scary. But tonight was breezeless and three-quarters of moon silvered everything. The path was macadam for a hundred feet, then became concrete, embedded with tiny stones. There was about fifteen feet of ivy-covered bank sloping up to the street. The pathway was three or four feet below street level. Without breaking into a run, she was moving as fast as she could, just on premonition. The tote bag felt like it held a cargo of granite.

Suddenly, she definitely sensed someone behind and above her, following her, stalking her, moving tree to tree along the bank like a black-cloaked Ichabod Crane rustling the ivy. Glancing up there she saw form and movement and broke into a trot, fright rising in her throat. As she was running she dug into her tote for the key ring, wanting to have the key in her hand the moment she reached the green VW bug. *Slam the door, lock it, roll.*

Near the last trees before the lot began, a wayward root had worked up through the pavement. Ellen's right heel caught it, sending her sprawling. Breaking the fall with her left palm, her right fist, clutching the bag straps, hit simultaneously. But the momentum drove her chin into the pebbled concrete and the man bounded up behind her, sinking a knee into her back.

For forty-eight hours insistent games had been on the mind of the owner of the knee, finishing up his long "See The USA" holiday. Whatever he did, wherever he'd gone, watching girls on Malibu sands or strolling down Hollywood Boulevard taking in the interesting sleaze, the games were exciting him, obsessing him, vivid pictorials of the past coming on suddenly, "projections of pain full of bliss," as he'd described them to Dr. Hoger, his therapist back home. Hoger was always fascinated with the pictorials, always asking for details. "All right, she was all in black leather and wore a lot of rouge and had a skull pin on her vest.

"Oh, yes, and tiny handcuffs for earrings."

"And what did you ask her to do?"

"That time, use the pussywillow branches. I was too sore for chains."

"I see."

2

DAZED FROM IMPACT AND CONCUSSION, feeling pain in both hands, something pressing into her spine, Ellen ordered herself, *Hey, girl, clear your head and try to think. Stay calm.* That's what daddy had said to do if she ever got into trouble like this. Stay *calm.* Think and play for time. Then do it. Fight back. The way he did in Vietnam. That's why he was still alive, he said. The man was speaking. "You vill do what I say." Accent distinctly foreign. "You vill . . ." European, she guessed. Wet, breathless quality to the voice. She couldn't tell if it was a young voice or old voice. Didn't matter, did it? His breathing was heavy, and there were two points of pressure, not one, she realized. Hand on the back of her neck as well, pinning her head, pushing her left cheek into the pavement.

Clear your head, Ellen. Hang on to the bag and clear your head. Try to get to your feet and hit him with the bag. At the same time try to knee him in the groin. What daddy had said to do. "Deball the a-hole." She knew she had enough strength to hurt him if she got the chance, but she warned herself not to struggle and waste energy. Not yet.

"You vill do it," the man repeated, sucking and blowing air. The sound was so scary. A few times she'd wondered what she'd do if this ever happened. Well, here it was.

Pressure on her spine, at the small of her back, stayed steady. Either a foot or a knee. She grunted a yes, tightening her grip on the tote bag. If she could swing it with those tennis muscles and it landed . . . there was enough weight to break his jaw. Hurt his balls. Break his ribs. It had to be his knee putting most of his weight back there. Then behind the knee she felt a hand go up under the denim skirt and move lightly across her buttocks, over her panties. She recoiled, tried to say "don't" but it came out a gargle. Blood welling in her mouth, she began to feel sick. A car came by, lighting up a swath of North Circle, but the bank and the trees hid the man holding her down like a heifer to be roped. The car approached and went away so rapidly that Ellen couldn't have screamed long enough for the driver to hear—if she could have screamed at all.

Oh, God, please send someone walking by. Please send the cops. Someone, please help me.

"I von't hurt you if you behave," said the voice. "I vant us to be frans . . ."

The "behave" sounded like "behafe." Not that it mattered. She grunted another yes. Blood was still leaking in her mouth, filling it. The impact of her chin had cut her tongue, she thought. Her whole face felt numb. She spit sideways. *If he lets up, roll away to the left and get to your knees, hit him in the groin with the bag.* Then she felt something cold and circular against her head just behind the right ear. Fingers also remained at the back of her neck. So both hands were up around her head. *Oh, my God, a gun.* A gun? Did this have something to do with daddy and the Marines? Maybe she was being kidnapped, daddy handled top secret papers . . .

The tote bag—four spiral notebooks, five hardback texts, forty-odd Xeroxed pages on the Bangwana, the Islamic tribe that aided and abetted slave traders, along with Clorets, lipstick, Kleenex, felt-tips and an apple uneaten at eight o'clock—must weigh at least twenty pounds. A weapon, her only weapon. The knee pressure on her back was suddenly released but his right foot came down heavily on the hand that held the bag as she tried to lunge up and hit him. She screamed as the shoe pressed down on her clenched fist at the knuckles. Two fingers snapped at the joints. God, the pain.

"Ach, entschuldigen, sie," he said apologetically. He hadn't meant to do that, he was just big-footed and clumsy. He pulled her to her feet, kicking the bag away into the grass, apple tumbling free.

The pain in her hand was excruciating, and she began to weep though fighting against it. Weeping was not like Ellen, except at the movies.

"Vee valk."

"My hand." She was sobbing now, breaking down at last. She had never felt such pain.

The gun against her head, fingers grasping the back of her neck, she began to move on rubbery legs like a hand-held puppet dancing on a board.

What daddy said to do couldn't be done. She still hadn't seen his face, nor could she judge his size as they went out on the macadam of the lot, but the thought kept occurring to her that it might be the heavy-set man in the library, the one who looked at her, looked away, looked back. He'd worn a safari jacket, and had that weird peach-colored skin.

Looking ahead she could see that only two cars remained in the lot. Her second-hand bug and another larger white car that seemed to be the last one in the metered visitors' row. They were moving steadily toward that one.

Fifty feet more and they'd be at the white car. *Oh please, God, where are the cops?*

And then all the strength vanished from the legs of Ellen Trenholm Hickel and she fainted, as much from terror as from pain, hitting her chin again. The pudgy tourist picked her up and carried her the last fifty feet, blood dripping from her open mouth.

Some ten minutes later the white Mercedes 500 SL series got underway and turned out of P-4 as a campus patrol car moved slowly up North Circle toward Bridge Road. Both the driver, Jack

Stapker, and his off-duty passenger, Howard Ames, saw the expensive car, wondering what it was doing at UCI this time of night. About 9:35. Yet they both knew that rich wheels came to campus.

Ames, who was going through a divorce, finding it cheaper to squander lonely time at night in a patrol car than in a bar, said, "Goddamit, this country is getting overrun by these turkeys. Ten to one that guy is Ayrab. Everytime you turn around some Iranian or a Chink or a Vietnammer is buying out a business. Who in hell in Washington is letting all these people in? Presto and they drive around in Caddies or a Mercedes. We're givin' this country away to foreign shits. I'd close all the gates tomorrow, lock up the borders, build a fence from here to Texas."

A few of the foreign students drove expensive cars and it was always galling to Ames, who had grown up in Oakland's black ghetto, to see them wheeling around. Neither officer noted that a green VW bug sat forlornly in the student permit section of the lot. They were too busy chewing out the foreign shits.

The white Mercedes turned right on Bridge Road and sped off. A moment later the squad car, as fully equipped as any metropolitan police vehicle—twelve gauge Remington to fire double 00 buckshot perched upright in the Electro-Lok; even riot gear in the trunk—turned left on Bridge.

Theirs wasn't a security-guard operation with longhairs and police has-beens. These UCI cops were fully functioning police, academy-trained and armed keepers of state and county law, enforcing it within a campus that had a daytime population of nearly twenty thousand; nighttime residency of about seven thousand. The UCI cops performed the same as any city department; had the same legal status. Tied into county and state law enforcement radio and computer networks, they were even equipped, with two trained detectives, to do on-campus investigations. Commit a felony and you'd go to Orange County jail, manacles on wrists.

Although there'd been a murder at the university hospital training facility, not in twenty years of UCI existence had there been a campus kidnapping. Most of the crime was theft, and most of the thieves weren't students.

18

3

KATTA TRENHOLM, mother of Ellen, had met Cole Hickel when he was still at Annapolis and she was at Georgetown U. for a bachelor of arts. She had been all the way across the room that Sunday afternoon in Shadyside, Maryland, early summer '63, with a glass in her hand, almost a head taller than the elderly couple who had cornered her. Cole had just arrived with four other midshipmen, all in gleaming whites, and suddenly there was this burst of female laughter and there she was. Easily the prettiest, sexiest female around. Low-cut dress flared at the hips with big bold red flowers on it. Blonde hair that he'd bet never suffered a drop of tint.

Feeling his stare, she turned.

Fine high cheekbones and brow to match, set off by long black lashes. Nose just right. All displayed in a deep tan.

Cole grinned, saying to his companions, "I got an errand," and wound through the drinkers.

Stepping around the elderly couple, he took hold of her elbow. "I must see you immediately, not a minute to spare." His face was grave.

Startled, but already propelled out to the side porch that overlooked Chesapeake Bay, she asked, "Who are you? What are you doing?"

"I must speak to you in private. It's urgent."

As soon as they reached the porch rail, he let go of the elbow and squared off in front of her. "Ma'am, you have the most glorious pair I've ever had the privilege to look upon."

Katta stood quietly. "Please repeat that. No, don't. Who told you to say that to me?"

"No one. But I grew up with my late father, an admiral, telling me that to achieve any objective you must attack, one way or an other. This attack called for truthful words."

"You're an expert on all this?"

"Well, I'm an appreciative observer."

"Who are you?"

"Cole Hickel, the second, of Fluvanna, Virginia, currently on loan to the U.S. Navy. Future uncertain. Who are you?"

"Katta Trenholm. Future very certain. Those people I was talking to, the ones you interrupted, are going to be my in-laws this fall. My fiancé is on a cruiser in the Med. He's an ensign."

"Unlucky ensign. He's about to lose his fiancée. Take a walk with me. There's an oyster shell road."

"*Midshipman* Hickel, the only walk I'm taking is inside."

"Better out here."

She moved around him, stopped. "How many times have you used this tacky do we know routine?"

"Four or five."

"What happened?"

"One hit me. Another walked off. One called me a stupid sex maniac. The former I'm not. You're the only one who laughed. Maybe we'll get along."

"I doubt it." She took another few steps, stopped again. "Are you the Cole Hickel who dropped the pass in the end zone two years ago and Notre Dame went on to win?"

"Nope, that was Jimmy Hickey. I just box. For fun. Club fights. But I think I've got a pretty good left hook."

"Wonderful. What's the point?"

"Not much, except you jab and the guy expects you to throw a right but you hook him with your left."

"Oh." She proceeded back into the house.

About ten minutes later she returned to the porch, carrying two drinks. They went up the oyster shell road, the tall pretty girl in the red print dress and the tall mishipman in his whites.

A year later, almost to the day, they were married in Virginia Beach. Seven months later he went off to Florida to learn how to be an aviator. He chose choppers over multi-engines and jets because he thought choppers were the coming thing in the Marine Corps.

He chose the Marines over the Navy because he didn't want to be known as the admiral's son.

She liked that.

4

ELLEN, regaining consciousness in the car, soon realized her wrists were tightly bound with cord, feet too, wrists strapped to her thighs just above the knees. Thought had been given to this trussing, he'd planned it well in advance.

They weren't on campus and the car was moving rapidly. On MacArthur, she realized, hardly traveled this time of night, headed toward the ocean. Tinted glass diffusing the light made it impossible for anyone to see in; dimmed the view out. To anyone looking at the car, she'd be just a "head" sitting there.

She glanced over at the driver and confirmed that she'd seen him before. The library. In the soft dash glow she recognized the baby-smooth skin, yellow and peach. One of those men who couldn't grow whiskers. Eyebrows a few random hairs. A blocky face, a sheen of sweat on the slick skin. There'd been several ritual murders in Southern California the last months. Girls hacked and mutilated and dropped into dumpsters. "Oh, God," she murmured out loud.

Trying to deep breathe, fill her lungs and calm down, she kept staring at the side of his face and head. It was *him*, no doubt. G Section. Suddenly she realized she'd seen him even before G Section. Newport Freeway! He'd looked at her several times from this same expensive white car. Stalked her, she now knew. Picked her out from all the cars whizzing along and stalked her. She fought against it, but she began to whimper. The pain from her broken fingers was overwhelming; her chin ached; her tongue hurt. There was the cold, sapping fright.

The man heard her this time. *"Mädchen, Mädchen, was wünschen sie?"*

The softness of his voice made it even more terrifying. She saw that one of his pudgy hands, with a ruby ring on it, was on the wheel; the other lightly on the gun, which was nestled in his lap. He looked middle-aged. Late thirties?

She began to have trouble breathing.

He soon turned north onto the coastal highway, where he'd been earlier in the day, venerable 101, El Camino Real, road of the mission priests. They glided past the subdued elegance of Fashion Island's new entrance with its arch of royal palms. Ellen turned her head over there, determined to keep track of where she was being taken.

She'd shopped at the mall occasionally over the last year, the time that the Hickels had resided in the area on their tour of duty. But only one of the stores was in her range. High-rent lawyer, doctor and investment offices; glittering metal and glass high-rises formed the backdrop for the squattier but equally glitzy peddlers of high fashion merchandise. The Amen Wardy, Neiman-Marcus crowd. What was happening to her now had the inelegant fabric of a nightmare.

A smell was in the car, one used to hide another smell. A perfumed deodorizer? "Could you please open the window," she finally asked, feeling sick at her stomach.

"I cannot do that," he replied without turning the yellow baby-skin face.

A laughing couple, about her age, did a little dance into Bobbie McGee's off on the left just before the intersection of Bayside. She'd been at the bar of Bobbie McGee's only last week with Phil Chiu. Laughing and laughing. Phil could be very funny.

"I may get sick."

He didn't answer. Instead he slipped a cassette into the tape deck.

As a violin solo—one she'd heard before but couldn't name— filled the Mercedes she glanced down on the seat between her and the man. A fan of light from under the dash picked out two magazines, one partially on top of the other. The top one was *Ouch,* with a cover picture of a girl in a long red cape beating a cowering man with a riding crop. The title *Bondage* crept out from the other magazine. She didn't know magazines like these existed.

As the haunting, river-running sound of the violin built, she closed her eyes, feeling her body shrink into the soft leather seat.

5

ELLEN HAD NEVER been in a vehicle with tinted glass, though she had often wondered who was in them. Why the hiding? Rock stars? Actors? Probably coke dealers, Phil Chiu had said. They put up the big money for the county real estate developers, he'd heard. Through the side windows, lights along the way were faint circles and blotches and blurs. The effect was to make the Mercedes more a prison.

Working her wrists, she strained against the cord bindings, discovering it was impossible to raise her legs. She could move her feet, bound at the ankles, back and forth, but no other movement was possible. Turning her bruised left cheek against the cold leather of the seat, she heard herself say, "Please let me go."

He glanced over, glazed look in his eyes; then quickly looked away.

As they rode on past the wide bridge over the east end of the boat harbor she tried to think of when and where she'd seen that glazed look before.

As they approached the restaurant and yacht brokers' enclave of Newport Beach she saw a police car up ahead moving in the same direction and thought about slamming her body sideways into the stocky man. Maybe force a wreck. Daddy had said to think things out in a few seconds, then make a move even if you took a chance. Do nothing and down you go. Sometimes in the air, in Nam, he said that's all the time they had to make a decision—a few seconds. Take the chance.

But then the patrol car turned off right. Only a few cars were rolling in either direction. The violin played on.

Klaus Hermann had spent an expensive hour, by appointment only, in the House of "W" on Melrose in Hollywood just the week before. "W" could always be found in a classy little ad in the Santa Monica *Fetish News,* published for those devoted to hurt or be hurt. After saying what he desired he was inked in, date and hour. A Mistress Trudy would be his dominatrix. But the professionals such as Mistress Trudy were hardly ever as satisfying as the amateurs like the one beside him . . . if they could be discovered and coaxed. Anyway, "W" was not up to the standards of the pain salons of New York, which he visited periodically, or of Amsterdam or Copenhagen, or when he was home in his own Hamburg.

"W" was nonetheless deluxe, with its three stylish bondage rooms and the dim red-lit chamber of Hades, complete with the usual racks for stretching, whipping posts and even a suspension harness that could "fly" a customer in almost any position for flagellation. He'd only tried suspension once, at Erebus in New York, wig flipping off to reveal a head slick as a pared turnip. Very embarrassing six feet off the floor, his dominatrix for the evening breaking up at the sight.

Klaus had come to "W" the Wednesday past, his coke furnace on a high stoke, with pictorials that fascinated Dr. Hoger so much. He'd requested a black silk diaper from Mistress Trudy, who was in a golden Queen Anne gown, and had enjoyed a keen Amish buggy whip until the lashes had sent him violent, no matter that he tried to control himself. Dodging around his contortions, Trudy had stepped outside the door for safety. Bones had been broken in "W" by the likes of Klaus, but she hadn't flicked him more than twenty times to the music of a symphonic tape he had brought along.

How nice it would have been if he could have talked to this girl beside him the way he talked to Mistress Trudy, explain what he needed done—those exquisite things he often saw in the pictorials; have her cooperate with a wide smile. But then there was always that thrill in doing it the other way, taking a captive, providing a costume for her, then trying to persuade or frighten her. One look at this pretty student and he knew he could never persuade her; not even if he put five hundred dollars in her bra. A thousand. Five thousand. Which made her all the more appealing.

Earlier this same *wunderschön* day he'd driven along Pacific Coast Highway after checking out of Malibu, coming a long way south on 101 looking for the right spot, one that was different.

Ellen tried deep breathing again. Maybe if she sucked in enough of the sweetened air she'd get sick all over his car. Anything to distract him.

Newport begins to get trashy on the north end. Beer joints and fortune tellers. Shabby motels. T-shirt shops. Self-service car washes and pizza parlors. As they cleared the city limits just beyond the Santa Ana River bridge Ellen remembered where she'd last seen that kind of glazed not-drunk look. It had been when she was about twelve and her father was stationed at Cherry Point, North Carolina. The boy next door, another military brat, was always a little strange. Raised rabbits—not that that was strange— but one afternoon, saying his family wanted a doe for dinner, he'd slit the white, furry throat in front of her, first looking at it with tenderness. A few years later, at USMC Kaneohe, on Oahu, she'd heard that same boy turned psycho. Flipped out. Tried to kill his mother.

Stay calm, don't get hysterical, Ellen told herself. Try to deal with him. Pretend. *Stay alive*.

As the Mercedes headed on toward Huntington Beach, another of the bedroom towns that sit on the Pacific shore every few miles all the way to Los Angeles, she noticed that the driver seemed to be searching for something on the right-hand side of the road. A street sign?

Finally, just past California Edison's huge steam generating plant, saturated with lights, high stacks ringed with red aircraft warning pulses, puffing thin vapor into the night sky, the car went right on Newland Avenue. On that side of Newland was the ten-foot high chain-link fence topped with barbed wire surrounding the power station. To the left was more fencing around a parking lot. Ellen knew this stretch of road by Cal Edison but had never paid much attention to it.

Where was everybody? Anybody? No cars on Newland. No one walking. The pudgy man would soon do what he planned to do, and she tried to see everything, fix it in her mind in case she could get away; know exactly what had happened to her and when.

They passed the Newland Edison gate, not even a guard in sight. The Mercedes turned right again behind the plant on an unlit street that proclaimed to be a dead end. She saw the sign, "Industrial Street." No one at home after dark.

As the Mercedes went on slowly a car-wrecker lot was to the left. Two huge German shepherds, paws on the gate, fangs exposed, ripped the silence. Ahead in the beams she could see a yard with heavy construction equipment; then an oil pumping rig going up and down like a mechanical crane drinking water.

Now he switched off the headlights, glancing back to see if anyone had followed him up the sandy road. He stopped, waited a few minutes. They were directly opposite the back of the generating plant. Humming high voltage wires were overhead. Parts of the plant looked like a spaceship, like the one sitting on Devil's Tower in "Close Encounters of the Third Kind." She looked over there, praying she'd see someone moving around, but the spaceship seemed uninhabited, and even if she could get away she knew she couldn't climb the barbed wire topping.

Another dirt road paralleled the wide-legged transmission towers that fed lines into the plant, and the Mercedes began to move along it, away from the small industrial complex. The erector-set towers were eerie in the moonlight.

Finally, some thousand yards up the bumpy road, the man carefully angled the Mercedes up under the legs of a tower and turned off the ignition. He had arrived at his own hand-picked House of "W."

———

Ellen sat rigid in the seat, eyes closed now as he moved out of the car. She wanted to melt until she disappeared. She'd reconstitute herself far from this place.

She heard him open the trunk. A moment later he got into the backseat and she heard cloth rustling. A door on her side opened. With eyes closed and her cheek planted against the seat, she could not see that he was holding a nurse's cap and a prayer rug in one hand, the gun in the other.

Nor could she see that he was naked beneath a long white doctor's coat, his penis sticking out like a grotesque hat peg.

6

ELLEN'S PARENTS were reading in bed at 311 Oakwood Terrace in the city of Tustin, not too far from the UCI campus, and not too far from where Colonel Hickel reported to duty at least five days a week, sometimes six and seven depending on what flight operations were underway, what training exercises.

Tustin, as middle-class as stir-fry, was yet another California orange grove town that'd had eighty-eight people and eighty-eight dogs and a few horses until the Santa Ana Freeway came through like a moving money tree in the nineteen fifties. Once the concrete in the exits had cured, Tustin grew backyards instead of oranges.

The two-story four bedroom tract house on Oakwood was shining white stucco, boxy but nicely done inside and out. The Hickels, who were leasing it from another Marine Corps family now serving on Oahu, were thinking of trying to buy a similar house down the street and hang on to it for retirement in about fifteen years. Not at all a bad place to live. Cole had served two tours at MCAS(H), Tustin, and knew the area well.

At half past ten he looked over the top of his reading half-glasses and said, "Wonder where the hell Ellen is?"

Katta, not putting her magazine down, said, "Oh, maybe having a wine with Phil . . ."

"This time of night? I'm sorry, I don't approve and I'll keep saying it."

"And I'll keep saying that she'll be twenty-one in less than a month. She can be with Phil as much as she wants to. In fact I'm about to suggest she move in with him."

"I still don't like it."

Ellen stopped at Phil's apartment several times a week, sometimes spending the night there. Phil was a commercial photographer, specializing in automobiles. Cole thought that was the best thing about him, taking pictures of cars. Maybe the only good thing.

"They like to talk, you know," Katta added. "Something we don't do much of."

The Hunt for Red October balanced on his knees, he peered at her, suddenly laughing. "You throw horse poop even in bed."

She smiled over at him, nodding.

A handsome couple now in their early forties—he with graying crewcut; she with shiny blonde hair that showed little aging. The other two occupants of the house, Jennifer and Cole, III, better known as Skeet, were in their rooms down the hall, insulated, for the time being, from all the evils writhing across the land.

Cole said, "I've got an urge to go call that Chinaman—"

"And embarrass Ellen? Go to sleep, for Lord's sake. And stop calling him a Chinaman."

He shrugged, reached over for her.

By a few minutes after eleven no light could be seen in the house on Oakwood. But the moon lit it up, beautifying it, making it almost stately.

Nearing two a.m., the white Mercedes passed over the border into Baja, California, entering at Tijuana. An immigration officer, Francisco Jurado, thoroughly chilled and red-eyed, Indian features, face the color of wet brown clay, had a blanket about his upper body over his uniform. Reaching a hand from under the blanket he waved the Mercedes on, noting that it had an oval D on the trunk and went off in the direction of Mexico 1, the toll road to Ensenada.

34

Jurado watched it. Two hours into his shift, tired as well as cold, he muttered, "Zonzo." With all that money, the *idiota* should be in bed with a young girl, not wasting the night driving in dirt-poor Mexico.

Klaus Hermann checked into a motel down by the beach when he arrived in Ensenada, then took a long hot shower, examining the fresh rosettes of teeth marks around his groin, the reddened slightly lacerated calves and thighs. The girl hadn't hit him hard enough. He would have liked her to whip his back but that part was still tender from the House of "W." Still, he had enjoyed her, better than those professionals who were so willing. And under those electric lines, it was a nice touch.

Putting on his red silk robe, KH embroidered in gold thread, Klaus placed a call to his mother in Spain. She demanded to hear from him every other night no matter where he was; no matter where *she* was. On this occasion she was on holiday in Alicante on the sun coast. He had to be nice to *Mutti*. She was always generous with him . . . a thousand Deutschmarks a week allowance that had enabled him to live well in an apartment at 21st and R just off Dupont Circle in Washington. On his government salary, even with the living stipends, he could never have afforded the apartment much less the cleaning lady or the fine restaurants to which he was accustomed, not to mention those trips to New York and the Erebus.

Twenty minutes later, when he was almost asleep, the phone rang and he said, *"Mutti, Mutti . . ."*

She asked what he'd been doing all day and he told her he'd been at Disneyland, in Anaheim, a good German name. She had been there, too, he knew, with Stefan Noll, her long-time companion and bodyguard.

"Ah, Disneyland, the home of Mickey Mouse," she said.

"Yes, mother."

"I liked that pirate's ride," she said.

"So did I."

They talked so long that Klaus fell asleep on the phone, mostly saying *ja* and *nein*.

7

AT ABOUT SIX-THIRTY, Cole could stand it no longer. "Look, Kot, I'm calling that boy. I just want to know that she's there."

They were in the kitchen and breakfast was in the making, decaf water steaming. This was oatmeal day. There was bran day; granola day; yogurt and fresh fruit day. Katta had long been a health nut. "Why this time, Cole? She's spent the night over there before. Suppose they're still in bed? How embarrassing for you to call. He answers the phone and has to tell Ellen, 'Your father...'"

"Well, I'm sorry all to hell about that. I just have a feeling, had it last night. Dammit, I'm calling. Get me the number."

She was tempted to say yessir, and salute. She'd done it before but not often. Cole did get carried away. One had to be careful with Cole. Don't push too far or the walls could come down.

She read the number off and Cole dialed Phil Chiu. The phone rang a dozen times.

Katta looked relieved. "So they went out to breakfast. Or Phil decided to take the boat out. They don't need to check with us, Cole."

"There's no wind, for Chrissakes." Kids should realize the anxiety they could cause. Especially girls. Even twenty-one-year-olds.

She ought to have her tail kicked a little, but what could you do nowadays? Katta minded, too, more than she let on, he knew.

Katta sighed. "Go to work." It was almost a plea.

Cole went on into the downstairs bath to shave and shower, leaving the master bath to Jennifer and her endless routines. Work was commanding officer of a MAG, Marine air group of combat helicopters stationed at the old lighter-than-air base. Cole headed up two support and eight chopper squadrons, two of which were always deployed in the Western Pacific. He was in charge of three thousand personnel who flew and took care of CH-46 Knights and CH-53 Sea Stallions, big chested whirlybirds for moving troops and cargo. Ever since Vietnam, choppers had a major role in landing and retrieval of assault troops.

Tustin Marine Corps Air Station could easily be spotted from the Santa Ana Freeway simply because the old blimp hangars were the height of an eighteen-story skyscraper and the length of three football fields. Largest wooden-arched structures in the world, they were so big that sometimes clouds drifted inside and rain fell, though the World War II sub-hunting blimps had long gone.

Slim and trim as his beloved oldest daughter, Cole Hickel was six-two and weighed in around one-seventy, only ten pounds more than when he got out of Annapolis. Hair the color of barn straw laced with gray, he made a striking figure whether in a flight suit or fancy dress blues, a man usually in full stride. Among the many decorations when he wore full dress were an Air Medal, Silver Star, Cross of Gallantry and the Navy Cross, not to mention the Purple Heart, unwanted remembrance of An Trach.

Katta was reading the Orange County edition of the Los Angeles *Times* and sipping Sanka when Cole came in to say, "I've got to go down to Pendleton for a few hours. Call me in Pete Cocelli's office when Ellen checks in."

Camp Pendleton to the south, almost the size of Monaco or Andorra, home of a Marine amphibious force, was always a roost for choppers participating in training assault troops.

Katta nodded. "That I'll do." She smiled up at him, offering her full lips, which he kissed. "Have a good one." He was always so intense in the early mornings, like a sprinter at the blocks, she once told him.

At the base, Cole got into a flight suit and piloted a Sea Knight down to Pendleton. It was generally felt in the flying part of the Marine Corps that Cole Hickel, II, would likely be a brigadier general in not too long a time and probably rise even further than that. He was said to have all the assets for major command—ability, understanding of fighting men, guts, intelligence and common sense, good looks in the younger John Glenn mold, and a very pretty, very sensible *non*-alcoholic wife. It hardly hurt that his late father had been a famous World War II air admiral, carrier man with Halsey. Other assets included a degree in aeronautical engineering and a stint as helicopter test pilot; staff time in the Pentagon; graduation from the Naval War College; presidential chopper pilot for a year. He'd been skipper of three different chopper squadrons, and it was said his pilots would fly up a gun barrel for him.

The two youngest Hickels were down by now. Mumbling a good morning, they flopped into their chairs for guava juice and oatmeal. Both were due off to school by eight. Jennifer was sixteen; Skeet, twelve. Perfect planned spacing. They were as photogenic as their oldest sister, father and mother. Golden Hickel genes. Katta remained almost as willowy as that day in Virginia Beach when she'd said, "I do," and she worked at staying willowy. The skill Ellen had shown on the courts at UCI had surely come from Katta. She played tennis and swam and jogged with Cole and mothered and wifed *and* was a congenial stateswoman for the other wives of the air group, both officer and enlisted—which wasn't always so easy and sometimes took its toll. Still, when Cole pointed out she didn't have to be superwoman, she told him, "no sweat" and he shut up fast, counting his blessings.

Cole had a little time to kill before seeing Pete Cocelli, who was in with the general, and dropped by a briefing for a night exercise —inserting fifteen-man sticks down in the landing zone. Cole stood in the back while the young pilot was saying it was going to be real dark and dusty in Combat-town tonight and safety was paramount. "Use night vision goggles and don't push your comfort level. We'll have six frogs and two snakes..." Landing troops. Inserting, extracting. *Crow, owl and hawk.* Over by moonrise.

Cole sighed and went on to Pete's office to say he wished to hell he was still a squadron skipper. Down there was where they had all the fun. They *flew.* They played meaningful combat games. Fun being with the guys every day. Fighting men. "I miss it, Pete. That's where the action is. They can have my job tomorrow." He was in his eighth month and already humdrummed out of his skull. Paperwork. Phone calls. Corps politics.

The phone rang shortly after ten and a female voice said, "May I speak to Ellen Hickel?"

Katta said, "She isn't here just now. Who's calling, please?"

"Lost and Found at UCI police department. Would you tell her we found her bag. We're on campus. On Bridge Road."

Katta felt a slight chill. "Found her bag? I don't understand."

"Officer Cates brought it in at the end of his shift. Her wallet was in it but I doubt if anything was touched. Some books and papers."

Katta asked sharply, "Are her car keys in it?"

"Minute, please."

Katta sat down on the high stool by the kitchen desk. Maybe Cole had been right?

"Yes, ma'am, they're still in the bag."

"That's strange," Katta said. "Could you please have someone check all the parking lots for a 1976 green VW bug? There's a Greenpeace sticker on the rear bumper. I don't know the license plate number."

"Are you Ellen Hickel's mother?"

"Yes, I am."

"Minute, please."

Katta could hear the girl asking for a parking lot check.

"All right, Mrs. Hickel, we'll do that for you and I'll call you back."

Katta said, "Thank you," in a tight voice; hung up and dialed Phil Chiu's number. No answer. She looked up Colonel Pete Cocelli in the Camp Pendleton base book, dialed his number. Cole was soon on the line.

"Hon, I, ah . . . just wondered when you were coming back?"

"You don't sound good. What's wrong?"

"I don't think anything is wrong. I think Ellen is with Phil, but UCI did find her bag, with her wallet and keys in it."

"That's not like her," Cole said. He'd start home in ten minutes, he told her. "What did you say to UCI?"

"Asked them to check the parking lot for the car."

"Good. I'll call you as soon as I land. Keep after Phil."

Cole, thank God, was operating, taking charge. Katta hung up, took a deep worried breath and blew it out. She realized her mouth had turned sticky dry. She poured a glass of water, sipped slowly. If Ellen's car and bag were at the school, and she wasn't with Phil, where in God's name would she be, and why?

Upstairs, she opened Ellen's dog-eared phone book, a book into which she'd never looked, and began with the first local name, Sandra Alpaugh, and worked all the way to the end, finding few at home; feeling drained after just five calls, mouth dry again.

Klaus Hermann woke up a few minutes after eleven, feeling irritable. He had a slight headache and runny nose. His first thought was to go down to the car, get the powder and take a snort. But he also knew there was not much left in the packet and wisdom told him not to go around Ensenada trying to make a buy. Probably easy to do but only if he bought from the right person.

He remembered talking to Mutti and telling her how much he regretted his holiday coming to an end. He did not say that he regretted even more having to come home again and be under her various yokes. She was such a strong person and her *jochs* weighed him down and made him feel helpless. *"Listen to me, Klaus . . ."* The past eighteen months in Washington—he'd only returned once to Hamburg, this last Christmas—had been heavenly so far away from her.

He lingered in bed a few minutes longer, thinking about Mutti and going home, decided to shower and, in the harsh Baja light not filtered by smog the way it was in California, once more examined his body. Turning this way and that, he looked at the dying marks of "W" and at the fresh trophies from the pretty blonde of last night. He especially liked her teeth marks around his groin. She did as she was told. He smiled at the memory of it. He showered long and leisurely and then went down to the desk to ask for the name of a good bar.

Hussong's, he was told. *"Famoso,"* said the clerk. A fine place for a fine gentleman.

8

OFFICERS JACK STAPKER and Howard Ames each got calls shortly before noon from Paul McManus, retired from the Los Angeles police force after twenty-five years and now having a second less stressful career. McManus, a burly, big-gutted, bald-headed man of fifty-four, had been UCI chief for three years and mostly enjoyed the campus peace and quiet, feeling on many days he was taking money. No wonder professors liked this cushy life. Mostly no strain or sweat.

Stapker and Ames were both at home, Howard asleep in the one-room hideaway-bed Santa Ana apartment brought on by divorce, spousal support and general lack of money. Stapker lived in Costa Mesa, a few miles north, and was awake.

McManus said the same thing to both: see anything unusual at P-4 last night? We may have ourselves a missing girl.

Both of them said the same thing: You kiddin', chief? Like McManus saying that the Anteater basketball team, starting to make a name around the country, just crashed at John Wayne. No survivors. *A missing student?*

Stapker was called first and informed McManus that Howard had ridden with him for a while off-duty to bitch about his wife's rotten lawyer. "No, chief, we swung into P-4 several times and the last time there was nothing left but a VW bug." Up to a dozen cars were sometimes left in the various lots overnight. Out of gas. Battery problems. A fair number of clunkers wheezed into Campus Drive every day. Old compacts mostly. Some were eventually towed.

"That VW belonged to her, girl named Ellen Hickel. We know she was in the library until nine o'clock. Pretty blonde. Her mother thinks she had on a denim skirt, yellow blouse and white golf jacket when she left home yesterday about five-thirty."

"Didn't see her," said Stapker.

"Can you remember when you checked P-4 last night?"

"Oh, I guess about eight the first time; then about nine-twenty, nine-thirty; then again about eleven-thirty. The VW was there the last two times, I know. Hey, wait a minute. When we did that nine-thirty check a white Mercedes sedan was coming out of the lot. I think I saw it there at eight over in visitor's."

"What year?"

"I'm guessin' eighty-four, eighty-five. Wasn't too old."

"Number?"

"Didn't look that close. We see a thousand cars a night. You know that. I don't look at the plates all the time. 'Less I got a reason."

"Yeh. See anybody in it beside the driver?"

"Nope. Wasn't really looking."

A few minutes later sleepy Howard Ames said practically the same thing. He had the miserable owl hours, twelve to eight a.m.

McManus had sent Detective Sergeant Louderholt and two officers to scour P-4 and every foot of real estate within five hundred feet of it, and they returned about twelve-thirty. Louderholt, oldest and most experienced of the trio, said, "I think we've got some dried blood on the sidewalk about six feet away from the south curb. I think we ought to lift prints from that VW." McManus nodded. Louderholt added, "There're some footprints along the top of the bank, I've got to find out the last time grounds maintenance was working along there."

McManus nodded again and then his door closed as Louderholt

went off. Thinking of the white Mercedes, a stupid car to use if you're going to kidnap someone, he decided to call the Hickel residence. He was afraid that all sorts of bells might ring needlessly. Few things whetted the press more than "Pretty Co-Ed Missing." From Hickel's student file on his desk he noted that her father was a bird colonel in the Marines.

Katta answered Chief McManus' first question by saying, "We think she may be sailing with her boyfriend," but the chief thought there wasn't much assurance in the voice.

"He's local?"

"Yes, and keeps his boat over in Newport."

"What kind of car does he drive?"

"I don't know. We . . . ah . . . really don't know too much about him."

"Your daughter ever mention a white Mercedes?"

"No."

"Any place she might be, aside from with him?"

"I've been checking her other friends and so far . . . ah . . . no one has seen her."

"Mrs. Hickel, has this ever happened before? I mean, dropping out of touch for several days?"

"Never."

McManus laughed gently. "You're lucky. I don't know many families, including my own, who haven't had a missing person for twenty-four hours or so. Ellen'll be home by day's end or less. I'll bet on that."

"Thank you," said Katta. "Please let me know if you hear anything."

"Immediately. I promise."

He hung up, thinking, truthfully—no bets. If that was indeed dried blood out there on the sidewalk, no bets at all. It shaped up as use of force, for rape, or worse.

Cole drove up to 311 Oakwood Terrace a few minutes later, hurrying into the house. Katta was still on the kitchen stool, guarding the phone.

"She call?"

Katta shook her head, biting her lip, struggling against tears.

"No answer from Chew?"

Katta shook her head again, then stood, off-balance.

Cole saw that she needed his arms and moved quickly to wrap them around her. "Hey, c'mon, she's all right, she's just goofed this time. Forgot to call us. I'll bawl hell out of her. Hell, she could walk through the door right now." He held his wife tight as she struggled to regain composure. She finally took a deep breath. "I'm damn glad you're back."

He moved away from her and became the bird colonel again. "All right, Kot, let's get to it. Do we have an address on that Chew boy?"

"He's not a boy, Cole. He's twenty-eight. And it's 'Shoo,' not 'Chew'—"

"Whatever, do we have an address?"

They had only met him once, an egg-walking ten minutes, and Katta knew that Ellen had felt uncertain about that situation. She'd known that her father, especially, didn't approve of her spending the night with Phil. To Katta, Chiu seemed to be okay. Even Cole admitted that Phil seemed to be okay aside from the sleeping-over thing. But in the seven months she'd dated Phil there'd been the usual minefield everybody tiptoed through. From the start Cole had said, "Look, I'm sure his people don't want their son marrying a white girl any more than—" "They're friends, they date and he's as white as you are," Katta would point out. "They may never get married . . ."

"He's at Breton Way, on Seaview Ridge."

Those were condos off MacArthur on the way to Fashion Island. Shiny new Yuppielands. Phil went to Detroit periodically to shoot dramatic photos of new Ford models. Ellen hadn't talked about him too much except to say he was very bright, very creative.

Cole parked his black '67 Austin-Healey, bought from the widow of another gunship man who didn't come home from Nam, in front of Chiu's place and pushed the button repeatedly. Finally he went next door to ask the neighbor, an elderly lady, out of place there, if she'd seen Mr. Chew around recently.

"Not for several days."

Cole went back to the 3000-MK-III, which he had restored and sometimes raced in antique meets, got a slip of paper out of the glove compartment and wrote on it: "Phil, urgent you call us. Cole Hickel."

He tucked the note under the bell pull of Chiu's door and headed for UCI.

Tinley Junior High unleashed its six hundred plus students at three o'clock, and fifteen minutes later Skeet came through the Hickel front door, almost knocking his mother down getting to the bathroom. A few minutes later he emerged, and Katta started to tell him that there was a family crisis but thought better of it. She decided to wait until Jennifer arrived and go through it only once. Besides, maybe by that time Ellen would have called.

Skeeter didn't really resemble either Katta or his father. There were no signs that he'd be tall. Hair dark and curly, not straw-colored. Rather large nose, not Katta's fine-boned nose or his father's puggish variety. Sometimes Katta looked at him and asked herself, Did I do that? Skeet didn't seem to have a drop of Swedish blood in him.

"What's the mail?" he asked.

"Mainly junk," Katta answered.

Then big-nosed Cole, III, went on upstairs to the wonderland of his Apple II and modem. At age twelve he was already a computer whiz.

The big sister relationship had always existed between Ellen, Jennifer and Skeeter, Ellen being almost five years older than Jen; eight more than Skeet. They'd looked up to her. She had been the built-in babysitter for a long time, and during the last year Jennifer had worn some of Ellen's blouses and jewelry, copied her sister's make-up. Ellen had been teaching her to play tennis. They were close.

If something happened to "Big Sis," as Skeet sometimes called her, it would take a long time for them to even partially recover, Katta thought as she went over to the kitchen window, looked out on the backyard, and put her fist to her mouth.

9

PENDING COMPLETION of a new building, the UCI police department was spread out between portions of the power sub-station and several long white house trailers parked behind it. In a trailer the chief was in no hurry to move. His force was running well in the makeshift headquarters. A pretentious man he never was.

And Paul McManus had learned long ago, up at LAPD, not to think out loud in front of worried next-of-kin; never verbalize suspicions. Oh, he might disguise some thought or idea and float it out obliquely just to see what might come up. But generally he smiled or shrugged and played a foxy game of wait. He listened to the tense, grim-faced bird colonel sitting across from him and white-lied when Cole Hickel asked, "Anyone see any other cars around that parking lot about the time Ellen left the library?"

"Last night was one of our quieter nights."

"Any sign of a struggle near Ellen's car?"

McManus said truthfully, "None." The blood spot was a hundred fifty-seven feet, four inches, away.

"Have you called in any other agencies?"

"No sir. We still don't know that she's missing, do we, colonel?"

"How long will it be before you do that?"

"Well, I'd say that we should wait until tomorrow morning. It's been my experience that it takes some time for the family to call friends, workplace, or other possible contacts. We're dealing here with an adult, colonel. Now if a child is missing we're walking the streets in an hour." Couldn't have been said better up at LAPD.

McManus wasn't able to see below desk level but figured Cole's fists were balled up, like his face. The man was a firecracker all ready to go bang. More than that—a cherry bomb ready to go bang.

"My wife has called all of Ellen's known friends or as many as she could talk to. No results. Ellen worked during late summers as a waitress at Five Crowns over in Corona del Mar but only works there weekends now. Katta checked there. We've already covered all bases except one. Phil Chiu. C-h-i-u. Shoo. Katta told you about him."

McManus nodded, touching his intercom and asking Sergeant Louderholt to come in. "At the moment we have only one investigator on the staff. The other one is in Virginia taking special courses. But Sergeant Louderholt is thoroughly trained and experienced. She could go to work for LAPD next week if she wanted to."

She?

The door swung open and in walked a plumpish redhead in her thirties. As introductions were made, McManus knew from his expression what the colonel was thinking. Bad enough to be involved with rinky-dink campus police. Now an overweight lady detective. They probably had to meet a state quota and Kay Louderholt had her correspondence school certificate. Now McManus will tell me she's got a karate black belt.

"Detective Louderholt came to us from the Baltimore police department. Seven years back there. We had a homicide a while ago over at our medical facility in Orange. She made us all proud by putting the pieces together and along with a sheriff's deputy made the apprehension. I think she could have done it alone. We're delighted to have her. She's already read all the reports on your daughter, has interviewed the night staff at the library and the Sri Lankan who found the bag . . ."

Kay Louderholt put in, "I'm sure you'll hear from Ellen soon." She had masses of freckles to prove she was a natural redhead.

50

Cole said, "Are you really?"

"Let's hope."

Cole nodded but directed his attention back to McManus. "I'd still like to know why we can't call in the sheriff, put out a highway patrol bulletin. Right now."

McManus said, "Okay, I'll make a deal with you. I'm not really wild about it at this point but I'll go public if the boyfriend shows up and can't be of help."

Cole shifted on the chair, obviously restraining himself. "Suppose he doesn't show for three days? Suppose someone has taken both of them? Ellen and Chiu? That's happened."

"Colonel, if we don't know anything by noon tomorrow I promise you we go public."

"If she's kidnapped, whoever has got her could already be in Arizona."

"New Mexico or further," agreed McManus. "But it hasn't been twelve hours since we found that bag. I promise you that if anything develops before noon tomorrow I'll call in every agency that might conceivably be of help. That includes the Federal Bureau, Colonel Hickel."

Cole stood, reaching down for the tote bag, which was on the floor beside him. "I'll bring Mrs. Hickel back in a little while and we'll take Ellen's car home? Is that all right?"

McManus nodded. Prints had already been lifted.

As Cole reached the door McManus said, "Do you ever handle out-of-the-ordinary top secret information in your job?"

Cole was startled. "I see secret material all the time but most of it can be read in *Aviation Week*. If you're asking if I have some sort of super-secret access, the answer is no." Was the cop thinking about foreign agents taking Ellen? Nonsense.

"Thank you, colonel," McManus said. "I promise I'll call you if anything breaks here. If Ellen or Chiu calls you—you know she might call him—please phone me immediately."

"You can count on it."

Cole told the redhead detective that it was nice to meet her, said goodbye and walked down the short steps of the trailer, simmering. The university chief cop might be a little too cool-assed and laid-back. All he needed to do was be sucking on a pipe in a tweed professor's jacket. Then again Cole well knew he'd rather not have a jumping-jack sitting there.

Though there weren't many students moving around in the warmish spring afternoon, Cole eyed the females among them with despair. They were talking, laughing. Carrying books. Young and so full of life. *Ellen, Ellen* . . . The sight of them only added to the steadily growing anxiety.

But as he walked toward the old car, Cole felt sudden anger . . . If by any chance she was out sailing with that noodle-eater he'd kick her butt for sure. His, too. No matter if she was weeks away from twenty-one, she still lived at home and the least she could do was to let them know her schedule. Katta was always sticking up for her . . . "Cole, she's a grown lady, very responsible . . ." So just pick up the goddamn phone . . .

As he reached the car door Cole realized he was talking to himself aloud. He could not remember ever having done it before.

Katta was sitting on the front steps when Cole drove up and her look told him something else had happened. She went out to the car. Phil Chiu had called from San Francisco asking for Ellen. "They had a date for tonight and he got tied up. He hasn't seen her in three days. I explained what had happened . . . finding her bag, leaving her car in the parking lot. I asked him if he had any idea where she might be. He didn't. He offered to fly back right away. Cole, I'm scared . . ."

"You got his number?"

"He's staying at the Clift House."

Cole unwound from the Austin-Healey and went inside to call McManus.

The chief promptly said, "Okay, I'll put the word out."

"All the way," Cole demanded.

"All the way," McManus said, then asked, "This Phil Chiu, did you ever hear Ellen say anything about him that caused you to think he might not be the right person for your daughter?"

"No. She said very little about him."

"You wouldn't think he's involved?" McManus asked.

Cole frowned over at Katta. Well, after all, what exactly *did* they know about Phil Chiu aside from his living on Breton Way, having a sailboat and shooting car pictures. "I don't know."

The chief said, "I'll keep in touch."

Jennifer came into the kitchen just as her father put the phone down. "What's *all the way?*" That tone wasn't particularly new when he talked to the base, but then she looked over at her mother. Katta's usually serene face was tight and drawn.

"What's going on?" Jennifer asked, frown starting over her forehead.

"Ellen's missing," her father said bluntly. No other way.

There, the words were out, hanging in the air.

Katta looked like she'd just been punched. "I was going to tell them together."

"Go ahead," he snapped. Katta, Jennifer, anyone. He dug down into Ellen's bag, which was resting by the kitchen desk, for the VW keys.

"Ellen's what?" said Jennifer, mouth remaining open.

"Missing," Cole said, more gently now.

"Come on upstairs to your brother's room," Katta said, moving out into the hallway.

Jennifer looked over at her father, disbelief and alarm in her eyes, then hurried out after her mother. "What is it? What's *happened?*"

Though his shift didn't start until midnight, Howard Ames was summoned to Bridge Road in midafternoon and went to the chief's office about four o'clock.

McManus said, "Howard, let's talk some more about that white Mercedes you say you saw last night. I've just issued an all-points on that Hickel girl. I think she's in a heap o' trouble."

"I already said all I knew. We got behind it on Circle and then it turned left on Bridge."

"License plate?"

"Didn't read it. Neither did Jack."

"Was it out of state? Blue? White?"

Ames shook his head. "If he did pick her up, he's crazy. Hell, that's like draggin' someone into a gold Rolls. That's like puttin' a sign on your back, 'I'm snatchin' someone. Big white Mercedes.'"

"We don't know that the white Mercedes took her, do we?" McManus said.

Ames said, "Maybe she just decided to screw off an' let nobody know..."

McManus shook his head and waved off the chatter. "You and Stapker want to go into a dark room for a while and just talk?" He'd used that up in LAPD.

"Hell, Chief, that won't do any good. We saw what we saw — a sixty thousand dollar white car leavin' the lot. I got mad at it. An Ay-rab student drivin' that much car—"

"How do you know it was an Arab student?"

"I don't, dammit. I was just pissed to see that much car on this campus. I get pissed everytime I see a shithead student drivin' one of those sixty-thousand-dollar cars whether they're white, black, yellow or green."

Stapker came in. McManus said to him, "We're talking about the white Mercedes..."

Stapker said, "You know, I been thinking about that car all day. I'll tell you what I did see just to the left of the license plate. It caught my eye. One of those white ovals with a black D on it..."

"Yeh, come to think of it," said Ames.

McManus stared at both men.

Stapker said, "You don't see those on cars so much anymore. That one was probably bought in Germany and shipped over."

McManus asked tersely, "You both agree? Black D in an oval on it, left of the plate?"

Stapker said, "Yeh," and Ames nodded.

"Well, that helps. If you think of anything else, get on the phone. And the next time you guys spot a car like that around here please *try* to remember the license number. Put it down, for God's sake."

Ames and Stapker left, wondering why the hell they didn't think about stopping the Mercedes just for the hell of it. McManus promptly added the "D" information to the previous all-points. He requested that any vehicle answering that description be checked for the possibility of involvement in the disappearance of Ellen Hickel.

He also sent Kay Louderholt over to Oakwood Terrace to obtain a recent photo of the colonel's daughter for dissemination to law enforcement agencies and the media.

About two o'clock, the Pacific Ocean sparkling, the sun lancing Colinas Chapultepec, the high hill overlooking Ensenda, the white Mercedes rolled onto Toll Highway 1-D at the intersection of Avenidas Castelum and Lopez Mateos heading north. Klaus' idea was to drive up and spend the night in Los Angeles, then head east. Denver, Omaha, Chicago. Perhaps Pittsburgh. A day or two in each place, then on to Washington. "Take it easy," as they said in America.

Klaus had been reintroduced to tequila at Hussong's, again impressed with the swift impact of the agave mash. He'd had it once before in Washington at La Fonda on R Street, not far from where he lived, but down here it seemed even more potent.

He had had lunch at El Rey Sol, Caesar salad and grilled *langosta,* and had bought a fifth of gold medal Cuervo, now on the seat beside him, to nip on, to keep the nice feeling. With a full and warm belly, he felt very good and looked forward to the drive north along the scenic road. The guide book said parts of it were quite spectacular.

He had not thought of the blonde student since awakening and examining himself.

She was ancient history.

10

JUST BEFORE DARK on that always lively stretch of San Diego Freeway north of Oceanside, twenty-six-year-old highway patrolman Glen Eberle was following a white Mercedes with blue-black tinted windows. He had swung in behind the gleaming 500 series about a quarter-mile back, attempting to determine whether or not the driver had had a little too much to drink. In the almost vacant slow lane, the car was wandering between the white lines. Not erratically, perhaps not dangerously, just enough to indicate the driver was either very tired or had gone a little past the alcohol content limit.

Over his left front fender was a long band of deep orange, last of the twilight sun. Time for a coffee break. Eberle had come on road patrol at three and had two more hours left until he logged in back at Oceanside. The day so far had hardly taxed. Weather good. One fender-bender and five speeding violations.

Eberle drew closer to the vehicle, which was rolling between forty-eight and fifty-two mph, and noticed, finally, that the red-and-blue plates read "Diplomatic." Letters "LW" were on it as well; meaningless to him. He murmured, "Son of a bitch." *One of those*. Bad news. State department issue maybe. Sometimes messengers drove those cars, having no immunity whatsoever. Consular cars had "CC" plates, four numbers on them, and a lot of consular people had no immunity either. But stopping a car with any diplomatic plate could mean a long evening. He also noticed a black D on the white oval to the left of the red-and-blue plate. *Deutschland*. The vehicle had likely been bought in West Germany and shipped over.

Not in four years of road patrol had boyish-looking Glen Eberle ever stopped a diplomat or even a consul person, but he well remembered most of what the instructor had said: "Extraterritoriality. You know it better as diplomatic immunity. Don't fool with those people unless you want your ass full of darts from Sacramento. Be polite. Be smart. Go by the book. You can't win. I don't care if they've molested children, beaten up old women, murdered, raped, tortured—they still may go free. That's the U.S. law so that our people aren't entrapped in Moscow, Bulgaria or similar places. It's good policy, like it or not. You don't have to grin but you do have to bear it. *Many of the people attached to all the embassies in Washington have full immunity, of course, as do some United Nations personnel,*" the instructor said.

Eberle shook his head at the rotten luck and radioed back to the dispatcher at San Diego that he was preparing to halt a white Mercedes for a possible under-influence; read off the plate inscription and gave his position, which was about three and a half miles below the San Onofre immigration checkpoint. Border patrolmen stationed there checked auto and truck traffic for illegals, mostly Latinos trying to sample the good life to the north.

Eberle remembered the diplomatic procedure to be followed by the book: Stop vehicle, request identification; request suspect to submit to standard roadside tests if drunkenness is suspected; if suspect *is* under the influence, detain him or her for their own safety as well as the safety of other motorists. Suspect may be handcuffed if fleeing, ramming or other physical violence is involved. But handcuffing is last resort. Officer's immediate supervisor should be notified as quickly as possible. If circumstances are extenuating, land line instead of radio should be used to contact the supervisor. He, in turn, will notify the State Department.

In the midst of mentally ticking off procedure, Eberle was startled when the dispatcher issued an all-points bulletin and described a vehicle identical to the one ahead. Missing person, a 1036.

"That's just great," Eberle said, face tightening. His gut tightened too.

A 1036 was a high-risk stop, one level below the most dangerous of all, the felony stop. For that one you tried to wait for back-ups and then went to the vehicle with gun drawn. You went carefully, ready to hit the ground and roll. Under usual circumstances Eberle would also wait for back-ups on a high-risk stop, especially at night, but the immigration station was not far ahead. Armed border patrol officers were there. If the scale facility for trucks was operating, other highway patrolmen would be there.

If the Mercedes didn't wobble out of the lane, or speed up, or sideswipe someone, Eberle decided it was best just to follow him and make the stop at immigration. If the driver did have a gun, a lot of help was handy.

Suddenly the white car ahead was forbidding. The heavily tinted back window prevented any vision into the vehicle. There could be several occupants, not one. Pulling up alongside the suspect was always risky. Easy for the suspect to wing a shot and take off. All cops hated tinted windows.

Pulling up within fifty feet of the Mercedes, Eberle called San Diego to say he'd decided to make the stop at San Onofre and got a brisk affirmative from the dispatcher. Any patrolman who stopped *any* car nowadays, no matter how routine, and didn't have butterflies was a jerk. Simply because California had more cars than any other state, the CHP had the nation's highest rate of attacks on highway officers; highest death rate.

Eberle removed the Smith & Wesson from his holster, pushed the safety to off and laid the .38 on the seat beside him. Yellow warning lights were flashing in the distance, giving motorists a quarter mile to slow and stop. Six lanes narrowed gradually to two, and border patrolmen at a spot opposite a cluster of immigration buildings glanced at the vehicles as they slowly approached. Those with U.S. plates and obvious lily-white or black occupants were generally waved on. Baja California plates and brown faces were another matter.

As the Mercedes, slowed now to forty, edged to the left, six lanes began to funnel into two, and Eberle weighed several problems. Stopping the car too early would eliminate back-ups; halting it just before the checkpoint might endanger other motorists if shooting began. Stopping it smack-dab at the feet of the flashlight-wielding border patrolman made the most sense. He was armed and the Mercedes driver might be a little more cautious.

Speed dropped in both vehicles to thirty; then to fifteen.

When the Mercedes was about twenty feet from the stop point, next up for the routine wave and pass-through, Eberle hit his powerful twin spotlights to bathe the white car in brilliant light, causing the immigration officer, in his old-fashioned Teddy Roosevelt peaked hat, to twist his head. Eberle also simultaneously switched on his roof lights and hit the siren button for two short bursts.

The skinny border guard yelled, "What the hell is going on?" and Eberle's loudspeaker countered, "Pull him over, pull him over."

Two immigration officers suddenly darted from around a large van parked at the checkpoint, blocking lanes into the funnel, and motioned the driver of the Mercedes to a parking spot. So far, so good, Eberle thought. It's working! Traffic slowed momentarily and then the steady northward stream picked up again as the border cop angrily waved them on.

Taking a deep breath, Eberle waved a thank-you to the traffic inspector, who shook his head, then shrugged and grinned. Turning in behind the white car, stopping about ten feet back, he kept the powerful spotlights beamed on the Mercedes, usual procedure, usually blinding whoever was in the driver's seat when he or she looked back. But it didn't work with tinted windows. Notifying San Diego that he had made the stop, he lifted the gun off the seat, put it into his holster and climbed out. He nodded to the border patrolmen, who were coming down each side of the car to help if needed; put his hand on the butt of the Smith & Wesson and carefully moved up along the right side of the suspect's vehicle, stopping about two feet behind the right front window. He thought he could hear his heart beating as he tapped on the window, waiting for it to roll down. It did. He said, "Good evening, sir. May I see your license, please? Take it out of your wallet, please."

Hands still on the wheel, thank God, the block-faced driver stared out at him with no expression. His skin looked funny even in the shadows, Eberle thought. Funny color to it. Creepy looking guy. Eyes dull, cold. Then Glen noticed the bottle of tequila exposed on the passenger side. If it was open that alone was a violation.

11

THE WEST GERMAN EMBASSY in the District of Columbia is on Reservoir Road, a multistoried black metal-and-glass building almost in the shape of a wedding cake. Behind it is a classic white mansion, the ambassador's residence. Just before noon His Excellency, a handsome elderly man with snowy hair and held in high regard in Washington, was preparing to lunch with a delegation of businessmen from Frankfurt when he received a call from his first secretary. He listened intently, frowning with disbelief at first, a look that quickly turned to shock and anger.

"Drunken driving in California?"

"Yes, last night."

"What's his status?"

"He's on holiday, pending return to Hamburg. His replacement is already here. You met him a week ago."

"Where is Hermann now?"

"At the consulate in Los Angeles."

"You know, I was always worried about him. This is all highly embarrassing." Klaus Hermann was a leftover staff member from the previous ambassador, departed five months earlier.

"I know, Excellency. But he did do his job. And, Excellency, he is the son of Gerda Hermann."

The ambassador's laugh was caustic. "He could be the son of Kohl, but if caught driving drunk, *out.*"

"Yes, Excellency."

The ambassador said firmly, "You know what to do. Make the proper notifications and tell the consul in Los Angeles that I want Hermann out of the United States by dinner. Instruct him to pay any fines or damages. Take care of everything. *Out by dinner.*"

The first secretary said he'd see to it immediately.

Four o'clock of the same day. "Like some coffee?" Paul McManus was asking Cole Hickel, dressed in civvies—jeans and a light jacket. His face was ravaged, drawn. He'd taken emergency leave. "I must have had ten cups last night, I'm coffee burnt."

You're much more than coffee burnt, McManus thought. Deep in his sleepless eyes was that thinly covered pain and fright that McManus had seen before in missing persons cases at LAPD. Not knowing whether the loved one was dead or alive was that cruel hammer that kept smashing down. A kind of insanity set in and with a man like this bird colonel, accustomed to running the show, the dangers of doing something unwise were many.

"You have something to tell me?" asked the colonel. There was a distracting tiny white pellet of spittle in the left corner of the colonel's lips. At this point he didn't look like a poster Marine.

"Yes, the CHP stopped a white Mercedes early last night at the San Onofre immigration checkpoint. It matched the description of the one that two of my people saw coming out of the parking lot about the time that Ellen may have disappeared."

The colonel sat forward. "Why the hell didn't you call me last night?"

McManus said, "I didn't know until mid-morning. It has taken most of a day for a lot of people to put a lot of things together."

The colonel came out of the chair. "Where is Ellen? Who knows where she is? Where is the goddamn FBI in this . . . ?"

The colonel certainly knew that the FBI had no jurisdiction at the moment. Only if and when ransom was demanded could they enter the case. McManus said quietly, "No one knows where she is. No law enforcement agency knows where she is. But a lot of people are looking for her. Please sit down and let me tell you what we do know."

The colonel slowly dropped back into the chair.

"Okay, follow me. The vehicle was stopped on a possible under influence after an all-points was issued and the driver was identified as being a legitimate staff member of the West German embassy. He was drunk. The CHP supervisor down there notified State Department security in Los Angeles. They called the protocol section in Washington. A little later the West Germans were notified. Everybody toe-danced. But the CHP did the right thing. Under Article I, Section 13, California Code, they detained the vehicle. They had it towed to Santa Ana for prints and a thorough search, turning it over to the Orange County Sheriff. Meanwhile, State's security people in Los Angeles, wishing that this particular West German had never left the District of Columbia, went down to San Onofre in a chopper, collected him, signed for him and took him to the consulate in Los Angeles. They breathed a big sigh of relief and I understand why. Nobody wants to fool with diplomatic immunity—"

"Get to the point!"

"Late this morning the sheriff's team found Ellen's prints on the dashboard of the Mercedes."

The colonel was beginning to breathe in short bursts, as if pumping his lungs up. "What else?"

McManus wondered if the colonel was going to have a heart attack and for the time being decided not to tell some of the "what else." Like a prayer rug and a rubber sheet, fetish magazines, and a batch of fetish photos in the trunk. A short, blood-stained leather whip. Then there was the gun, a Walther P-38. Not a real automatic but one made by a company called MetRep. Their guns looked and felt like the real thing except the barrels were plugged at the firing-pin seat. He also decided, for the time being, not to tell the colonel about the spot of blood on the right hand seat of the Mercedes. Might be Ellen's; might not. In time the colonel would know everything. Not now, he couldn't handle it, McManus

65

thought. One thing, the forensic people in Orange County had the latest equipment and techniques. Better than LAPD or San Francisco by far.

"We don't know too much more at the moment and..." Now was the part that McManus had been dreading for more than an hour, selected words certain to turn the colonel into lava. "...and we might not know too much more for a while—"

"What do you mean?"

McManus took a deep breath. "Klaus Hermann left Los Angeles in the first class section of a Lufthansa 747 at 3:25 today, bound for Frankfurt. He was put aboard by his consul, sent home. He was the third commercial attache at the embassy in Washington and has full diplomatic immunity. Unless he volunteers to return or unless the West German government determines it could step in at a later time and deliver him back here, well, he can't be touched... I'm sure you're aware of diplomatic immunity."

The colonel was stunned, as McManus had anticipated. What little color had been in his face drained out.

"Was he asked about Ellen?"

"I don't know that State asked him anything. I don't know that they were aware that your daughter is missing. I doubt it. It went down fast. It's all happened in less than twenty-four hours from the time Hermann was stopped near San Clemente."

"He's *gone?*"

"That's what State said."

Silence for a moment, dead silence. Then the colonel repeated, "Three twenty-five," as if mulling a price. He swallowed several times, then asked, "Did he say *anything* at all about Ellen before he left?"

It was such a pitiful question that McManus found himself groping for words. "I don't know" was what he decided on. Of course, the German didn't say anything about Ellen.

"Oh?"

It was bad to see this proud tough man down so far. "Colonel, State wasn't notified about the fingerprints until nearly two-thirty. Wheels don't grind all that fast. You know that. By the time they likely called the ambassador, Hermann was already in the air."

The colonel was coming around a little, beginning to try to sort out his thoughts. "Why didn't State call the airport police and have him held for interrogation?"

"It wouldn't be that easy. As I said, he has full diplomatic immunity and you know what that means." McManus opened his palms.

The volcano began to bubble. "Goddamn, no way. No *way* is that Kraut not going to say where my daughter is. They can stick diplomatic immunity up their asses." Color was back in the colonel's face.

McManus said quietly, "The only proof at the moment that she was in that car are those prints."

The colonel slammed his fist on the glass desk top. "Proof enough for me. I want someone to question that son of a bitch the moment he lands in Germany. Now, how do we go about it?"

McManus said, "This kind of thing is brand new to me but I'm guessing you'll have to work with the State Department."

"Those people are gutless, you know that. I flew them a few times in Nam. They're schooled in gutless."

McManus went on, trying to soothe. "I still think State is your best bet, maybe your only bet. Even though she might have been kidnapped, the Justice Department will move very slowly on this one, is my guess. An international thing. They'll let State be point man—"

"Jesus Christ, there's no *time* to move slow. I want that bastard arrested and held for questioning the moment he steps off the plane."

"Colonel, he'll be on West German soil and when that happens you lose ninety-nine percent leverage. But try to raise someone in State protocol, is my advice. There's a duty officer, I'm sure, taking calls at home if not in the office. We had to work with State protocol a couple of times when I was with LAPD."

Cole leaned over toward McManus, placing both hands on the desk. "You know what I'm thinking? I've got friends who have access to fast military aircraft. I can be on the ground in Frankfurt with a gun in my hands when that son of a bitch walks off . . ."

So you're going to set up refueling all the way across the country and over the Atlantic? Get a man-hunt flight cleared? McManus didn't know much about the military or supersonic airplanes but this one didn't sound like it would work. He nodded, though, going along. "I'm sure you could, Colonel, but I'd think that the consequences might not be to your benefit. I'd think that the West Germans would take a very dim view of that, not to mention the Marine Corps. You're a high ranking officer—"

"Well, you can damn well sit there and rationalize all you want but it's my daughter who's missing. Maybe dead? I want to know, dammit. I demand to know. . ."

"I understand, I understand."

"Bullshit."

Cole continued to glare at the only target in sight, then kicked the chair back and almost dove through the door.

Chief McManus sat at his desk a moment longer, knowing that he'd probably be reacting the same way if it was his daughter missing. Seams coming undone. Sadly enough, the toe-dancing hadn't really begun.

Outside, Cole ran across Bridge Road and into the parking lot, almost knocking down a cluster of students.

One yelled after him, "Hey, jackassary. . ."

That night Jennifer kept coming downstairs, the last time to cry in her mother's arms. Skeet was up and down three or four times, saying, in different ways, "Can't we do something to find her?" Cole finally shouted. *"Goddammit,* Skeeter. . ." then went over to hug his only son.

None of them had reckoned with the impact of television. When Ellen's smiling face from a recent photograph flashed on the tube at eleven, Cole pounded the wall.

On Saturday morning, in the highlands above Dana Point about twenty-five miles below the power station at Huntington Beach, two small boys playing the old-fashioned, almost obsolete game of cowboys and Indians discovered a rapidly decomposing nude body in a field of greening foxtails. Terrified, they ran down the slope to tell their father what they'd seen.

———

By late afternoon, about five, in Santa Ana, just about the time sailboats were tacking toward shore off Dana Point, Cole Hickel stood rigidly in the county coroner's work area and with a quick, devastating glance identified what remained of his older daughter.

No autopsy had been performed as yet but the deputy examiner on duty already knew that her neck was broken. Whoever had done that must have been a powerful man, he judged. One blow.

At the same time Orange County sheriff's technicians were making a cast of tire tracks on the narrow rutted dirt road near the spot where the small cowboys and Indians were playing. It was a waste of time, they believed, since the freshest tracks on a road like this seldom belonged to the vehicle that was connected with the crime. This looked to be more a motorbike trail than a standard vehicle route. It just went from one paved east-west road over undeveloped land to another paved east-west road an eighth of a mile away.

"Mutti, Mutti, I swear to you that I did not do it."

It was night in Hamburg. Frau Hermann was still in Alicante. "But did you have her in the car?"

Klaus squirmed on his end of the phone at the university hospital in the Eppendorf district. "Yes."

"I've had four calls from the foreign ministry, one from the ambassador in Washington. He was very angry. He sent you home without knowing about the girl. He has already apologized to the American Secretary of State without knowing any further details. Do you understand what you have done? A girl is dead and her fingerprints were in your car."

"Mutti, she got into the car, and then I don't remember . . . I don't remember, I *swear* it."

"Klaus, you promised me. After the other girls you promised me never to do that again. You promised."

"Mutti, it came over me. That bad thing, that spell. I could not control it. Mutti, come home and get me out."

"I have just talked with Dr. Hoger. He said you are a very sick man and you must stay in Eppendorf for tests."

"But they have me in a locked place, Mutti."

"And maybe that is where you belong, Klaus. Why do you do these things to your mother? Here I am trying to enjoy myself—"

"I did not mean it."

"Oh, Klaus, you have told me that before and it happens once more. You told me that in January with that other student and look what we had to pay."

She hung up, only to call him again in five minutes to tell him he was a bad boy but she still loved him.

Eyes red-rimmed, Phil Chiu was shaking inside as Katta opened the front door. "Come in, Mr. Chiu."

"Phil, please."

"Phil . . ."

She closed the door and called for Cole, who was in the kitchen on the phone.

Chiu said, "I had to see you . . . to talk about this in person . . ."

Katta nodded, waiting for Cole to come out. "Please sit down," she said as they went into the living room.

Cole came in and Katta said, "You remember Phil . . ."

"Sure," Cole said, but he hadn't remembered the man being this tall. Six feet, at least. Maybe the fact that he was slender made him look that tall. Most Orientals he'd met were short. And he was white, not yellow. He shook the extended hand.

Chiu began, "I . . . I . . ." and had to start all over again.

"We understand," Cole said, hoping to end this quickly.

"I don't think you do, sir." He shifted a tense look over to Katta and then back to Cole. "We were very much in love and had even talked about marriage. And children. She wanted three . . ."

Marriage to Phil Chiu? Three children?

Katta said, slowly, carefully, "Ellen didn't share all of her thoughts."

Chiu nodded. "She was afraid to. She thought it needed a lot of time. But I did want you to know that I loved her very much and she loved me . . . and it just needed time."

What he meant, Cole thought, was that her old man didn't approve of Orientals. But who cared about that tonight?

70

Katta's eyes were full. "If she found happiness with you, that's what counts."

Chiu nodded. "Well, that's about all I have to say. We loved each other . . ."

Okay, okay, Cole thought. Please just go. I've got to get down to it. I've got to think about killing.

With First Lieutenant Cole Hickel II, USMC, in the right hand seat as co-pilot, little monkey-browed Mike Goody, good old Goody, aircraft commander, lifted the Bell "Huey" turbine-powered UJ-1E gunship off the Navy carrier deck, crabbing toward the beach and Marble Mountain in a thin September drizzle, start of the monsoons over Vietnam.

Below, the South China Sea was so smooth it looked like mud gruel. Everybody had said that Da Nang, not far over there, was full of rain, smoke, garlic, whores, rice and death. In that order. So it was, they soon discovered.

The Huey had machine guns and rocket pods to fire at Charlie, and back in the deck space, vibrating behind Goody and Cole Hickel, was a green crew chief and a green gunner. First time to Vietnam for them. Well, everybody aboard was first time. They were green gunship men. Everybody was looking over at gray Da Nang.

The squadron's operations officer, Major Phister, had kindly discussed Charlie-land while they were still on the flattop. Twice before Phister had come to Vietnam, first time in '63 for a short advising time. Second time, shot down. He didn't like LBJ very much and said so. The tall Texas asshole either wanted to win a war or didn't. Who knew?

"Now, gentlemen, let me show you something here on this goddamn map. South of here is Hoa Vang district an' then the Song Cau Do river . . . Phong Le bridge, which carries railroad tracks an' Alternate Route One. An' pay attention now if you really want to keep your ass in one piece. *Everything south of the river is pure Viet Cong territory.* Charlie land. Pucker your scared anus when you go that way because Charlie is gonna be shootin' at you. He loves to punch holes with small arms fire, an' bigger, hopin' he'll hit some fuel or fix your rotor. I'll tell you already that this is the shittiest, no-account, no-win LBJ war ever fought . . ."

Cole wrote Katta about that spooky session in the wardroom, then tore the letter up. With new baby Ellen at her nipples, she had enough to think about just watching those guys on the nightly news.

Cole flew a lot with good old Mike Goody—Coley and Mikey —that first tour in Nam, and when they met again at Quantico years later, both majors now, Mike, sitting at the long bar in the O Club eating peanuts and sipping bourbon, said, "Cole, 'member the night we had *the* drunk, the-eeee drunk? Oh, lordee, lordee."

"Never forget it. Wild Turkey and Peppermint Schnapps on the rocks. Snowshoes. Dynamite."

"Hey, we gotta be crazy drink that stuff."

"Classic brake fluid," Cole agreed.

The time they were talking about Cole and Mike had flown groundfire suppression down in Elephant Valley, escorting two medical evacuation choppers. The medevacs brought out eleven dead Marines in body bags, none over twenty, seven of them black. Their bloody balls were stuffed into their mouths like turkey dressing, the corpsmen said. Charlie had done it. VC had done it.

Cole said, "You know, I'd heard about that kind of thing but I'd never quite believed it."

Next morning, skulls compressed from the Snowshoes, guts twanging, eyes like those red antholes in Marble Mountain dust, they put on chest armor and got into their seats under which was nice steel and ceramic lamination. They took their Hueys up, wop-wopping south on more groundfire suppression. Back to Elephant Valley on an assigned mission and shot every VC they could flush. Fourteen certains and seven maybes. Stumbled into a patrol.

"The old Wild Turkey shoot," Cole said, recalling all of it. "You know that was the single worst hangover I ever had in my life and I lost it the very second I saw that first Charlie start to run."

"One helluva shoot that day, huh?" Mike Goody said. "We paid 'em back for those eleven gyrenes with balls in their teeth."

"We did," said Cole.

In time he told Katta about the Wild Turkey shoot. He said that's what "whar" did to you. "Made killing easy. Easier than you'd ever believe."

12

THE PHONE RANG all day on overcast Sunday. Some calls had to be answered. Family, close friends. Katta's mother. Cole's sister from Maine. Mike Goody called. Thomas Paddington called. Also superiors. Commanding generals at El Toro and Pendleton; even the commandant of the Corps, from Washington, a surprise.

Art Hoberman, Cole's skin-and-bones executive officer, a gangling man with a huge Adam's apple, a light colonel, was manning the phone, and about three o'clock stepped in from the kitchen to say, "Another from Washington. A man named Wally. Said you'd remember him."

Cole was on the stairs, bottom step, reading cards of condolence that had been hand-delivered. People from the base. Hoberman's wife was in the living room, talking to Katta. She'd put lunch together from an alp of food sent by pilot's wives and friends. There were enough salads to start a restaurant.

Cole nodded, glad to hear from Wally, following Art back into the kitchen, then suddenly deciding he wanted to be alone to talk to Wally Stonebridge. He said, "Art, mind stepping outside and closing the door?"

Hoberman went on out and Cole said, "Glad you called, Wally," having thought about Wally several times in the last twenty-four hours.

"I can't tell you how sorry I am. My heart goes out. I'm truly stunned by it and I think I know how you feel."

"I'm a real mess, Wally. So are Katta and the kids, of course. But I think I cried myself out last night. I've been a raging ass for four days. Really got drained. Everything got sucked out of me for a while and I still feel like a hollow shell. But I'm better now, I think. My head is better. I don't walk around and break into tears with no control. Of course, I may do it again right now."

"I understand."

"Wally, you know anything about this? Anything at all?"

"Only what I read in the *Post* this morning. They hinted that somebody from the West German embassy might be involved."

"Might be involved? *Is* involved. The only problem is that he's home safe. I'll never sleep another full night on this earth knowing that. I don't think diplomatic immunity was meant to protect a son of a bitch like that guy. We're not talking about rape and murder. We're talking about Ellen. Her fingerprints were in that car. That's enough for me—"

"Don't blame you a bit. But you know the so-called longer view. It's a two-way street. You've served overseas. Who knows, for example, what the Soviet bloc would do if we didn't have some immunity. But there's no question how you feel when it comes down to a personal situation, I realize that . . ."

Cole could feel Wally's reluctance. "I only understand that Ellen was raped and murdered and I want the guy back here in Orange County for trial. Or I'm gonna go over and persuade him to come back."

"Can't blame you feeling that way. If I had a wife and kids I'd feel the same."

"Okay, Wally, a long time ago you told me that you owed me a big one. Now I'd like to start collecting. Beyond that, you're my friend and I need your help. I know it already. I've had two calls from the State Department and those A-holes are scrambling for cover."

There was a snort from the apartment in Georgetown. "As ever," Wally said.

———

"I want to know everything there is to know about one Klaus Gustav Hermann. Everything. Right down to the size of his socks. Right down to whether he eats his eggs scrambled or over-easy. I've got a hunch that these people out here and at State aren't telling me all they know. Not even half. All they do is talk about diplomatic immunity."

"I can't do it officially. You know that," Wally said.

"I know."

There was a pause from Georgetown and Cole thought he heard a small sigh. He ignored it. "All right," said Wally, "I'll get a file together for you but I'll lie in your face if you ever connect me to it."

"Only person I'll tell is Katta. But you could stick hot needles in that Swedish lady, she wouldn't crack."

Wally was silent.

"I've found out in the last four days that she's a helluva lot tougher than I am."

Wally said, with reluctance, "Okay. You've got my home phone. It's safe. Just don't call me at the office."

"Agreed."

"I want to tell you again how deeply sorry I am and that my thoughts are with you and your family."

"Thanks, Wally, we'll need them."

Cole hung up and went back into the living room.

Katta said, "Who was that?"

"Guy I met in Nam. Tell you about him later." She already knew a lot about Wally. A husband usually doesn't get a Navy Cross without the wife knowing why. But in front of Art he didn't want to mention CIA. Nor even the name Wally Stonebridge.

In Georgetown Wally walked away from the phone, now wishing he'd sent a condolence wire and flowers instead of calling. Of all the young females in the whole USA, why did that Kraut son of a bitch have to pick out Cole Hickel's daughter? That was like pissing into a working two-twenty socket. Wally had met the Hickel family. Beautiful little girl, as he remembered. Whole family was good-looking, he remembered. Family-of-the-year type they use for Thanksgiving stories, sitting down for the turkey dinner, all smiles. Now the colonel was going after the German, Wally knew. His thoughts, like Cole's earlier, went back to how he got into this bind with Cole Hickel . . .

13

THE GRAY, HUMID MORNING had begun with a platoon getting shot up: "Robin Hood, Steel City 2–1 is taking fire, 9 o'clock, 500 meters."

"Roger, Robin Hood 4–11 in hot with rockets. You copy 4–12?"

"Robin Hood 4–10, this is 4–11, I'm in shootin', cover me."

"Roger, 4–11."

Thomas Paddington, the crew chief for Cole Hickel, had painted "Paddy's Punch," which wasn't much of a name for a killer ship, in white on the chopper's belly, and Paddy's Punch 4–11 Huey whirred out over some rice paddies and then back over the jungle.

On this second Vietnam tour, not really wanted since he'd started a family, Cole was now a captain, aircraft commander, with a first lieutenant named Flexner in the right hand seat. Mike Goody was safely back at Camp Lejeune.

Rulak was the gunner this time. They were up there chattering bullets and rockets, and then the VC quieted down and sneaked off into the green tangles. Thirty minutes later 4–11, voice call of the day, refueled and rearmed hot and lifted off again, going up to three thousand feet just in time to hear a jittery Avalanche, a major, Direct Air Support Control, say that a chopper was down with VIPs on board; give the coordinates.

Cole checked his map. They were in the area and reported in. Four-ten was still on the ground, taking on fuel and rockets.

Avalanche said, ". . . there's a congressman plus two CIA riding it. Proceed to crash site and inspect same."

Flexner said, "Wouldn't you know we'd have been away from here in another five minutes."

No landing zone near. No troops near. Whoever piloted that crashed Huey should have his head examined if it was still on his shoulders. With a congressman on board, plus CIA, why the hell wasn't he where Charlie couldn't reach him? "Damn the luck," said Cole. This was a mission for an empty medevac, a *slick,* a troop carrier, not a gunship.

Flexner just cast his eyeballs up. "Maybe the goddamn thing exploded an' no one's left. We could get shot down jus' tryin' to take a look."

"I know, I know," said Cole, and then called Avalanche to say, "We're going in to try and find him." He was ticked and nervous.

Avalanche had changed voices. A light colonel was on the air now. "That's not good enough, 4–11. Congressman James Stafford, of Mississippi, is on that aircraft, or what's left of it. Now, I want you to land and bring him out, dead or alive. Understand?"

Was he insane? Gunships, with all their armaments, were too heavy to do this kind of work. Avalanche *was* insane, announcing this in the clear, not in brevity code. Charlie would love to get his hands on a U.S. congressman.

Out of one side of his mouth, Cole clipped a Roger to the Avalanche light colonel and then the other side said, "Sheeee-it . . ."

Smoke was soon below, curling up through the trees as Cole said to Flexner, "There he is," leaning to check out the chart, see if the coordinates were right.

"Okay, let's take a look," he said, telling Paddington and Rulak to hang on; watch for ground fire. He pulled the plug and the Huey dove three thousand feet for a sideways glance through the branches.

Flexner murmured, "Oh, Jesus," as the bottom dropped out. A pile of green spaghetti down there.

Cole was busy flying, expecting to hear VC bullets bong off the fuselage.

"Don't see a soul," said Flexner as Cole swooped up again. "He just flopped and burned."

Cole nodded. "Avalanche, this is Robin Hood 4-11. We're on top of that congressman and don't see a soul."

Avalanche said stubbornly, "4-11, I repeat. Land for on-site inspection. Dammit, land for on-site inspection."

Where? Where? Cole said to Avalanche without saying it.

Just then 4-10 came wopping into sight, fully fueled and armed. Baily could at least cover them. Or try.

"Roger," Cole said to Avalanche. Nerve of the bastard sitting back there safe as a desk general. Nothing but a postage stamp clearing a quarter mile away. Chopper graveyard. A lot of times you had to hop and skip these things on their skids just to get them off the ground. Fully-loaded gunships just didn't go up like they were in an elevator.

"Avalanche, I just hope Charlie isn't down here under us."

"I hope so, too, buddy," said the light colonel metallically.

Paddy's Punch curled up and away while Cole talked to Baily over in 4-10. Both Hueys went up to twenty-five hundred, wopping in orbit. "Keep 'em off our ass, for God's sakes," said Cole, and circled out to fire his rockets, lighten the load a little bit.

"Roger, and good luck," said Baily. He wasn't the best chopper pilot in town but he had guts.

Cole went down fast toward the oval clearing that appeared to slope gradually to the south, thinking about Katta and baby Ellen. He glanced over at Flexner. His co-pilot was lard-white. So was he, he knew.

Robin Hood 4-11 sat down and everybody aboard waited for the mortars to begin, the chatter of machine guns. He was ready to feed fuel in and lift off at the first thud of one of those heavy red rounds from a Russian-made mortar. But there was only engine-sound and the *whump-whump* of the main rotor, noisy enough.

They sat for two or three minutes, looking out, looking around, awaiting attack from the jungle, and then Cole nodded.

Thomas Paddington, who'd lived through thirteen months of action up in the Hue-Phu Bai area on his first trip, almost as big as an NFL lineman, shiny tarred as most, always kept a sub-machine gun and a personal canvas bag of grenades back in the cargo space. "Jus' let one of those lil' fuckers mess with me . . ." That was just fine with Cole. As long as it didn't weigh too much, bring anything aboard that would spit. He loved big black Paddy.

Cole said he was going to take Paddington and look.

Flexner said, "Shouldn't I be doing this?" The aircraft commander was not supposed to leave his machine.

"Nope, you sit tight," said Cole, trying not to act heroic. Paddington and Rulak should go, according to rules. But with a congressman involved, rules bent. He said to Paddington, "Bring that burp gun an' come on." What made Paddington so nice to have around anywhere were his muscles. He did weights back at base.

Four-ten was now orbiting above them, and Cole told Flexner to send him over where the chopper was down. That's where they might need some firepower.

Cole saw that Flexner and Rulak were staring as if they might never see him again. He said, "Hell, just keep this thing in flying condition," afraid he was sounding heroic again . . . off into the wild wild jungle stuff.

Standing there with his burp gun, a black hulk, crisp goatee beneath shining teeth, Paddington even grinned. "Just like the movies," he called to Rulak. "Give you half my medal."

They moved off in the direction of the crashed Huey, not once seeing Charlie, and in twenty minutes found it, smoldering mangled metal, sickening sight for anyone who rode choppers. There was a civilian thrown clear, babbling and in a state of shock. His left foot was crushed and who knew what else might be busted up inside him. Another body was on the ground and five were still in the burnt chopper, or what was left of it, over on its side.

Thomas Paddington picked up what they agreed was the congressman from Mississippi, or what was left of him. Pretty well charred. Flesh was already rubbing off on Paddy's shoulders in black and red ribbons before he took a step.

Cole piggy-backed the babbling survivor. Someone else could go in with body bags for the rest of them. Maybe drop a squad to hack out a landing zone closer to the crash site.

Arms and legs trembling, Cole floundered through the vines and trees behind Paddington and his burden. How much did this guy weigh? Hundred-ninety? Two hundred? Felt like double that toward the end. It took them thirty-five minutes to get back. Cole had put his passenger down once—he had to rest—and the man yelped in pain as he was lifted up again.

Finally Cole sat, exhausted, in the right hand seat as Flexner lifted up from the oval, the Huey lurching from the extra weight, and headed home. It took three or four hours to discover they'd left the congressman behind. The corpse that Thomas Paddington brought out belonged to the CIA. Cole had selected the oldest looking civilian but it turned out that the late Congressman Stafford, of Biloxi, was only in his thirties. Well, hell, they'd tried, Cole told the CO, who agreed. It was just another fucked-up part of this fucked-up war . . .

Two days later Cole got a message from a doctor at the base hospital that his patient, a Mr. Stonebridge, would like to see Captain Hickel if possible. Cole wasn't flying that afternoon and went off to see Mr. Stonebridge, whose left extremity was under one of those little white tents shaped like a pyramid.

The patient said, "I'm Wally Stonebridge and I'd like to shake your hand for saving my life." He was CIA, Cole already knew.

Cole said, "We were glad to do it."

"I understand you carried me out."

"Yeh. Mind if I ask you how much you weigh?"

Stonebridge allowed a smile. "When we left Ky Ha, I think about a hundred-fifty. In the States, usually weigh about one-sixty."

Cole nodded. "By the time we got you back to the chopper I swear you felt like three hundred. How's the foot?"

Stonebridge shook his head. "Don't have it anymore. I'll be walking on high-tech plastic. But I'm lucky to be alive and know it, thanks to you."

They talked a few more times before Wallace Stonebridge was flown back to the States and the last time Wally said, "Cole, I owe you one. If you ever want to collect, let me know. I'll try my best."

Collection time now.

14

MEMORIAL SERVICES for Ellen Trenholm Hickel were held in the small base chapel on Tuesday morning, filling it to standing room only; then flowing outside. Mostly Marines, some in their dress blues, some in flight suits, and dependents. They stood as the chaplain talked about how cruel life could be, how sometimes superhuman strength was required of those left behind. How Ellen was in peace, in the loving arms of God. Amen.

Mostly the same things that Chaplain Coombes or some other sky pilot before had said when a hearse was needed at Tustin. The Hickels held hands. They were dry-eyed. Phil Chiu sat with them. Even Skeet was dry-eyed. They were all spent, drained out mentally, wrung out physically. No longer did they have the stamina to cry at hearing words. Earlier Jennifer had said, "I don't think Ellen would want it to last too long. She didn't like church much anyway." They smiled a little about that, and it hurt.

Commander Coombes went on and on in a somber tone, finally ending the service with a prayer. Then the daughter of a sergeant in HMH-462, heavy lifters, sang "Memory" from the Webber musical in a clear sweet voice and the Hickels came apart again, Cole's whole body shaking. The third and perhaps cruelest punishment for the family, but one which they all understood, came immediately after they walked out into the sunlight. Twenty-one choppers of the air group thundered across the chapel at low level and then four El Toro jets, F/A-18s, swept over, one splitting off to rise toward the sun as far as the eye could see.

When the man from the mortuary had asked Cole and Katta whether or not they wanted Ellen cremated, Cole had quickly answered for both of them, "No, she's suffered enough already."

So she was buried an hour later in a plot with a sea view behind the town of Corona del Mar, south of all the fancy yachts at Newport Beach.

The hushed-tone mortuary man, who was making Cole grit his teeth, offered to drive them all back to Oakwood Terrace in his stretch limo but Cole declined. Art Hoberman had brought the family Dodge wagon over, parking it at the cemetery. The sooner they shed some of the reminders, the better, said Katta. They said goodbye to Phil Chiu, Katta saying they'd keep in touch, and ducked the offer of air group wives to have a potluck lunch. "Please, let's try to close the door," Katta said.

She was right, Cole knew. To an extent. That extent did not include the German, who was free to do what he pleased. Now it was time to concentrate totally on that son of a bitch.

On the way home Katta said abruptly, "Let's go away for a week or two," turning in the seat to look at the children. "Wouldn't you like that?" Immediately they said they would.

Cole looked at Katta. "What?" Was she out of her mind?

"How about Maui? We've never been there," said Jennifer.

They'd gone to the big island and to Kauai when they were stationed at Kaneohe on Oahu. Never to Maui.

Cole said, "We'll talk about it later."

Katta frowned at him. "Okay," and there was deep silence the rest of the way home.

At Oakwood Cole parked in the driveway and Katta said, "Stay out here a moment with me, Cole," as Jennifer and Skeet went on into the house.

Mind already made up, Cole sat against the front fender. "I've got things to take care of."

Katta nodded. "Like the children, I hope. They've been under as much pressure as you and I."

Cole took a deep breath. "I tell you, my mind isn't on Maui. My mind is on a place called Hamburg. Look, I can't sit on the goddamn beach and think about what was done to Ellen. Jesus Christ, Kot, I've got to do something about him. Don't you understand that?"

"That's you. But Jennifer and Skeet would like to think about something else. I guess I would too. We need a break. You, darling, more than any of us. If you don't come off it for a while you'll go nuts."

Cole took another deep breath, sensing defeat. "Why don't we wait? End of the summer?"

Katta said gently, "Why don't we just do it now? I know the kids won't want pitying looks in school. I should think you wouldn't want to be a tragic figure around the base for a while."

"Katta, Jesus Christ . . ."

More forcefully she said, "I've been thinking about this for two days. I'll take the children and go somewhere if you won't go. But I think it's bad if you don't go. You owe it to them. You owe it to me. We need some healing, all of us. Don't you understand that?"

Cole looked at his wife for a long minute. "All right. *But* just for a week. No more."

Katta nodded. "A week. Can we leave as soon as possible?"

Cole nodded reluctantly.

"Go commercial?"

Cole shook his head. "Get a MAC flight out of Norton to Hickam, then take commercial over to Maui."

"Can all of us fly MAC?" There'd been, after all, new restricting regulations for dependents on vacations.

"Yeh. There's a nonstop out of Norton to Hickam. We just can't fly over the continent."

"Will you check this afternoon?"

He nodded, unhappily. But he knew he had to go along. For her sanity, and the kids. But not, damn it, for long.

Art Hoberman had assigned a corporal to stand phone watch

during the funeral and now she had a list of calls, one of which was from Wally Stonebridge. Another was from Nyall Kinnick of the office of the Assistant Secretary of State for European Affairs. Cole remembered the name from somewhere.

Due to a time difference Cole couldn't call Wally until about five, Pacific clocks, at which hour Wally would likely be back in his apartment. But he did place a call to the 634 number at the State Department. Kinnick came on, introduced himself. "Colonel, I'd like to take the redeye out tonight and meet with you and Mrs. Hickel tomorrow to discuss a mutual problem." The voice sounded very New England.

Cole was almost curt. "It'll have to be soon. We're taking off for a week. May I ask what the subject will be?"

"Klaus Hermann," said Nyall Kinnick in a Cambridge-Quincy-Peabody accent. "It'll take me a little while to get from Los Angeles to Orange County. Will two o'clock be all right? On the base, in your office?"

"Two o'clock will be fine but I'm on leave, Mr. Kinnick. I'd prefer to meet you in my home. I live at—"

"I have your address."

Well, now . . . "See you tomorrow then."

Maybe it was the New Englandese that rubbed him wrong . . . then suddenly it struck him who Nyall Kinnick was. No wonder. The face and name came together. TV briefing officer for State several years back. The man who stood up every day and told reporters how the USA felt about the rest of the world. At every crisis he'd been there reading statements and answering questions. Smooth Nyall Kinnick.

Walking into the dining room where Katta was huddled with the children, he said, "Nyall Kinnick from State will be here tomorrow. Remember him, the fancy Dan who did the TV briefings? He's coming at two."

Katta's eyes were wary. "To tell us what?"

"To hold our hands, I'd guess."

Katta slowly turned her chin back toward the yellow tablet. "I'll allow you a new bikini, Jennifer. Your trunks are still okay, Skeet . . ."

Cole walked back to the kitchen to finish the calls and contact MAC at Norton. Two were from the press, which he ignored; another from the CBS station in Los Angeles, which he also ignored. Both reporters and camera people had showed up at the base for the memorial but the military police corralled them, keeping them at a distance.

At five Cole dialed Wally in Georgetown. "I just fixed myself a Manhattan with two cherries," Wally said.

"I remember. You're the only one left on earth who still drinks Manhattans."

"That's me. How you doing?"

"We survived. Ellen is in a pretty place up on a hillside with an ocean view. I doubt we'll ever leave here. I feel very close to her, Wally. That may sound morbid to you but it's the truth."

Wally let that one alone. "I'm going to be sending something to you. Copied them myself in the local stationery store and'll mail them on the way to work tomorrow."

"Hold 'em for a week. We're going to Maui day after tomorrow..."

"Just the thing."

"But give me a little taste of that bastard. I can't wait."

"Right. Let's see here... born in 1943 to a very rich shipbuilding family, old Hamburgians. Money and land dates back to the German confederation in the early eighteen-hundreds. They had an estate in exclusive Harvestehude with gardens going right down to the water; they had a summer home in Blankenese on the Elbe. You didn't build ships for Hitler unless you were a Nazi, so the Hermanns were Nazis. The old man didn't stand trial at Nuremburg or anything like that but he was a party member. Mother Gerda, second wife of Ernst, married him when she was nineteen, took baby Klaus to Sweden, place called Karlstrand, late in 1943 when things began to fall apart. Stayed there in safety until 1946. Three stepchildren by the first wife were killed. Youngest in the firestorm of '43. Other two at sea. One on the *Bismarck*. Not long after VE day Papa Ernst got some contracts from Uncle Sam, wouldn't you know, to help clean up the Elbe. And before he died in '55 Hermann Werft was damn near as big as it was before the war. Gerda holds the purse strings now, and Klaus is the rotten apple of her sharp Bavarian eyes. She's as tough as a pair of old *lederhosen* and no one wants to tangle with her. She's sixty-five."

"That doesn't tell me a helluva lot about *him.*"

Wally went on. "Gerda also has deep and wide connections in the Bundestag, even into the Chancellor's office. Klaus wanted to live for a while in the United States, and *voila,* an embassy job opened up. Answering correspondence mostly. Third assistant commercial attaché. All he did was shuffle papers. Didn't meet the public. They put a bag over him. He isn't the classiest looking guy, it says here. Has some rare type of alopecia . . ."

"What's that?"

"No hair, no whiskers. His skin is as smooth as a coat of fresh paint, kind of light peach-colored. He was born without hair and wore a wig all through childhood. School kids no doubt laughed at him."

"I'm heartbroken."

"Never been married. Girls don't usually fall for billiard balls. He likes to play the violin, likes to oil paint and sometimes sails small boats in *die Aufen Alster—*"

"What's that?"

"Lake in the middle of Hamburg."

Cole had had a mental picture of a big German butcher with hamhock hands. Violin player? Painter? "You get the right guy, Wally?"

"Yep. Lonely guy, I'd say. Kinko in the sex department, as you might expect. Very kinko."

"Specifics?"

"I don't have the details. Like I say, it's no surprise . . . some weird streaks run through most of these rich old Europischer families. Take a look at the Hohenzollerns some day."

Cole shook his head. "Violin player?"

"I'm just skimming for you. I don't think today is a good time for all this and on second thought wish I hadn't called you. You'll have it all and more when you get back from Maui."

Cole thanked Wally for all the work, then added. "Had an interesting call today from Nyall Kinnick."

———

"State," said Wally instantly. "One of the glamor boys."

"I guess. Flying out tonight. Wants to see us tomorrow."

"Take my advice and hold your temper. Won't be easy. Nyall Kinnick and the lot of those career diplomats have an annoying mind-set. By my lights they're schooled in appeasement."

"All right, I'll try my best not to throw his ass through the front window."

"Do, and, hey, try to have some fun in Maui. Wish I could come and sit in the sand with you. Never been there, they whisk me through Honolulu every time."

"Wish you could, too. I need your advice."

"I'm not sure you do. You may need Nyall Kinnick's more than mine. Take care."

Both Katta and Cole liked to sleep in a flow of cold fresh air. Tustin seldom provided any real cold but it was cool a lot of the time at night. So now both wide windows of the master bedroom were open and from far off they could hear freeway whine. A light wind was carrying it westward into the tract. They'd been in bed about ten minutes, both thinking about the day. Neither had spoken. Finally, Katta said, "Wally Stonebridge called you again today, didn't he?"

"Uh huh."

Her warmth was close against him, her cheek was touching his right shoulder. His left fingers caressed her back, moving slowly upward from her buttocks.

"What about?"

"To tell me something about Klaus Hermann. I asked him to find out."

"Why? I'm not sure I want to know."

The hand stopped moving. "Because I don't think he'll ever be brought back here for trial."

"And?"

"We have to deal with that, Katta. That's what I was trying to tell you this afternoon."

After a silence she said, "And I was trying to tell you that we just buried Ellen and now we need time to put the pieces together.

Our pieces. Let's just think about going to Maui. Nothing else. I wish you'd told that man from State that we didn't want to talk to him until later."

"But I do want to talk to him."

Silence, an abrupt shudder that ranged along Katta's body. "Cole, make love to me. Do it all night. I have to get lost."

The urgency in her voice pushed Klaus Hermann away. Cole's hand went lower to reach the hem of her cotton nightgown. Within moments he discovered that he needed Katta's body just as she needed his. This healing need had not occurred to him.

Dr. Hoger said, "As I was saying yesterday I'm your doctor, not a police official, and anything you tell me will stay in this room. I'm not taking notes, as you see; I'm not taping you. Whatever you did over there, I'm only interested in helping you." Thick-lensed glasses magnified and intensified his gray eyes. Probing, set in a small sallow face dominated by a black brush of mustache. There was an oval of baldness on his head. No matter how he looked, Dr. Franz Hoger was the best psychiatrist in Hamburg and probably one of the best in Europe.

Klaus thought for a moment. "Nothing happened over there."

Dr. Hoger nodded. "Well, let's talk about it again anyway. You were walking along toward the parking lot at that university and began to talk to this pretty girl . . ."

Klaus nodded. He was comfortable in a deep chair across from Dr. Hoger. Living green plants were all around them. There was a soothing, friendly atmosphere in the office.

Outside in the waiting room Stefan Noll was reading the latest issue of *Stern,* pages turned to an article on hunting in New Zealand. It was morning in Hamburg, 9:15, and Klaus was Hoger's first patient.

"I forgot to ask you yesterday, why a university? Why did you visit there instead of Disneyland, where you told your mother you had visited?"

"I always do when I'm near one. I like to look at the architecture. I visit the libraries. You know I graduated from Heidelberg."

"I thought it was Stuttgart."

"I attended Heidelberg but graduated from Stuttgart. I keep forgetting that. I majored in music."

"And so you met this pretty girl while you were walking along toward the parking lot . . ."

"And we began to talk."

"Just like that?"

"Just like that. I told her I was an official of the Deutsche embassy in Washington, on holiday, seeing her country. Then she told me what she was doing and by that time we had reached my automobile. She admired it and I asked her if she wanted to take a ride. She said she did and off we went."

Hoger's eyes read Klaus Hermann's face like a sensor can read fire. And it didn't take a skilled therapist to know this miserable, hopeless creature was lying. "Where?"

"We just rode all around near the university. She was like a tour guide for me."

"Just rode around. You didn't stop anywhere."

"No. After an hour sight-seeing I took her back to the university."

"And you didn't harm her?"

"I did not."

"You didn't touch her?"

"No, I did not."

Dr. Hoger tapped his polished fingernails on the glass coffeetable top that separated him from his patient. "Well, you haven't changed your story to me."

Klaus smiled widely. He always looked best when he was smiling, almost perfect white teeth against the Aztec skin.

"But you told your mother something different, Klaus, as I mentioned yesterday . . . that you couldn't remember anything and that you'd had one of your spells."

Klaus kept on smiling widely. "I remember now and the spell I was talking about had happened the week before in Hollywood. I was confused."

"Oh?"

"Yes," Klaus said, positively radiant.

"'We've talked a lot about those spells, as you call them. Ah, are

---

they any more intense now? This one that you had the week before, was it a bad one?"

"No, I don't think so. I didn't break anything at that place."

"Anything? You mean like a table or chair?"

Klaus nodded.

"You've told me before but tell me again, Klaus, during one of these periods of high stress where you lose control, and then seem to lose memory, have you ever hurt anybody?"

"Only once, as I told you, that I know about . . ."

"That you know about. Where?"

"Here. In Wandsbek. That television actress."

Dr. Hoger nodded. "Yes, you did tell me about her. You broke her shoulder and arm."

"Yes." Klaus was not smiling now.

"And when did that occur?"

"Four years ago."

"Why?"

Klaus shrugged. "She was whipping me and I lost control. Don't you remember?"

"Yes. That was when your mother sent you to me." Dr. Hoger rocked back in his leather chair, gazing at the son of Gerda Hermann, one of the most interesting patients he had ever had. "Klaus, are you quite certain that you didn't have one of your spells with that girl in California, and suffered loss of memory as well?"

"No, *no.*"

Dr. Hoger stayed in his rocked-back position studying Klaus Hermann with those magnified eyes. "Klaus, let us cut the bullshit. You are a highly intelligent, talented man, and the only way I can help you is for you to tell me the whole truth. What happened with that girl in California? Did you have one of your spells, and break more than an arm and a shoulder?"

Klaus sat looking back at him, his face revealing nothing of what he felt . . .

15

COLE HEADED OFF THE BASE, having gone over a few last minute priorities with Art Hoberman, who would run the group for the next two weeks. No major exercises were scheduled down at Pendleton; the squadrons all had capable commanders. Air Group Commander was a paper shuffling job anyway.

Coming to Red Hill, he took a sharp right and aimed the antique car into midtown Tustin and the Orange County Public Library at Centennial and Main in Civic Center. He wanted some special reading material to take to Maui. Oh, yes, he'd hide it from Katta and the kids, if he could. But the library had only one book on Hamburg and that was mainly pictures with brief English and German text. But midway through it was a color plate of a huge shipyard with cranes, scaffolding and half-completed hulls. The German caption said, "Schiffsneubauten in der Hermann Werft."

He studied it a moment, then turned to the plate text, scanning down to ". . . second largest of the five big shipyards on the Elbe is Hermann Werft." It proved Wally was on the right track. The size of the yard indicated that Gerda Hermann probably called in a lot of favors on the Federal Republic.

The Tustin library was of little help when he asked for something on diplomatic immunity. "You'll have to go to Santa Ana Law Library for that," the reference desk said.

Back in the antique car, he scooted back along Red Hill, headed for home. Katta had said to try and forget the German for now. How? Slick-skinned peachy Klaus Hermann would be riding along in the next seat, standing at the next stop sign, driving the car just ahead. If it wasn't Hermann, it would be Ellen. Or rather it couldn't be Ellen so long as there was the murdering, raping Hermann.

". . . plays a violin." Paints pictures.

Nyall Kinnick pushed the button at almost precisely two o'clock. Chimes rang and there he was, holding an expensive briefcase. High forehead and fine, thinning ivory hair. Almost as tall as Cole. Shoes gleaming. Right out of Central Casting, the way he'd always looked on TV. Crease in his pants was sharp, flawless, a knot in his silver-and-gray silk tie, set off by white collar wings. He looked like a *Gentleman's Quarterly* ad. Fiftyish, probably. Yale or Harvard? Kinnick said, "Colonel Hickel?" His gaze was immediately one of assessment.

Cole nodded, asking him to come in, please. "I'll call Katta down."

Kinnick said, "I can't tell you how extremely sorry all of us are, and the Secretary asked me personally to extend his deepest regrets. It's a terrible, shocking thing that has happened to your family."

"Thank you. Let's go into the living room." He showed the way, calling upstairs to tell Katta that Kinnick was there.

Skeet was off somewhere; Jennifer was up in the guest room ironing things to take to Maui.

Kinnick's pale eyes took in the room. "You have some nice pieces in here."

Yes, they were. "Mostly hand-me-downs from my parents." Fine antiques from all over the world.

"Your father was an admiral, wasn't he? World War II hero?"

"Yes."

Katta came in, looking cool, composed. She always made a good entrance, Cole thought. She took Kinnick's hand so briefly that he probably wasn't even sure she'd touched it. He repeated the condolences, including the Secretary of State's personal regrets. Katta just nodded. "Please sit down, Mr. Kinnick."

Cole and Katta waited for Kinnick to speak. It wasn't the time to discuss weather in Washington or Tustin. No chitty-chatty was wanted this afternoon.

"Colonel and Mrs. Hickel, this tragedy has placed us all in a very delicate situation."

Really, now? thought Cole. *Us?*

". . . and we hope, your government and mine, that it can be resolved without becoming a media event. May I say that all of us in the Secretary's office are extremely grateful for the remarkable restraint both of you have shown so far. Our relations with the West German government are extremely good, and we do have a lot at stake there, as you of course well know, Colonel. Thousands of troops stationed there. Air bases, missile launch sites . . ."

Cole and Katta sat deadpan.

". . . and when such incidents occur, on either side, there is a strain and we make an all-out effort to contain the damage—"

"What's the damage to the West German government in this one?" Cole asked.

"Great embarrassment internationally. The nature of what may have happened. Your rank in the military. . ."

"Oh?"

Katta said coldly, "What *did* happen?"

Kinnick nodded and shifted his shoulders in the large wing-back and lowered his voice as if afraid of being taped. "Colonel and Mrs. Hickel, I cannot tell you this officially but I am telling you confidentially that both the West German chancellor and the foreign minister have conveyed to our secretary their deepest and most sincere sympathies to you and your family members."

"Why can't *you* tell us officially and non-confidentially?" Cole said.

"Because that would be an admission on the part of the West German government that Klaus Hermann is guilty, even before an investigation."

"He's guilty of rape and murder," Katta said with such ferocity that it momentarily startled Kinnick.

Cole said, "You're aware that her fingerprints were found in his car."

"Obviously, he has some explaining to do—"

"One helluva lot, Mr. Kinnick," said Cole. "And we want him back here for questioning. The fact that he ran home within forty-eight hours of Ellen's disappearance speaks for itself. Does anyone in Washington actually think Ellen willingly got into his car?"

"Well, in confidence, Colonel and Mrs. Hickel, the people at the embassy consider Klaus Hermann unstable. They've been worried about him for quite a while—"

"Why didn't they send him home when they started to worry?"

"I can't answer that, colonel. But I can tell you that the new ambassador is a man of integrity. He was also the West German ambassador nine years ago."

"I want answers," said Cole.

"We've asked Justice to contact every agency out here to give us as much information as possible—"

"You do that. Get all the information you can," said Cole. "Meanwhile, we're going to have the county make a request to your boss, an official request, to have Klaus Hermann returned here for questioning. Flat-ass extradition. And as much as I resent the press for what they did to us in Nam, I'll use them for a lever if there's no action."

"Which is partly why I'm here, colonel. To persuade you not to do anything of the sort, at least not until the matter can be thoroughly investigated. You already know, I'm sure, that the West German government can refuse any such request, and to be very honest may well do so. Diplomatic immunity is a keystone of behavior between countries—"

"Refuse the request because of Gerda Hermann?" Cole asked.

Kinnick's pale eyes flickered. "You know about her?"

"A little."

"I deal with the West Germans every day and I can assure you that Gerda Hermann will not play a decisive role in this—"

98

"Katta and I really couldn't care less about who plays what role. We just want that man returned to the United States to stand trial in the courts here in this county."

"Conceivably that could happen. After investigation, of course, and hearings." Kinnick cocked his head slightly. "But suppose it doesn't happen?"

Cole said, "Well, we'll probably take some action and do what is necessary to throw gasoline on what could be a pretty messy situation with a former unstable member of a friendly foreign embassy."

Kinnick frowned, cocking his head the other way, sizing Cole up in earnest. "That sounds vaguely like a threat."

Katta got right into it. "Nothing at all vague about it, Mr. Kinnick. That is exactly what my husband and I will do."

Kinnick responded as if he hadn't heard her. "Colonel, I talked to the commandant yesterday morning and he said you were one of the brightest officers in the Marine Corps. He remembers you from when you flew the presidential helicopter a while back. He said you had great potential for flag rank . . ."

Cole moved up to the edge of the sofa, muscles in his jaw working. "Hey, wait a minute. *That* sounds not so vaguely like blackmail. And as for the commandant, I'll make bet he'd never be any part of a game you people want to play. I'll have a star pinned on me if and when I'm ready for it."

Kinnick nodded. "The general was just making an observation. A very accurate one, I'm sure."

The nerve of the bastard to call the commandant. "Let's don't get what happened to Ellen mixed up with my career. Okay?"

After a beat Kinnick said, "Let me ask you a question. What would satisfy . . ." He paused, thought a moment and started all over . . . "For the moment, just for the moment, would an account of that evening, a deposition from Herr Hermann delay your request for his return? Our relations with the embassy officials, with the ambassador himself, are such that we might even be able to have him make his deposition under a lie detector. I can't promise that, but it may be possible . . ."

Cole looked over at Katta and read in her eyes that she was

noncommittal. He looked back at Kinnick. "We won't do anything until we get back from Maui. If you have a deposition by then, we'll read it."

Katta added, "With great interest, Mr. Kinnick."

He stood. "All right, that's the way we'll do it for the time being. I'll send it here, providing I can get the other party to cooperate. I'll call you two weeks from Friday. I hope you enjoy Hawaii."

"Sure," Cole murmured.

Katta stayed seated. "Goodbye, Mr. Kinnick."

Cole showed him to the door.

When Cole returned to the living room he said, "You know he's setting us up. He'll weasel us."

"Can he do it?"

"Not unless we allow it."

16

TWO HOURS out over the Pacific the MAC C-141 was treading along smoothly at thirty-four thousand feet, both Katta and Jennifer were asleep, Skeet was trying to figure out Satanix, a bedeviling new game something like Scrabble, letters on rotating rings instead of on a board. For this military flight to Hickam there were sixty seats. Strapped behind them were two large cargo containers bound for Guam. MAC flights always carried freight, which took precedence over passengers. On occasion not more than ten were aboard, sometimes only four or five. But the fare was right. Ten dollars.

Last week's havoc was on Katta's face, even in deep sleep, though few except Cole would have caught it. Under her eyes was dark; her skin was tired. She was curled up against the window, pillow providing a white foreground for the light blue backdrop of sky. Katta was aging slowly, actually growing more lovely. When she awakened she smiled sleepily, moved against him and took his hand.

"Still got two hours to go but this bird is gettin' lighter every minute. Burnin' that good kerosene." Soon, they'd be going downhill.

After shaking off the drowse she sat bolt upright, looking across his body. Skeet had joined Jennifer in sleep, curled into a tight ball.

She stared at them for a moment. "I hope I never again take them for granted. I sometimes did with Ellen . . ."

"Hey, none of that," Cole said.

A few minutes after arrival Jennifer, looking down the green lawn from the condo porch toward the beach and ocean, said, "Ellen would have loved this . . ."

Cole and Katta exchanged hopeless glances. Quietly Katta said, "Yes, she would have. Well, what about changing and hitting the sand." Which Skeeter was already doing.

Through a friend of a friend of the general's they were staying at the condo near the Kaanapali for free. Four hundred feet from the Pacific with hibiscus showing reds and yellows in front of the porch. Palm fronds shimmied on the edge of the beach and out in the water a baker's dozen wind-surfers scooted across wave-tops like multicolored butterflies.

"Yeh," said Cole absently, thinking about what McManus and Louderholt might have learned; whether or not the Germans had agreed to a deposition.

Lugging beach chairs and towels and a thermo bag of cold drinks, they marched to the sands, Cole dropping his load to spring off and splash through the light breakers. He swam out several hundred yards and then came back shoreward, meeting Katta at about half that distance. She said, "Isn't this great?"

He spurted water and said it was, not meaning it.

They treaded for a little while and then went back to the beach and flopped down.

Jennifer was already into her paperback, and Katta got out her needlepoint and Cole returned to *Red October*. He'd left it with the *E. S. Politovsky* doomed, her core melting down, and the *USS Pogy* listening to her death rattles. It was the most exciting part of the book yet Cole found himself lifting his eyes seaward and thinking about Klaus Hermann.

That night, he eased off Katta after making love to her, rolled on his back and cupped his hands behind his head, staring up at the ceiling and thinking of Hermann rather than the exciting woman beside him.

All the sunshine and warm wind and ocean and guitars and pine-apple drinks at sundown stayed in place but they still talked about Ellen, coming on to her suddenly, thinking how much she would have enjoyed all this. Finally, on the third afternoon, Cole said, "We should go home," and even the kids agreed. Katta nodded. They were all worn down by Ellen's absence, or maybe it was her presence, finding it increasingly more difficult to speak of her without choking, feeling guilty to be here while she was there . . .

Though he was on Cole's mind most of the waking hours, Klaus Hermann wasn't mentioned until the last afternoon, number four, when Cole and Katta were on the beach in front of the Kaanapali. Jennifer and Skeet had gone into Lahaina. They seemed much closer than before, and Jennifer wasn't putting him down the way she sometimes did.

Katta said, "Suppose the Germans refuse to extradite him?"

Cole took in the horizon and held on it, knowing exactly what he wanted to say to Katta but not sure he wanted to say it just now. Maybe it was too soon. Yet he'd never made a practice of holding back on her.

It was another one of those Hawaiian days made for hotel brochure photography. Everything perfect. Sand, sky, sea. Big fluffy clouds were sailing around. A day for dark-skinned girls going topless. Paradise on the beach. Under the palm fronds. On the buffet line. Paradise in bed.

"If that happens, I'll feel like going over there."

"And do what?"

Still staring at the horizon, he took a while to answer, then thought, okay, I'll say it. "I'll feel like killing him."

Katta looked over at her husband of twenty-two years. "You say that so calmly. No rage in it. Would it be that easy for you?"

"I probably killed two, three hundred VC in Nam just by steering choppers around. I didn't know any of them. So it was just a job. I don't know this man, either. But I suppose it would be harder . . . *looking* at him and shooting him . . ."

"You'd be committing murder, Cole."

He took his eyes off the fluffy clouds. "Well, he did. And more."

"Are we sure?"

"Her fingerprints were in his car, weren't they? No one can tell me she got in there willingly. You and I know she didn't. And the next thing we know for sure is that two little boys found her in a field. That's enough for me."

"Maybe Hermann will tell us what happened—"

"It's all up to them. I mean Kinnick and the West Germans. If he can prove he's innocent, if he has some convincing explanation for those fingerprints, for the fact that he was at UCI that night, he can catch the next plane home."

"If he can't do that?"

"Then it's my guess that they won't send him back here."

"This sounds like that Charles Bronson movie." Katta got up and ran to the surf, cutting through a wave and driving her long body out to sea.

Cole remained on the beach, wondering if he really could do it. Killing from a gunship was like spraying ants. But this man had destroyed his daughter.

Katta and her mother were talking in Swedish. Mrs. Trenholm still preferred her native language.

"Mother, if I said we were doing okay I'd be . . . oh, well . . ."

"It's going to take a long, long time, Katta. Even then, until you die, Ellen will come back at the most unexpected times. How long has it been since your father died? Sixteen years? But no week goes by that he doesn't visit me one way or another."

Katta's mother lived in Port Wing, Wisconsin, on the shores of Lake Superior. She refused to move to California, or Oahu or Cherry Point, or Virginia or any other of Cole's stations because she liked the bitter cold of the winter and she was always afraid that if she did move the Marine Corps would send Cole somewhere else. Katta's father had gone down on an ore carrier in a winter storm, which was the main reason Ulla Trenholm wouldn't leave Port Wing. Katta called her once a week.

"How are the children?"

"Doing the best they can. I'm very proud of them."

"How is Cole doing?"

"Not very good. I didn't know he could be so emotional. I never saw Cole shed a tear over anything until the moment we knew Ellen was gone for good. Now I catch him crying three or four times a day. He hides, if he can. I mean that he'll just walk out of a room to do it. I'm sure when he's alone in the car or somewhere else it takes him by surprise. I guess we all do it, but Cole . . . you'd think he'd be the last to break."

"Has he been to the doctor?"

"Sure. They gave him a pound of Valium at El Toro but I don't think he's taking it. He says he wants to stay sharp."

"Well, you should leave there. He should ask for a transfer. Be less reminders."

"Mother, with his rank that's not easy. There aren't that many jobs for a full colonel in aviation and his air group is the most prestigious helicopter outfit in the Marine Corps. I think we'll be out of here in six months, anyway. Normal tour here is fourteen months."

"Well, go away again for a while."

"Can't do that, either. Jennifer and Skeet are still in school. It's important that they. . ." Katta felt herself breaking. She said, "Just a minute," and held the phone away from her mouth, taking a deep breath. She cleared her throat. "I'm sorry. . ."

"Nothing to be sorry about. Ever."

Katta took another deep breath and again fought back tears. "It's all so mixed up." She took another deep breath. "I have to talk to you about something. *I have to talk to someone about it* and you must never repeat what I'm going to tell you, no matter what. Cole may be thinking about going to Germany after that man who took Ellen's life."

There was a long silence. Then, finally, Mrs. Trenholm said, "Well, he can't do that."

"Oh yes, he can. That's been his business, mother. Killing an enemy or helping to kill an enemy. He did his share of it in Vietnam—"

"But this is different. This isn't war."

"This may be Cole's final war. But the awful thing is that sometimes I agree with him, without even talking to him about it. All I have to do is think about Ellen. She should be alive. So I want that man's life as much as Cole does. I want him dead, if he's guilty of killing her. But then I think about us as a family, and what it would do to Skeet and Jennifer, as well as to Cole and myself. I don't think it would ever be the same for any of us. But it can't be the same without Ellen either. So there you are. Is it any wonder I'm mixed up?"

"You must talk him out of it."

"I don't know that I can, or really want to. I'm not encouraging him but I'm not really discouraging him. It's almost like a game we're playing. Some game . . ."

"You *must* discourage him, Katta. Or have some close friends talk to him. Maybe his commanding officer."

"He won't do that. He's a very private man, you know that. And what could be more personal than this?"

Her mother said calmly, "I'm sure he's going through this terrible time the best that he can and I understand his rage. But he'll come to his senses soon and realize he just can't go around the world and do away with somebody—"

"When he dedicates himself to something, that's it, mother. He goes all the way. I guess that's why he's such a good Marine."

"He'll come to his senses," Mrs. Trenholm insisted.

Oh, mother, you have no idea, thought Katta. She'd heard some Vietnam stories about Cole Hickel from Mike Goody. In combat, so Mike said, he could be savage.

Nyall Kinnick sent the letter to the air station, perhaps wanting to keep communications in channels, weighted down as much as possible; remind Cole that he was active duty military in long-term career commitment to the government, just like Kinnick was. Cole was sure that civil servants like Kinnick eventually got to believing that the government owned the people. Either way, it was damn annoying. Art Hoberman had called to say that an envelope from State had arrived; did Cole want him to send the messenger over with it? Nope. Cole went over, staying no more than ten minutes before heading back to Oakwood, wanting to see no one.

A thousand yards from the base he pulled off on the side of Red

Hill to read what Kinnick had to say, marked *confidential*, putting an official twist on it. It occurred to Cole that maybe Kinnick had sent a blind copy to the commandant.

Dear Colonel Hickel:

I do hope you and your family had a pleasant and relaxed stay in Maui and only wish that I had some positive news to tell you on your return. I've spent hours trying to persuade our West German friends that Klaus Hermann should be returned to California for questioning. The same with your request for a deposition under lie detector equipment. After due consideration, they have decided that such actions would not serve a purpose. They base this decision on medical evaluations.

A team of psychiatrists examined Hermann and came to the conclusion that he is mentally diminished. It seems he has a Jekyll and Hyde personality and the latter dominated him the night he allegedly visited the UCI campus. He has been dismissed from the diplomatic service of the Federal Republic and is undergoing treatment, restricted to his residence. I am told that such treatment will continue until he is no longer a menace to society, in any country.

Unfortunately, considering his mental capacity, the attitude of the Federal Republic officials, and the sanctity of diplomatic immunity, the State Department regretfully can no longer be of help in this matter. I have enclosed a summary of the psychiatric evaluation.

So *Klaus Hermann was home free*. Cole had a muscular reaction, a facial spasm.

Obviously a translation, the one page document was signed by a Dr. Franz Hoger. Klaus Hermann was crazy, it in effect said, once you sliced it thin. Not all the time, Dr. Hoger was careful to say. Klaus went in and out like Swiss clock cuckoos. After his kinky sessions were over he couldn't remember all that he'd done. Because of the skin problem he had suffered psychologically. Societal rejection. As a child, little girls had tip-toed away, saying "eek." Then big girls, later on, had done the same thing. Klaus hated himself, said Dr. Hoger, and that was part of the whipping and humiliation.

Klaus was, literally, home free, just as Wally had predicted.

How about Ellen?

"Allegedly visited the UCI campus . . ." Kinnick must have been a lawyer at one time. *Allegedly.*

The little car sprinted away from the Red Hill roadside in a screech of rubber, and Cole was doing a smoking seventy-five before he slowed for a right turn. "Diminished capacity"—more lawyer bullshit. What about Ellen up on that hill, cold stone dead? Very goddamn diminished capacity.

". . . the State Department can no longer be of help." When were they, anyway?

The Austin-Healey soon mounted the sloping driveway on Oakwood, and Cole went inside, calling for Katta. A muffled voice came from the backyard, where he found her. On her hands and knees, cultivating an impatiens bed. Give Katta some good dirt and seeds and she was off in gardener's heaven.

"Read these," he said. "Those sonsofbitches, Katta. Kinnick and State are ducking. They didn't take two weeks to duck it. They don't want to hassle the West Germans."

She stood up, shedding muddy gloves. "I have to get my glasses."

"Use mine."

He took off on an angry walk around the big grassy yard, trying to simmer down, then came back to stand beside her. "How do you like that one line . . . 'treatment will continue until he is no longer a menace to society.'"

She read, frowning.

He went to the back steps and sat down beside her. "Take your glasses," she said, passing the letter back to him.

"Is that all you have to say? Take my glasses?"

"We both knew what might happen, didn't we? This isn't a surprise. We knew it the minute he came out here to warn us to keep quiet and not cause trouble. That's what he was really here for, wasn't it?"

"I guess."

"And, Cole, if we start raising hell—going to the newspapers— Kinnick or someone back there will drop this doctor's letter in our laps. They'll give it to the press. There are a lot of crazy people in the world and sometimes they sexually abuse and kill nice innocent people like Ellen. Isn't that what they'll do? And some people will say don't violate his civil liberties—"

"Hey, I'm not about to take the word of some double-talking German doctor that he's actually crazy. And I'm not sure it matters if he is or isn't. Anybody who rapes and murders is crazy in my book. And screw his civil liberties. How about *Ellen's* civil liberties?"

"It's supposed to matter in the civilized world. People who are crazy do crazy things and the law protects them. Isn't that right?"

Cole's laugh was brief and harsh. "Civilized world? Where is it, Kot? Tell you what I just made up my mind to do. I've got nineteen days of leave left and I'm going to track down every single person who saw Hermann or talked to him from the time Ellen disappeared until they hustled him home."

"Then what?"

"Then we'll make a decision. We go to the press and go after State, or do something else. I said *we*, you and me, will make the decision. Okay?"

She studied him. "Remember that, Cole. *Us*. We make it. We all have as much pain as you do."

"That's a promise."

She waited a few moments, then reached over and put a hand on his knee. "You thought about letting go? Releasing both of us, all of us, from it?"

Cole frowned. "Is that what you're suggesting? Letting the son of a bitch go free? Sanctity of diplomatic immunity?"

"Well?"

"No! The goddamn diplomats stretched it too far this time."

Katta said quietly, "I'm just asking if you've thought about it?"

"Yes, I've thought about it. For about ten seconds."

He got up to go in and call Wally Stonebridge. But then he remembered that Wally played raquetball every Wednesday night and didn't get back to Georgetown until nine.

He was burning up inside.

17

THE COFFEE SHOP was on El Camino Real, on the once benign road of Father Serra, now a snake cage of traffic at five o'clock. The Miramar, with a neon sign that had survived three wars, a kitchen that had survived a dozen grease fires, was now surviving the boots of hardhat workers on their way to the nuclear plant at San Onofre. The nuke plant, which always seemed to be under construction, was a few miles to the south. Nothing uptown about the Miramar, in midtown San Clemente. Bacon, eggs, biscuits, gravy and beef stew. The menu had not changed since 1940, nor had the decor. Faded, slip-of-the-lip WW II posters were still up. Ancient white tile on the floor; battered counter stools and cigarette-scarred red formica for booth table tops. In mid-afternoon there were still fifteen or twenty customers. Day's special was three twenty-nine. Liver and onions and white bean soup. Plus all the sourdough bread you could eat.

Officer Eberle ordered coffee and Cole asked for a Bud. "I'm dried out," he confessed, blaming it on the Santa Ana winds. He knew better.

Cole had expected an older highway cop to come through the door, one who might have an insight into so-called psychopathic killers. Surveying Glen Eberle, Cole thought he looked around the same skin-head age as most Marine recruits, kids barely out of high school, barely free of pimples. The way Eberle looked he'd fit right into basic training.

"How long can you spare me?" Cole asked, depressed by the youthfulness.

Eberle was on duty. "Oh, thirty minutes more or less. Less if I get a call." His mobile radio receiver was hooked on his belt. "I told the dispatcher I was ducking in for coffee."

"I appreciate this, Officer Eberle," said Cole.

"Call me Glen. I'm more used to that."

"Okay, Glen. I'm taking a look at the sheriff's investigation reports up in Santa Ana tomorrow. I guess being a Marine helps. I mean, letting me look at things. But like the reports I have to write, they don't always tell gut feelings. That's hard to put down sometimes. For me, anyway. I guess I'll see all the facts I can stomach tomorrow and what I want right now is a verbal picture of that son of a bitch."

Frowning, Glen thought a minute, obviously trying to recreate Klaus Hermann. Looking over Cole's shoulder in the front booth. Looking out at the cars rolling along El Camino Real. Biting his lip. Then his gaze met Cole's eyes. "Well, he's scary to look at the first time, as you've probably been told, and I would have crapped if I'd known he had a gun in that vehicle. I was about to, anyway. A 1036 stop."

Cole was startled. McManus hadn't mentioned a gun. "No one told me that."

Glen shook his head. "Wasn't real, a guy in sheriff's told me. But it looked and felt real. If he'd pulled it on me, he'd be dead now. If I hadn't shot him, one of those border patrol guys would have, I'll bet you. Walther P-38. I've never seen one to my knowledge but I've heard about 'em. They look and feel like the real thing. If someone held it to your mouth a lot of bells would ring."

"Why in hell would he have a toy gun? A diplomat on vacation . . ."

"No toy," Eberle said. "Exact replica. A man like that might have trouble buying a real gun, being a foreigner and not knowing where to go. A lot of people are taking guns on vacation. It scares hell out of me."

"You think he's a murderer?"

"Hard to tell about anybody. We've had guys had their brains blown out by guys who looked like preachers. This one looked strange enough. You don't see too many around with his face as smooth as glass and light red and yellow around the cheekbones."

"What else about his face?"

"Kind of pudgy and square. Talks with an accent, of course. But he could be a beer salesman or a barber. I only saw him that night, of course, and he was half drunk."

"He's fat?"

"A square face. He isn't what you call a beer belly, flopping over his belt. He's heavy-set, that's all. Oh, chunky, I guess."

"Know anybody who looks like him? Politician? Movie star?"

Glen thought again. "Just ordinary, except that skin. You could see him on a TV commercial, easy, except for that skin. They seem to be picking ordinary people nowdays."

"Did he give you any trouble when you arrested him?"

"Not really. He was sort of mild but he insisted on placing calls and that was his privilege. He spoke in German so I don't know what he was saying. But he wasn't all that excited. Not shaking or anything like that. He was calm, like nothing had happened. Like he wasn't any suspect for what happened to your daughter."

"Did he speak any English to you?"

"Enough. He sure as hell was quick to let me know that he had diplomatic immunity. I called on land line to my supervisor and he called a State Department security officer in Los Angeles. Within twenty minutes we had ourselves a bonafide diplomat identified. And, colonel, we sure as hell didn't want him. Neither did the sheriff."

"You question him?"

Glen shook his head. "Only about his blood alcohol concentration. I asked him if he'd been drinking and he said, 'A little.' That was bullshit. It had been a lot, I knew. I spotted that fifth of tequila when he rolled the right window down. So after he got out I asked him if he had any physical problems. That's routine. Like bad legs or some kind of disease; was he on medication? Then I said I was going to tell him how to do the tests. I gave him the Nystagmus where you follow the finger back and forth, checking for lateral eye control. He failed it. Then I had him close his eyes and watched for weaving. He weaved. I had him stand on one foot with the other up and try to balance. Failed that one, too. It's a damn wonder he didn't run off the road. So I radioed back that I had detained the driver and was holding the car. . ."

"Was he complaining?"

"Mumbling in German. Not much, though. Not near as much as I've had in the past. He knew I'd seen that quarter empty bottle of tequila on the seat next to him. Or I think he knew. He'd been drinking the stuff straight and warm."

"But he didn't refuse to cooperate? Didn't do anything wild? Anything crazy?" More and more, Klaus Hermann was beginning to sound pretty damn sane to Cole.

"Not a bit. He behaved. He was polite. No trouble at all. My orders were to detain him until we had instructions from the State guys in Los Angeles. Just keep him there in the lounge of the immigration station. That I did. I thought about putting cuffs on him but that wasn't necessary. There's no way to run, anyway. He finally stretched out and went to sleep, as if he didn't have a care in the world. I was mainly interested in the vehicle by that time, after I heard the all-points. My supervisor said not to touch anything and stay with it until it was towed to Santa Ana for a check by the Orange County people. They've got the best investigative equipment in the country. Laser capabilities and everything. But I didn't know about any of that stuff he had in the trunk until two days later when I found out about the gun."

"What stuff?"

"Oh, a prayer rug, a rubber sheet. Nurse's cap. Doctor's coat. Whip. Ropes. Length of inch chain about four feet long. He's a weirdo, colonel. Oh yes, little less than a gram of coke in the glove compartment."

Cole closed his eyes. Only God knew what Ellen had gone

through. He suddenly wanted to run from the liver and onions smells of the Miramar and hear no more from this baby-faced CHP.

"A real weirdo to get his kicks, is my guess," Glen went on.

"Any sign at the time that Ellen had been in the car?"

"I didn't even touch it. After he got out I closed the door with my elbow. And with those tinted windows I couldn't really see into the backseat. About forty minutes later Detective Sergeant Louderholt, from UCI, comes screaming up. She wanted to roust that German and question him. Madder'n trapped badger when the State Department people, who got there about the same time, refused it. They'd come down by LAPD chopper. She yelled at them, 'Whose side are you on, goddammit?' Didn't do her any good."

Suddenly Cole was impressed with the lady detective from the halls of academe. "Tough, huh?"

"She was that night. Blew her top that a suspect in a kidnapping was about to slip out the front door, never to return. Took it personally that a student could be missing and that maybe the suspect would talk. Yelling at the State security guys while the chopper was taking off, calling them dumb bastards. From what I hear, as soon as they got him to Parker Center they turned him over to the West German consul and up, up and away he went the next day. It really pisses me, colonel, when people can duck the law like that. I was pissed myself when he got free of the blood alcohol count and possession. So I know how you and your family must feel that he got away without a scratch on him."

Cole was tempted to tell the baby-face that Klaus Hermann had a very uncertain future but then thought better of it. Stick to why you're here, he told himself. "Did he act at all crazy?"

"Not crazy at all. In fact I think he was in complete control of himself after he took that nap. Why do you ask?"

"The Germans won't send him back. They say he's nuts and under psychiatric care. They're off the hook."

"Oh, man. Last time I saw him, just before he got on that chopper, he turned around and looked at me. Right through me. He was sober by then. But he's no gibbering crazy man."

"A Jekyll and Hyde. Crazy one minute, sane the next."

"Well, maybe."

"I got a confused picture of him," Cole said, shaking his head. "Son of a bitch."

"That's a good description," said Eberle, not smiling.

Cole nodded. "Hey, I want to thank you. You ever get up around Tustin, look me up. I'll take you to the O Club. Mongolian Barbecue Wednesday nights."

Officer Eberle smiled and shook the colonel's hand and left. Cole sat in the booth a while longer wondering how much to tell Katta. Rubber sheet, whips, nurse's cap, doctor's coat? Cole tried not to think of what Hermann might have done with all that sick stuff. He slapped two-fifty on the table and fled the smell of fried onions, even going down the street to make a call. Detective Sergeant Louderholt said she would wait for him. No, she didn't mind.

Staying off the freeway and the five to six p.m. traffic in both directions, Cole drove El Camino Real northward along the San Juan Capistrano beachside and the state park at the foot of Dana Point. It could not have been a finer early evening. Ocean a blue lake. Sun over the port bow. Ellen was still standing on the curb at every stoplight. Cole had to wipe his eyes twice.

The Austin-Healey turned right on MacArthur in Corona del Mar, a mile or so from Ellen's grave, and headed on east toward UCI. Ten minutes later Cole was in the white trailer where Kay Louderholt had her desk. She was wearing a green softball suit and the deep green contrasted nicely with her flaming hair.

"Hope I'm not keeping you from something," said Cole.

"Not at all. I catch for the Orange County Policewomen. We're in a pretty fast league. Game isn't until eight." She grinned. "The *Register* did a story on me. Rough and Ready Red. It's fun."

Cole had a mental flash of her squatting behind the plate, throwing to second for an out, or blocking home. Solid barrel that she was, she was probably a heavy hitter, too. He said, "Glen Eberle described him as ordinary, aside from his skin."

116

"I saw him maybe two minutes. They were walking him, one on each side, to the LAPD chopper and he didn't know I was there until I began yelling at the people from State. He turned and looked at me then, like he was sort of puzzled. It doesn't make a damn bit of difference how he looks, does it? It's how he acts."

Right. Looks didn't mean a damn.

"I did stay around and shined my light into that vehicle before they towed it. I saw the bottle of tequila on the seat and then what appeared to be a stain right at the edge. Had no idea what it was. But it tested out over in sheriff's forensic as Ellen's blood. Then her fingerprints under the dash. She did that on purpose, I'd bet . . ."

Cole exploded. "First I've known about any blood stain."

"Hers. Couple that with those prints and there's no doubt that she was in that vehicle sometime during the night. Now after seeing the tequila on the seat I went to the border next day on a hunch, thinking maybe he'd gone to Tijuana or Ensenada. Foreigners usually like to go down there. So I found an immigration officer who'd been on the midnight to eight shift at the Tijuana gate." She checked a pad. "Name is . . . Francisco Jurado. He remembered seeing the vehicle about two a.m. but saw no one but the driver. That's what I was trying to find out. Whether or not she was still alive at that time. I talked to our people at the main entry gates but no one remembered the white Mercedes coming back across about five-thirty or six. That's the beginning of the peak time in the afternoon."

"Any idea where he went in Mexico?"

Sergeant Louderholt shook her head. "My guess is Ensenada and it would only matter if someone saw Ellen with him. I'm going down there day after tomorrow and check all the motels and hotels just to see if anyone remembers the white Mercedes and the man driving it. I'm not sure any of this will do us any good but I'll keep trying, colonel. I blew it when they were rushing him to the chopper. I had a Minolta in the car but didn't have time to get it. It was all going down so fast. There are no pictures of him, I've heard. At least, not out here. Eberle didn't take one. Some CHP have their own personal cameras along but Eberle didn't have his that night. I'm sorry about that."

"Don't be," Cole said. "You seem to care, that counts. Mrs. Hickel and I appreciate it."

In a way her situation reminded Cole of the carrier doctor on the way to Vietnam. The whole ship was so healthy that the doctor had nothing to do. He prayed that someone would fall down and break a leg. On the crew's lounge bulletin board he offered to remove warts, do circumcisions. Like a discount clinic. Kay Louderholt didn't have many felonies at UCI to handle.

"This one wipes me out. First ever kidnapping on this campus. Last, I hope. But Ellen raped and murdered? You have to know I go to sleep at night thinking about it, thinking how it might have been stopped if Officers Stapker and Ames had had a hunch."

Cole nodded. He'd gone over and over not getting out of bed that night. How easy it would have been to put on a jacket and go to the campus. He was always first to pay attention to any warning light in an aircraft. Why not one at home?

Louderholt went on. "Some things bother me and I don't have any explanation for them. The autopsy indicates a terrible struggle. Most of Ellen's fingernails were broken. Her knuckles were badly bruised. Two fingers on one hand broken. She'd hit and clawed and there was blood under the nails that wasn't hers. So she must have scratched Hermann good. I didn't see any marks on him, but I was about thirty feet away. I asked Glen Eberle about it. He didn't see any on that smooth skin and he was up close to him, doing the tests. No face scratches, at least. Of course she could have gotten him in the chest and shoulders. We've seen that in rape cases. If we could provide forensic with Hermann's blood type . . ."

"Yeh," said Cole, shaking his head miserably. If . . .

"Another thing puzzles me is Hermann's profile. Someone who is mixed up in fetishes and bondage doesn't usually go in for rape. Now we know that they can get carried away and get violent enough to do anything. Rape, batter, kill. Especially if they've been free basing."

Hesitantly, Cole asked, "Sergeant, as a woman and as a detective, do you have any idea what else he might have done to Ellen?"

118

Kay Louderholt looked at him. "Aren't you punishing yourself? Wouldn't you rather not know?"

"Put blinders on? No. I can't do that."

"Okay . . . fellatio, maybe. I'm not sure about anything, aside from penis entry. The autopsy supports that. With all the kinky equipment he was carrying your imagination will tell you other possibilities. Before my marriage broke up . . . I was married to a cop . . . I was on the Baltimore police force for three years. We had some beauts roaming around East Baltimore Street. A few rubber sheet boys. They had prostitutes chaining them until they bled all over the place. Whip games. But I don't know how you do that kind of thing if you have to hold a gun on somebody. That's another puzzler."

"Lot of puzzlers here," said Cole.

The sergeant said, "I admit I'm obsessed with this case. I keep seeing Ellen on her knees on that Moslem prayer rug, begging for mercy, and him naked under that doctor's coat. Goddammit, I'd like to kill him myself."

Cole suddenly realized that tears were in his eyes again. He hadn't seen that particular mental picture, hadn't thought about it that way. He looked off into a corner of the room. "Wish I hadn't called you." *Ellen begging for mercy.*

Sergeant Louderholt looked away, not wanting to watch the Marine colonel while he bent his head down to hide his eyes. Like a cancer doctor, she said, "I'll do everything I can, colonel. Believe that."

He did.

It was past sundown when Cole walked back to his car in P-6 lot.

18

"DADDY, Mr. Stonebridge returned your call."

"Thanks, Skeeter. How's it going?"

Katta was at the commissary. Jennifer was down the street with a friend. Only Skeet was home.

"Okay," said the boy who didn't look like anyone else.

Cole went into the kitchen and closed the door. Dialing Wally's number, he wished his head wasn't so mushy. Start taking notes, he told himself, instead of relying on memory. But he didn't want to get into the business of hiding pieces of paper; neither did he want them around unhidden.

Wally answered, "Sorry I didn't get back to you last night. Couple of things happened. Didn't play raquetball, didn't even get home until one-thirty. Goddamn North Koreans."

"Busy, huh?"

"Yeh. First, what's on your mind?"

Cole told him about the letter from Nyall Kinnick. Wally said, "Prick." Cole then told him about the conversation with Eberle and Louderholt.

"Wally, I know where I'm going with this now. Made up my mind driving home tonight." Which wasn't quite true. He was still thinking about making up his mind. Right now, he was fishing . . .

trying out on Wally, hearing what Wally had to say, hoping Wally would say, "Go, tiger..."

"You probably made it up before you went to Maui."

"On and off."

"We'll talk about that later. I know a bit more myself. K.H. was on a holiday. You know how Europeans feel about their holidays. He knew he was going back to Hamburg soon so he decided to see the old USA first, and not in a Chevy. Drove all the way across, zigzagging, Illinois to Texas to Utah and Arizona, sending postcards back to the embassy. Little time in Vegas, little in Reno, then to San Francisco. Have no idea whether or not he got his rocks off in those places or how. Then to Malibu and Hollywood, and finally down to where you are. I think some embassy people have known for quite a while that K.H. was bad news. They didn't know how bad. Believe me, what you just heard is on the best authority. One of his fellow krauts hates him. Anyway, seems he got involved with a reluctant student from American University in January. Some Deutschmarks converted to dollars at Old Dominion Bank paid that one off. This new ambassador didn't know about it until last week. As to that letter you have from Germany via State, I don't think there's any doubt that his head is afloat some of the time. He does drugs, in surges. Likes to puff on cigarettes dipped in hash oil and perfume. Likes to toot or smoke a little coke. That, of course, doesn't make him a psycho. He's also a first-class kink, as your highway cop reported. That doesn't make him a psycho, either. But there's enough evidence on the other side of the pond, about which his dear mommy may know everything, to give you a profile of a sometimes nut. The German doctor seems to be right."

Cole was tamping it all in, but the portrait of Klaus Hermann was still about the same. "How much chance do you think we have of ever getting him back here?"

"Nil, Cole. Absolutely none."

"That's all I hear from everyone."

"That's all you're going to hear, my friend. Check the U.S. codes on extraterritoriality. Go to a law library, check 'em out. You won't even get a justice of peace to sign a writ. But because of what happened to that coed here, you may have someone contact you who has nothing to do with the Federal Republic and offer you quite a sum of money as a gesture."

"Gerda?"

"Someone close to her, maybe."

"She can shove it."

Wally said, matter-of-factly, "I knew that would be your answer and don't blame you. But think it over, think about it as an alternative to what else you're thinking about."

"Forget it."

"Okay. All right. I'm speaking as a friend . . . I haven't told you everything. He's now at home in Hamburg, like Kinnick said. Under psychiatric treatment and has a companion named Stefan Noll. Not a very nice fellow."

"A male nurse?"

"Bodyguard, really. Noll joined the Hermann company thirteen years ago and worked up to head of security. He has a Hamburg police permit to carry a gun and does so. I'm also told he's a bullyboy and likes to slap people around. He supposedly worships the old lady and will do *anything* she asks. That includes, I'd guess, making it very uncomfortable for anyone who makes her errant son uncomfortable."

"That includes me."

"At the moment, especially you. She's well aware that the so-called alleged victim was the daughter of a combat-skilled Marine Corps colonel. Need I say more?"

"What's that alleged shit?"

There was a pause. "I said so-called, didn't I? The point is, you'd be very foolish to make a try on him. If you were successful you'd have to find a way to get out or face German courts. I've seen a few of their jails. Killer dogs loose in the courtyards at night and no one moves until daylight."

Katta came shoving through the door carrying two bags of groceries, put them down, kissed Cole's cheek and returned to the driveway. Cole called for Skeet to help his mother.

"Cole, what you're thinking about could be first degree stuff.

You call it revenge. Rambotime. They won't see it that way, though they fully understand and may even sympathize with you. But this isn't the movies. I'm guessing that someone from the shipyard security staff would set up surveillance the minute they get a call that you've passed through immigration. They'll be on your tail night and day until you leave, alive or dead. It's my guess that Noll would try very hard to kill you. You'll end up as fish bait in the Baltic."

Katta returned with two more overflowing bags. "Help me, Skeet. Charcoal's in the car." She put the bags down. "Who are you talking to?" she asked Cole.

"Wally Stonebridge."

Katta shook her head in dismay.

Cole picked up Wally's voice again. ". . . what you should consider is help. You don't speak German, do you? Don't have any contacts. This isn't the Old West, Cole. Ride up a single canyon to a guy who lives in a shack. This kind of help is costly."

Katta paused in unloading the first bag, continuing to look at Cole with a frown.

"We'll afford it."

"I'm trying to discourage you, Cole. I'd like you to stay healthy, for the sake of your family and . . ."

With Katta hovering about, Cole wanted to end the conversation. "I'll think about what you said and call you in a day or two. Thanks for the info. Take care, Wally."

"You, too."

Cole did hamburgers on the grill, medium rare for all except Skeet, sipping at a vodka-Seven and thinking about Wally's call while the meat was charring on the outside. They ate in the dining room. Potato salad from the commissary deli; tortilla chips and pickles. Like old times, which made it hell for all of them once again. No one at Ellen's place.

After Jennifer and Skeet turned on TV, Cole said to Katta, "Take your wine and let's go out on the patio. We can clear this later."

"I need a sweater."

When she came out and sat down beside him Cole said, "I'm not going to Santa Ana tomorrow to the sheriff's department. I've had it, Kot. Takes too much out of me. Hurts too damn much. I know enough already. I'm through playing detective."

"What'd you find out?"

Cole knocked off the rest of his vodka-Seven. "Too much. The highway patrol guy told me he had a toy gun."

"Toy gun? Come on now. Toy gun?"

Cole eyed his wife. There was no sturdier woman on earth. He'd flown with guys who didn't have her guts. She could handle it. "Prayer rug. Rubber sheet. Whips and chains. Nurse's cap. Doctor coat."

Katta suddenly had horror on her face. "My God. Oh, my God. What did he do to her?"

Maybe Katta couldn't handle it . . . "My reaction, too, Kot. Oh, my God."

"I don't think I want to know anymore."

"I asked Eberle how he looked and he said he was chunky and ordinary aside from that skin disease, that rare alopecia thing I told you about. I asked him if Hermann looked or acted crazy and he said no."

Katta picked up on the nurse's cap, turning it over in her mind. "Nurse's cap?"

"That hung me up, too." He took another drink. "Then I went back to see that lady detective over at UCI. She's got balls, Kot. She went after those State Department guys."

"I'd like to meet her."

Cole told Katta about the Mexican crossing but not about Louderholt's guess at what Hermann had made Ellen do. He planned never to tell Katta about that.

Wincing, she said, "Do you think he made Ellen put that cap on her head?"

Yes he did. And he thought Hermann dressed himself in that doctor's coat. "I don't know."

"I don't understand anyone like that."

"Who the hell does . . . ? And who at this point cares . . ."

It wasn't a question. His words hung there. After a long silence they got up to go to bed, and once again sleep was a losing struggle.

Over the years Cole had seen Mike Goody, good old monkey-browed Goody, a dozen times and had talked to him more than that. Mike had departed the Marines long ago when it looked like he would be stuck at light colonel, facing a pass-over for bird colonel. But he had done fine selling stocks and bonds to rich Leisure World old folks. Mike had called that terrible Sunday after Ellen's body had been found and now was sitting across from Cole in Delaney's oyster bar on El Toro Road.

"Well, I'll tell you exactly what I'd do about it, Coley. I'd go over there and blow that son of a bitch to the backside of the moon. I'd empty a .38 right between his fucking eyes is what I'd do."

Cole thought, That's exactly what I expected Mike Goody to say. Go get him, tiger.

Mike added, "Anybody do anything like that to any member of my family is a gone gosling. Bingo."

An antidote to all the naysaying he didn't want to hear. "I've been thinking about it, Mike. I didn't go to sleep this morning until four-thirty, five."

Mike nodded. "It can drive you crazy unless you do something about it."

Cole sighed, catching himself at it. He had done quite a lot of that lately. Almost as if it might bring some solution, at least relief. "I feel like I'm in a tug-of-war. With myself, with Katta, with the kids . . ."

"Sure you do," said Mike, signaling the waitress for more drinks. "And the only way to get over it is to go get him."

"I know," said Cole.

"For God's sake, you look like you just drove cross-country without stoppin' . . ."

"I know, I've used a quart of Visine the last two weeks."

"Look, Coley, you asked for my advice and you got it . . ."

"It's not going to be easy," Cole said, more to himself than his friend.

———

"Nothing like this is. You plan an operation. Go about it like you ran that air group. You got a target and you get into position to hit it . . ."

Cole shook his head. "I can't do it while I'm in the Corps. You know that."

"True," Mike said. "But I got out and haven't exactly suffered. Made eighty-two thou last year. I miss flying and you guys but I don't miss that government check. You'll never get rich being a gyrene, Coley."

"It's a way of life. I like it . . ."

The waitress brought two chilled seafood platters.

Cole was not really hungry.

There was no easy way to tell her. So just tell her. "Kot, I'm putting in for retirement tomorrow."

Shock was in her voice before it could register on her face. "What? Have you lost your mind? *Retirement?*"

Cole nodded. There *was* no other way. Wait ten years to get him? Retire on thirty and then go hunting the son of a bitch? By then Hermann would have forgotten what he did.

Katta shook her head. "Cole, you can't mean it, you have such a bright future ahead—"

"I'm a desk-jockey. I can make twice as much money on the outside . . ."

Katta shook her head frantically. "You'll be a general soon, your whole life has been the Marine Corps, you just can't—"

"Kot, stop it. You have to understand. I'm burnt out—"

"You're also bulling me, Cole."

She'd either accept it or she wouldn't. He didn't answer. Yes, she damn well knew the reason why but didn't want to get into it.

"If you retire what'll you do to make a living?"

"Pension won't be too bad and I'll triple it in no time at all. Lots of jobs in aviation. I've got a degree in aeronautical engineering, remember?"

Katta was terrified. And not because the dandy Marine Corps domestic rug was being jerked out from under her. It was what she knew he was thinking of.

"Hey, Kot, we've talked about this before, getting out, getting a civilian job. Don't worry about me making a living. I'm over-qualified, I can go to work for Hughes or Bell next week..." What the hell other way was there? Having made the final decision after talking to Mike Goody he felt better than he had since Katta called him at Pendleton to say she thought Ellen was missing. No more hand-wringing. No more embarrassing tears. No more rolling around on the bed. No more talking to himself. No more sighing. Now go over, kill the son of a bitch and get on with living. Do everything for Kot and Jennifer and Skeet that he couldn't do as a Marine. Forget the Academy, forget Admiral Cole Hickel, the first, and all that family tradition stuff. Just go *do* it. "Bingo," as Mike Goody had said.

"Please talk to General Ferguson before you do anything we'll both regret."

Christ yes, of course she knew.

Joe Ferguson was COMCABWEST. Commander, Marine Corps Air Bases, Western Area. Friend, as well as superior.

Cole said, "Just because he's charming to all you wives doesn't mean he's father confessor to anyone. Joe's in Washington for the next week."

Katta kept staring at her husband. "Don't rush into this, for the sake of all of us."

She knew, but she was ducking it. "Not rushing, it'll take a few weeks to get me out. Meanwhile I'll start looking for work."

"Make me some tea, please."

He went inside. The kids were into another show. He lingered by them a moment, then asked his usual question. "Homework all done?" He still had to try to be daddy.

Skeet sighed. "Nope."

"You?" he asked Jennifer.

"Yep." She got up and headed for the stairs anyway. She'd been very quiet, withdrawn lately.

Another toughie. How to deal with them? Daddy is getting out of the Corps, going away for a while. When he comes back, if he comes back, daddy will be a hit man. Put that to soft rock, Jennifer. He returned to the patio with the tea.

Katta said, "You've been thinking, all right."

"That I have."

She sat in silence for a while, then turned to him. "Back off," she said. "Please back off, Cole. Ellen wouldn't want you to destroy a career."

Cole was watching a passenger jet begin its descent into Orange County airport, lights blinking.

"Are you listening to me?"

"I'm listening, Kot, but I've also decided."

In the morning, trotting briskly along the tract streets, weaving around Ivy and Birch and Ironwood and White Oak, Cole collected his thoughts, phoning Art Hoberman after getting home and taking a shower. They chit-chatted a few minutes about things in the group—no problems, said Art—and then Cole told him. "I'm bailing out, Artie."

"Bailing out from what?"

"From Mother Marine Corps. She's been damn good to me but it's time to go—"

"Whoa."

"I've been thinking about it a long time, Artie. You know that. Hell, we've talked about it. No fun anymore. Only time I fly is to go to Pendleton or get my hours in."

"We've never been serious."

That was true. "Well, I am now."

"What does Katta think?"

"Scared, I guess."

"Don't blame her. What'll you do?"

"Some consulting work to start?"

"Who with?"

"West Germany company."

There was a great gap of silence on Art's end, then he said, "Oh? West Germany. Well, I'll be damned." Cole could picture Art's shovel jaw, those dark eyes. Consulting work, my ass, he was thinking. Cole Hickel was going hunting.

Cole said, "A company over there is thinking about building some helicopters. I'll consult."

"They've picked themselves a good man to consult with," Art said, thinking sure, consult, with a forty-five.

"Thanks, buddy."

"Big decision, Cole. You've really thought it out?"

"Sure have."

"Well, then that's good enough for me," Art said. "When are you putting the paper in?"

"Today. I don't know how long they'll take to get a replacement. Maybe they'll let you have it?"

"No way. Too many standing in line. I'll be temporary until the wheels grind." No question, Cole was going hunting.

"We'll talk later, Art."

Cole put the phone down. Good man, Art Hoberman. Accepted it, even the phony reason. Didn't ask questions. Even said, between the lines, I understand, buddy. There were things in life bigger than the U.S. Marine Corps.

Not many. But some.

For sure, this one.

19

"COLE, this is a helluva surprise," General Ferguson said, tapping the retirement request. It was on his desk for endorsement. "I don't want to sign this thing. You've got ten terrific years ahead. You could be sitting here by then . . ."

"General, I appreciate everything you've said to me and all you've done for me over a long time. But I have to get out now."

Traditional Marine, never a politician, Ferguson would never go higher than El Toro. He wasn't built for Pentagon power struggles. A stubby, florid man with powerful-looking hands, white hair stubble-cropped as far back as Cole could remember, Joe was always at home in the *fighting* Marines. Carrier pilot in Korea; Vietnam vet.

"This have anything to do with Ellen?"

"Right now, it seems that everything has something to do with Ellen."

"I'm not going to ask you what, but I hope you've really thought it out and talked it over with Katta."

Divorced from an alcoholic wife, Joe had come over for dinner several times.

"I have, sir."

"Well, that's good enough for me."

The sharp eyes searched Cole's face. "You know what you want to do when you get out?"

"Yessir... I'm going to do some consulting work, with a West German company as a starter..."

Ferguson nodded. "You'll be very good at that, Cole. Very good."

"Thank you, sir."

"Good luck and give my love to Katta and the children. And, Cole, be careful."

Joe Ferguson knew right away. "Yessir."

Cole felt Ferguson's eyes on his back as he closed the door of COMCABWEST. Go get him, Cole silently heard.

The details of what had happened to Ellen Hickel, embellished, Cole was certain, had traveled throughout the Tustin and El Toro bases down to Pendleton. Everyone knew. Wincing when they heard about the whips and nurse's cap and doctor's coat. Somebody did that to the MAG colonel's daughter? So beyond the need to revenge Ellen, Cole felt the need to be a Marine in the eyes of Marines.

Katta said, "You talked to Joe Ferguson?"

"He said give his love to you and the children."

Katta nodded impatiently. She'd resigned herself to the story about the West German company wanting to consult on chopper building. She even told her mother, and Ulla believed it, not connecting West Germany to Ellen. Well, it was better than thinking about the other thing, Katta rationalized.

One part of her actually wanted Cole to go over there and avenge their daughter... but reason said it was wrong, that they'd all regret it forever. All day long the two parts were doing ritual dances like those plumed birds down in the San Diego Zoo.

"Are they really going to build helicopters over there?" she asked Cole. The charade had its consolation. Maybe she could even learn to convince herself it was real.

"Of course," he said. Playing along.

* * *

132

Three weeks later the retirement party at the O Club in Building 39 brought out every MAG officer not on leave, plus some friends from El Toro, and their wives. General Ferguson and other brass came. The Pendleton chopper bunch drove up. Soon there were about two hundred and fifty people at the no-host bar drinking and talking and saying goodbye to Cole Hickel. They knew. *They all knew.* Consulting job in West Germany? Believe that and you believe in tooth faries. But only one, Major Farrar of HMM-268, the Red Dragons, flying CH-46s, said anything direct. Mike had a snootful and advised, "Cut his balls off, colonel, like Charlie did to a lot of good Marines."

All the rest just said good luck. Chaplain Coombes, who would never step on a snail, said, "God be with you, colonel." Cole suspected he knew too.

Nobody asked anything about that West German company, and these were chopper people. A new German chopper? Not a word did they ask.

On the way home, driving up to Santa Ana, Cole thought of how the guys supported him, at least didn't ask questions, and said to Katta, "Let's go on over and visit Ellen."

She extended a hand to his shoulder. "Why do you keep making it so hard on yourself? Let's *don't* go over there."

Cole began growing the beard the next morning, knowing it would eventually be one of those gray-brown mottled jobs that looked like an aging airedale's back. Wally had said that it was still the easiest way to change a face. He got up early, didn't wait for Katta, and ran three miles, planning to build the distance to ten or fifteen as the weeks went by. He was puffing heavily by the time he got home and realized he really wasn't in too good shape. All right, do something about it. He got into the Austin-Healey and went to El Toro, feeling strange for the first time when the guard at the gate saluted him. But the car sticker said he belonged and the Chicano Pfc whom he'd seen before waved him through.

In the weight-lifting and exercise room a black sergeant said, "Mornin', colonel."

Cole replied in kind but couldn't bring himself to say he had retired the day before. He knew there would be a change in attitude on the sergeant's part. The difference between active duty and retired was like the difference between the Grand Canyon and a ditch.

"I haven't done any weights in three years, sarge."

"You got to start slow then. Do some stretches and then I'll give you thirty pounds . . ."

He had talked to other people who had gotten out and they said they had felt naked without a uniform. Well, he'd never felt that way in civvies and didn't intend to now. What *would* bother him was not being able to walk out to the apron and take off. Next to losing power of command, knowledge that you were running an operation, the biggest loss was not being able to fly, at least to get those hours in. That was the joy part of the job : . .

"That's the way, colonel. Stretch high. Get up on those toes. Get that left arm straight to the sky. . ."

An hour later Cole was floating in the jacuzzi thinking what a fine party had been thrown for him. Not often did over two hundred people come out to say so-long to a bird colonel. Most of the time they said thank God that miserable SOB is gone. In the heat and steam his eyes watered. Got to cut that out, he told himself. *Got* to.

After lunch he went out to the patio with the two cassettes and phrase dictionary he had checked out at the base. They were standard Defense Department issue. "Speed Up" language-learning tools. Even Tagalog or Serbo-Croatian or Swahili tapes could be checked out. German was nothing.

The lady on the cassette said, "I shall come back soon," then translated, "Ish KAWM-muh bahlt tsoo-REWK."

Cole tried it twice and it sounded like robot gibberish. He called to Katta to come out and listen. "Does she know what she's talking about?"

Katta came, listened and said, "Just sit and listen ten times to each phrase, then try them one by one."

"There's at least six hundred—"

"There's a ton more than that."

About six he called Wally from the upstairs phone. "Well, I'm committed."

"Committed to what?" Wally asked.

"I'm out of the Corps."

Why, Cole? You're tearing your whole life apart. What about the rest of your family?"

"There's only one way to put it back together. I can't go over there on active duty. Land there as a U.S. Marine and do what I have to do? You know that."

"I wish to hell you'd called me before you put the papers in."

"So you could tell me not to."

Wally didn't answer, but three thousand miles away Cole thought he could feel his disapproval, to put it mildly.

The rest of the conversation tailed off, Wally saying he had another call to make. At that time of night? "Talk to you later," Cole said.

"Sure." Wally's voice was chilly.

On the fifth day, Skeet, at dinner, asked, "What's all this stuff going on with Germany? And speaking it?"

"Right," said Jennifer. "You have a job lined up over there? We get to go?"

Katta looked over at Cole. Well, daddy?

"I won't be long. You know me. I do my homework, which is more than I can say for you."

"Aw, come on, daddy. Official business?"

Her father was always going off somewhere. Two of the squadrons were always deployed in the Pacific. "I'm a civilian now. I'm a consultant."

"What does that mean?" Skeet asked.

"I suggest things," Cole said, wishing the phone would ring or that Katta would help him out. She didn't. Just sat there while he struggled.

Surveying him, Jennifer said, "I don't know whether or not

you'll look good in a beard. Is that what happens when you retire? You grow a beard?"

"Come on, Jen, I'll look distinguished. Like a professor."

"I don't know," she said . . .

Twice a week he went to the firing range east of El Toro, off toward the low mountains. He had had to turn in his own forty-five to the armory and had borrowed Art Hoberman's for practice.

As the days got warmer he was running eight and then ten miles and pressing two hundred pounds in the weight room. The beard was now out a half inch, gray and brown as expected.

Afternoons, there were those miserable language lessons with the nameless voice on the cassettes; evenings, until he fell asleep, the guide books on Hamburg. "Katta, did you know Mendelssohn and Brahms were born there?" No, she didn't know that. About 1000 A.D. there was a river crossing and a fort called Hammaburg sixty miles up the blue misted Elbe . . . Because it had the health of a blacksmith and the laughter of barmaids it even survived World War II. Cities such as Hamburg crawled out from under the rubble to survive and defy the world. So the book said.

Studying the detailed map, Cole was beginning to feel he knew the streets, from the Alsters all the way to suburbs. He kept coming back to look at the shipyards. Hermann Werft.

Stefan Noll was fuming to his secretary about the Spanish in general and the Spanish telephone system in particular. She had placed the call to Gerda Hermann at the Sidi San Juan Sol in Alicante more than an hour ago. In return she had had two broken connections and a flimsy excuse. Despite the fact that Germans had settled all over the Costa del Sol, spending bundles of money, most of the operators spoke no German at all. Infuriating.

In the yard outside the office blue welding sparks flew in all directions, and big red mobile cranes crawled along tracks dangling assembled bulkheads or steel plates. There were three active building contracts and eleven major overhauls this late spring, putting Hermann Werft nearly at capacity.

Gerda usually spent May and some of June in the best suite of the luxury hotel, sunning herself on the balcony, walking her poodles along the rocky beach, taking a daily swim in the pool and at night staying nearly even at *chemin de fer*. Her short late summer holiday was always divided between a modest villa on Lake Geneva and the cottage at Karlstrand, Sweden, to which she had a deep sentimental attachment.

Stefan Noll had visited her in all three places, liking Spain the least. Aside from bullfighting, olives, cork and fresh fruit, Noll could not think of a single contribution that Spain had made to the world. Not even that insane Picasso. Especially not.

At last the secretary, who always wore too much lipstick and blue eyeliner, said, "Frau Hermann is on the line," and Noll moved swiftly to shut the door, though he knew there would still be a busy ear in the outer office. The only reason he had never fired that farmer's daughter from Husum was that she knew much too much about the Hermann family. She also had actually surmised he had murdered that Lubeck doctor. He had given her a fat raise after that.

"Gerda, Gerda, how are you, how *are* you, my dearest? I do hope the weather has been good and the casino exceptional..."

There was no click to indicate the secretary had hung up. Noll's eyes narrowed as he stared at the door.

Gerda laughed. "The weather has not been very good and the casino was a tragedy last night. I lost twenty thousand pesetas but I am even for almost the last two weeks, so..."

"Luck will change with both the sun and the casino, you will see."

"Where are you?"

"At work. I had things to do here this morning. Herbert Richter is with Klaus. He is a good man."

"Klaus seemed so unhappy when I talked to him last night. He—"

Stefan interrupted, lowering his voice as if it was possible to avoid eavesdropping simply by lowering decibels. "That lawyer from Los Angeles, the one..." He was still studying the door and said to Gerda, "Moment, please," and arose, stepping quickly over to the door, springing it open to be greeted by an innocent smile. Her phone was down.

"Go to lunch now," he said.

"Yes, Herr Noll," she replied, smile widening. God, she had enough teeth for two mouths.

Stefan closed the door and picked up the phone again, sitting down, ". . . the lawyer, the one you have on retainer, said that the colonel has retired. He sent news clippings."

Gerda asked worriedly, "Do you think he will actually come over here? Harm Klaus? Even after the medical reports? Is it possible?"

"He is a combat officer. I know the type. After such a career, he would not leave the military unless such was on his mind. He may be very dangerous. Vietnam, you know."

"Oh, Stefan, if only these silly girls would behave and take his money none of this would happen. He can't help himself sometimes, poor boy."

Stefan could picture her stroking one of the poodles, sitting in that large chair by the coffee table in Suite A. The Mediterranean could be seen from that chair, he remembered. White-haired, she refused to accept the condition and always carried a formula that kept the strands honey blond. For a woman of sixty-five, her body was not at all bad. But the damn poodles, they yapped and got under his feet. Of all the breeds on earth, they were the most useless, just like the Spaniards.

Stefan said, "The house in Blankenese is not safe. Three entry doors. Windows are low. If you go out the back you have to take the alley out. The other way deadends. I was thinking about it yesterday. There is a position to the left where he could control both doors if he had a sniperscope—"

"I *don't* want to hear about those things, Stefan. But I do know that Klaus is unhappy being penned up in Blankenese. He's such a dear boy."

"He had a good time Sunday night. I took him out . . ." Yes, and I had to rub salve on the back of the sorry bastard when we got home from Ottensen and the whip girl.

138

Gerda was saying, "He wants to return to Denmark and play in that group two weeks from now. That always makes him happy. As I've said before, he might have had a fine career as a musician."

Or a fine career cleaning toilets in whorehouses, Stefan thought.

"Do you want him to go to Copenhagen? Okay with me. He'll be much safer there than in Blankenese. I'll tell Dr. Hoger we are going, though I doubt that he will approve."

Gerda said, "Tell him to call me. And what about Karlstrand after Copenhagen? It's so soothing there. I'll join you."

"All right," he said. "Copenhagen and then Karlstrand."

"And now that you think that man may come over, you must stay with Klaus every minute, Stefan. Is Richter the one with the hole-in-his-head?"

"Yes."

"I'm sure he's all right, but I feel much better if I know you are with him constantly, my love."

With a desolate look at his antler collection on the right side wall, Noll said, "All right," and they went about "dears" and "my love" a moment longer and then Gerda hung up from Alicante.

Stefan had been in bed with Gerda Hermann dozens of times over the past thirteen years but now her appetite, thank God, had dropped off to almost accidental couplings. Right wine, the right place; degree of loneliness. She hadn't remarried after Ernst Hermann had died in the fifties, not wanting to share the wealth, and Stefan hadn't married at all after he had become personal security guard to Gerda and then chief of security for the shipyard. It was not difficult to remember the night in Montreux eight years after Ernst had died when Gerda, then fifty-three, had called him to say, "I seem not able to open this drawer in my nightstand. Could you help me, please?" Stefan, six months into his new job, had checked the knot in his tie before going next door. An ivory see-through nightgown was nicely lit up by the table lamp, and the dark patch between her legs beckoned. He immediately cast aside any difference in age as of no consequence. The pampered body he soon saw was still rich in curves, and desire. As was the pent-up thrusting and moaning of Gerda Hermann. In his twenties then, the security

---

man sometimes wondered if Gerda had not screwed her elderly husband to a splendid death. Stefan was now amply mentioned in her will, specifically in the amount of a million Deutschmarks, which he recognized as a stud fee. He was also quite decently paid for the anti-crime welfare of the shipyard. Protection of Klaus was part of the job, insurance that Gerda would not change her will.

He sat in the office a few minutes longer, looking at the twin rows of small antlers. Bavarian deer were shamefully under-pronged. He had accompanied Gerda to the United States on two occasions but never had the chance to hunt over there. He was squiring his employer about and servicing her when required. He had never taken a big American buck into his sight. He longed to do that. Perhaps in Wyoming or Montana. They were marvelous hunting places, or so he had heard.

The secretary from Husum soon slid into her chair in the outer office as if she had never left it, and Stefan soon returned to Blankenese on the Elbe to relieve the man with the hole-in-his-head who was nurse-maiding Klaus.

In her suite in the Sidi San Juan Sol, Gerda poured herself an aperitif and settled into the depths of the couch, thinking of how unfair life had been to Klaus. She still blamed her late husband for the terrible skin problem. Old Ernst had some kind of impurity in his semen, she believed, although there was not one specialist who had agreed. It was not *her* fault, she was certain.

She sat idly rubbing the head of honey-colored Puppe, the more loving of the two poodles, wondering what would happen to Klaus after she was gone. He would be at the mercy of the world, always needing someone like Stefan Noll to protect him. She only hoped that Stefan would take on that responsibility out of kindness. And she had been considering, for a while, having a will drawn up for Klaus naming Stefan as his guardian, with proper compensation as long as Klaus lived. Something of that sort.

What a dear, suffering boy, she thought. In Karlstrand, he could work again on that portrait of her that he had started before leaving for Washington. Gerda thought his preliminary sketches had been quite good. He had such talents that had survived despite the cruelties. What a dear boy. She took another sip of the Dubonnet light and then called the head waiter to make sure her table would be available at 1:30.

"You said you wanted to talk to me about Ellen in private," Cole said to Phil Chiu. "Well, here I am."

They were in Coco's in Fashion Island for coffee.

"I saw in the paper that you'd retired."

"Yes, I wish they hadn't done that. Now, let's talk about Ellen. What did you want to tell me?"

"I haven't thought of much else lately."

"Neither have I," said Cole, becoming annoyed.

"I was born in this country, in San Francisco, but I was raised very Chinese. My parents still speak very little English. They think Chinese, and some of the time I do too."

Cole shifted around in his seat. What did that have to do with Ellen?

"When I do that, I try to think back and then analyze forward—"

"I don't follow you," Cole said abruptly. He wasn't too fascinated by how the Chinese went about thinking.

"Ellen used to tell me how much you loved the Marine Corps and that someday she was certain you'd be a general."

Cole frowned. "Yes?" Get to the point, boy.

"Thinking about it," said Chiu, long face as expressionless as a Beijing stone dog, "I decided that the real reason you resigned was because you plan to avenge Ellen's death. We Chinese understand that."

Cole felt sweat rise. He fought not to react. "You have the wrong reason, Phil," he said, trying to keep his voice steady.

Chiu nodded. "If you say that, sir, I must believe you, but I came here to offer to help. To go over there with you . . ."

"Wait a minute, Phil. Your imagination is running away with you." Cole lifted his cup, needing something to hide behind for a few moments. He drank, wiped his mouth. "That would be pretty dumb, wouldn't it?"

"No," Chiu said, unblinking. "After what he did to Ellen, no."

Cole stared at the young man across from him. "Did anybody tell you I was going over there?" Could Katta possibly have said something, hoping to stop him?

"No, sir."

Cole nodded, knowing that Chiu must be telling the truth. Chances were a thousand to one he was in contact with any Tustin Marines who might be second-guessing aloud. And, of course, Katta, regardless of her feelings, would never have compromised him.

Chiu said, "Well, if you ever *did* decide to avenge Ellen, and don't want me along, then I'd at least like to help financially. I'd like to contribute a thousand dollars toward expenses."

Cole shook his head, liking this young man more and more.

"I hope you'll reconsider, sir. I find it damn hard to sleep these nights knowing he'll never be punished."

Cole nodded, pushed his cup away. "Well, Phil, I've got a dozen things to do today, but I do appreciate your offer. Highly unusual as it is . . ."

"I mean it."

"I believe you . . . but I hope you won't go around speculating about why I retired."

"Certainly not, sir. I keep my thoughts to myself."

Out by the Austin-Healey, saying goodbye to Phil Chiu, Cole suddenly hugged Ellen's boyfriend, something way out of character. Imagine hugging a Chinese boy? The antique car went away quickly.

While Katta was making dinner Jennifer came out on the patio and sat down on her father's knee, the way Ellen used to do. She looked him straight in the eyes. "I know Ellen was always your favorite and I understand. She was born first."

"Hey," Cole said, "I don't have any favorites. I love you just as much as I loved Ellen. Skeet, too."

Jennifer said, "That's not what I want to talk about, daddy. I loved Ellen. You don't know how close we were."

142

"I think I do." Cole was beginning to feel uncomfortable and not because of the weight on his knees. She did have something on her mind other than favorites.

She said, "I think you're going to Germany to get the man who killed Ellen, and I'm glad. That's what I want to tell you."

"Come on, Jen." His cheeks felt hot. "That's crazy talk."

She said earnestly, "I'm going to pray for you."

"Up!" Gently he shoved her off his knees. "Have you talked about this with your mother or Skeeter, I mean this nutty idea of yours?"

She shook her head.

"Well, hey, that's a wild thing you've dreamed up. It's scary. It scares me."

"I don't think so," she said, her eyes holding his.

Cole didn't know what to say. Sixteen-year-old daughter talking like this . . . His forehead was burning. He wished Katta or Skeeter would walk out. "All right, Jen. I've had some thoughts, but doing is something very different."

She nodded. "I understand, daddy, but I just wanted you to know how I felt about it, before you went."

He was still speechless.

She leaned over and kissed his forehead and began to walk away.

Cole called after her. "Jen, not a word about this to anyone. Not Skeet. Not even your mother."

She paused and nodded and went on into the house.

It was the closest Cole came to not going.

20

EARLY MORNINGS the Orange County airport was always in a
state of high flux. Businessmen to San Francisco, Oakland; politi-
cians to Sacramento. Commuters to Los Angeles for connecting
flights east. The airport was built to take care of bedroom towns
along the flight path, not the rambling metropolises in the making
all around it.

Cole and Katta stood near the entrance to CommutAire, which
flew Dutch prop-jet STOLS to Los Angeles on the hour. Against
the muraled inner ceramic tile wall, bodies touching, Cole's sparse
luggage at his knees, her right hand fingers on his chest, they
waited. In a blue poplin jacket, red Lacoste cotton shirt, jeans and
polished brown boots, nobody from MCAS (H) would have known
Foxtail One. The beard was a neat inch, beginning to curl here and
there, old gray-brown airedale fur. Though he was blond, the beard
and eyebrows had always come out dark brown. There was hair on
the back of his neck for the first time since Nam. He fit right in
with Orange County's elder Yuppies. But around his gut was a
green cloth money belt with forty-eight hundred in it. Yuppies
didn't usually wear money belts.

Katta said, "That was good love we made last night."

Cole smiled. "Didn't last long enough. Like ice cream."

145

Voice suddenly dry and tight, Katta said, "I don't know what a wife-lover-friend should do at a time like this. I've thought about it for days, always hoping you might back off. Then again, I know Cole Hickel the second."

He didn't answer. A finger was on the side of her neck, touching her gently; he was looking over every inch of her face, wanting to remember it clearly.

Her sudden laugh was thin. "There's no script for this, is there?"

"Sure, there is. I'm back in two weeks, job done. That's the script."

"That, I'd like. I didn't tell you but Jen asked me a devastating question yesterday morning."

Cole already knew. "Oh?"

". . . she said, 'Is daddy going to Germany to find the man who killed Ellen and bring him back for trial?' She thinks you can do anything. I said no but she's so bright. That's why she's been so quiet lately, I think. That's why she avoided you this morning. She's frightened for you."

Cole nodded. "Be sure and keep telling her how much I love her. Tell Skeet too."

The flight was called.

Katta said, urgently, "I'll go crazy unless I hear from you every night."

"I'll call."

"Cole, I keep hoping you'll get there and just turn around and come home . . ."

He didn't reply but held her hard and close, kissed her, and then moved quietly into the security check.

Wally had suggested they meet at Tyson's Corner near Vienna, Virginia, where the Dolly Madison road slices the turnpike that rolls on toward horsey Leesburg, Kennedy country once upon a time. About noon, he had said. The plowed earth smell, where there was still plowed earth to be smelled, was rich this late morning. Dogwood was long gone but new honeysuckle creepers were reaching fragrantly over hand-hewn fences. Cole had always liked this time of year in Virginia, land of his birth. This time, and the fall. Wally had not, of course, suggested the Langley woods, the CIA's quiet wire-meshed hundred and twenty-five acres just eight miles from the White House in McLean, Virginia.

Cole parked the Honda rental, cheapest he could get, on the left at Tyson's and waited for Wally, breathing in the cool, smog-free air. Horse country would be an awfully nice place to live except in the summer. As his father had said, Virginia had true gentility that couldn't be matched anywhere except Vermont and New Hampshire.

Soon Wally drove up in an Olds Cutlass, which faintly surprised Cole. Living there in snooty Georgetown, Wally ought to be driving an Aston Martin or Alfa Romeo. Wally grinned. "Like your beard. You look like one of us now, not a jarhead."

"I feel like I'm wearing a mask."

He got into the Cutlass and they headed for Leesburg on the pike. After about twenty miles there was a small creek off on one side, and alongside it, almost on the banks, was a shady pull-off. Seeing no other cars around, Wally bounced the Cutlass over the shoulder and parked.

"I come here now and then for lunch just to get away." He lifted out a styrofoam take-out carton. "Pastrami on rye and Heinekens. Got to be back by two." Wally was one of the major operations officers on the Far East desk. He limped now toward the stream.

No doubt Wally's long conditioning had brought them to a secluded place like this. All those intrigues played all around the world. At the time he'd been in Vietnam Wally had been known as Plover, Cole recalled. He even looked a little like a plover. Wally had started in naval intelligence in the late fifties, after being in UDTs for two years, just in time for Vietnam.

Cole sat down on the sandy bank of the creek, out of the blue thinking about crawdads of childhood. Lovely, peaceful days in Northern Virginia. Wally joined him, spreading a piece of plastic under his pants. The water, clear and swift, babbled over rocks at their feet. A red and gold leaf, strayed from autumn, lost soul shook loose from a November hiding place, plunged bravely down the stream. Here they were in the proximity of McLean meeting clandestinely over an affair that had nothing to do with Laos or Elephant Valley or the Komitat Gosudarstvennoi Bezopasnosti.

Unwrapping his pastrami, Wally asked, "You learn anything since I last talked to you?"

"Haven't even tried. Been so busy coming up to shuck that I haven't asked anybody anything. I told you I was through with the detective business six weeks ago. That prying around isn't for me. It's too painful, Wally."

"Glad you found that out."

"But you're sitting beside a dude, as they say on TV, who is fit and ready to go. I've worked my ass off on the road and in the gym. I know Hamburg as well as I know my navel. I can even speak a little of the language . . ."

"Okay, okay," said Wally, fidgety. "How are the kids?"

"They've done real well, Wally. Better than I've done. So has Katta. She's been . . . well, magnificent. I don't know how I got so lucky, I keep reminding myself of that."

"Smart boy."

"But lets get back to Hamburg. What have you found out?"

"Cole, I didn't bring you out here to get back to Hamburg. The reason I brought you here is to try one last time to talk you out of it. Why don't you get the red-eye out of here tonight, go back there and tell whoever you need to tell that retirement was one helluva bad mistake. Or can you do it here in the Pentagon . . . or wherever you do it—"

Cole broke in. "Listen to *me* for once—I'm going, with or without your help."

Wally shook his head.

"Cole, you're asking for a hole between your eyes. Or in your lower regions. You won't be wearing a flak jacket and helmet this time. You're going to operate in a country you know nothing about . . . and don't tell me that forty days of reading guide books and jogging will make a pisspot of difference. I worked in West Germany for three years and was just beginning to know a few things when they hauled me off to Greece. What I'm trying to tell you is that you don't have much of a chance to put him away and come out. If one of the shipyard security people doesn't nail you, the Hamburg *polizei* will. Cole, you're a professional soldier and a good one, but you're an amateur hitman and the amateurs usually get killed in this business. So, chances are you'll be killed. You hear me, Cole?"

"I'm deaf."

"I'll try again. Hamburg has one of the best police forces in Europe. Ten thousand cops. And I tapped a little on the computer just for the hell of it. In homicides, they've solved ninety-two point five of the cases. They make New York and Los Angeles detectives look like a bunch of Clouseaus. So if Noll doesn't get you, you'll no doubt go to Glasmoor on a murder charge."

"I'm still deaf."

"You ever seen those "Death Wish" movies with that Charles Bronson? I see movies a lot. I sleep better after seeing 'em. Anyway, in the first one, he plays vigilante after his wife and daughter are messed up. Shoots a bunch of punks. In the sequel, he does it all over again after his housekeeper and vegetable daughter are messed up. He shoots another bunch of punks. Maybe eight or nine. I lost count. He walks away free after doing in fifteen, twenty guys. All he gets is an arm wound, as I remember. Walks off free, both in New York and Los Angeles. That's movies for you. In real life, odds are that one of those punks would put a bullet in his mouth."

"I know a little about real life, Wally. I just got through a piece of it."

The stream babbled and they chewed. Silent for a moment.

"How did you leave Katta?"

"What do you mean?"

"What kind of state was she in? Do your kids know?"

"Katta hasn't said much about it since I quit. She's tried to talk around it as if she believes the consulting thing. One day she wants to see it done, the next day she's begging me not to do it, all without saying a word. The kids? Maybe Jen suspects . . ." More than suspects.

"Did you really pull all of your savings out of the bank?"

Cole nodded.

"What the hell can I say to you? Your goddamn head is on ass-backward, colonel. What you're going to do isn't going to bring Ellen back. That's the oldest statement in the universe, but goddammit, the truest. I'm sure Katta has said that. Why do I have to say it?"

"Why do you?"

Wally took a frustrated gulp of beer and wiped his chin. He didn't answer.

"All of those Marines back there, the guys I served with, knew exactly why I was retiring and not one questioned it. Not even the general. Not even the chaplain. In fact, they were starting to take up a collection until the general stopped them. They're behind me—"

"I've always thought Marines should have their heads examined..."

"Yours is on your shoulders because of one Marine... Sorry, a cheap shot."

Wally looked over. "I deserved it."

"Wally, if you had a daughter and someone did to her what Hermann did to Ellen, and got away..."

Wally breathed in through his nose.

"Well?"

After quite a while Wally kicked some sand into the creek. "I'd try to take him out."

"So..."

"I don't have a wife and kids. They can be the final losers."

"They can lose either way. I wouldn't be a fit husband or father. I'd drink, smoke dope. Hide from myself."

Wally just sat there, looking at the creek.

"You know, there are a lot of fathers who *couldn't* do this. I'm trained for it. I can take out that son of a bitch without a second thought."

"You can?" Wally looked over, his eyes saying more than words.

"Yes, I can."

Wally nodded, then said briskly. "Okay, I got the Bureau file on

Hermann. I got a shipment out of Bonn for you on Stefan Noll. Someone did me a special favor."

Cole was relieved that the talk had changed. Apparently Wally was giving up the fight, no matter how much he disapproved.

"He's the only dangerous one?"

Wally ignored the question. "I want to tell you what you're up against and then I'll keep my mouth shut and help you in every *unofficial* way that I can. I want to see you come home."

"Tell me about Noll."

"About seven years ago a Lübeck doctor, a plastic surgeon named Rensch, found out some Nazi activities that could have brought Gerda Hermann down; could have cost the company millions in litigation. Dr. Rensch decided to do a little blackmail. And one day, while he was driving from Hamburg back to Lübeck, his Porsche got behind a truck loaded with steel construction rods. Two other cars apparently boxed Rensch in and the truck stopped suddenly. The doctor got the rods through the windshield. About a ton of them. He was decapitated. What a way for a plastic surgery expert to die."

"Next chapter," said Cole.

"The man who put the brake on in the truck was Stefan Noll."

A car bounced over the shoulder and let out three small children who ran joyously for the creek. Wally watched the car with suspicion. A woman got out of the right-hand door and a man walked to the back of the car, pulling a picnic basket from the trunk.

Wally muttered, "Let's go. First time I've ever been interrupted here."

"It's a family on a picnic."

Wally nodded. "But they could have picked someplace else." Checking his watch, he said, "I've got to get back anyway."

"It won't take an hour to get back."

Wally stared at the family again. "How about tonight? My place. You remember where. Eight o'clock. I should be home by then."

"You still live in the same apartment? Same building?"

"Number Four."

They picked up the trash and climbed back into the Cutlass, Wally limping to it on that plastic foot.

151

21

COLE PARKED THE HONDA two blocks away and walked about for twenty minutes until it was eight, then went to Number Four in the fashionable old Georgetown building renovated to look older than it was. Handmade bricks-and-gas lighting. Wally opened the door and Cole saw that the apartment hadn't changed much since the late seventies when he last was there. Maybe a few more books in the floor-to-ceiling shelves. Some of the furniture was probably circa Mary Lincoln. A few good paintings, one in particular, a Grammie Moses. No visible feminine touches.

Wally asked casually, "What did you do this afternoon?"

"Went down to Quantico to see a few old buddies. They were bitching. They don't want to go to war but it seems peace stinks."

Wally grunted. "You like my Whispers, I remember."

"They hurt the next day.

Wally mixed a couple of British gin martinis with only a quarter eyedrop of vermouth in each, then offered a choice of Mexican or Italian dinners or left-over beef pot pie. "I didn't get home until ten minutes ago."

"Pot pie if you made it this week."

"Last night. I had company."

Cole thought it would be interesting to know what kind of company Wally Stonebridge kept.

From the kitchen, which centered around a chopping block, he called out, "Where you staying?"

"Motel off Shirley-Duke. It's clean and twenty a night."

"Bed's a bed, so long as it's safe."

Cole stared off toward the kitchen. The meat block dominated it and garlic festooned from the ceiling.

Like Joe Ferguson, Stonebridge would have been a disaster as a politician but on a second level well below the Director, not in daily contact with State or National Security or the White House or other sensitive offices, he was a wise cobra. Packed under that bristle of thick shining gray hair was intimate knowledge of the intelligence community from Moscow to Tokyo, with stop-overs in Belgrade, Berlin, Athens, Rome and Seoul, not to mention the District of Columbia. He once said he was a student of weakness. That's where the counter-operations always rode, he said. On the other man's weakness.

"Pot pie's on," he announced, emerging from the kitchen in a red apron. "Twenty minutes at three-fifty. Masterpiece the second night, always. Want another drink?"

Cole held out his empty glass. "Who's my contact in Hamburg?"

"Schade. S-c-h-a-d-e. Gunther Schade. *Privat detektiv.*"

"German private eye, yet."

"I used him several times for small errands when I was in Bonn. Paid him cash. He didn't know who I worked for and didn't care. He doesn't know anything about you except you're in real estate and you need to contact someone in Hamburg. International real estate. You don't need to be an expert to do that. You can lie like hell . . . properties in Mexico, the Caribbean. You've been down there, huh?"

Cole nodded.

"Be careful with money. He knows I'm not involved and he'll take everything he can. Don't tell him anything more than you need to."

Wally went back to the kitchen to make two more Whispers and Cole went to the bathroom. Except for the addition of an electric shaving plug and a French phone by the tub it probably hadn't changed since the twenties. Lion paws on the bathtub legs. Washing his hands, Cole noticed an expensive negligee hooked on the back of the door. Even in the mirror it looked expensive. Girl with credentials, likely. Good for Wally.

Coming back into the living room, sitting down to sip his drink, Wally said, "The best source in Hamburg that you can tap may be a specialty prostitute. Girl named Teddi, spelled with an 'i', Hagner. H-a-g-n-e-r. She speaks English. Put Schade on her. Unless you go door to door, I doubt you'll find her by yourself."

Cole wrinkled his forehead. "My idea of this was just go over there, find the son of a bitch. Pop him. Get out."

Wally kept a straight face. "All in twelve hours?"

"Maybe forty-eight. I'm serious."

"He's in hiding, Cole. And Hagner may be one of the few outside people who knows exactly where he is. He may not be in Hamburg as of tonight. Until he got that attaché job, he stayed in Copenhagen a lot. May like the whip girls over there."

"Denmark?" As if he had never heard of it.

"That's right next door, if you'll look at a map. Did you really think you could just walk in and do a job like that on him? Professionals can't even do that."

Cole knew he was beginning to come off dumb.

"Okay, I've got a file for you to take back to the hotel. Read it. Memorize it. Then get rid of it. Tear it into pieces no bigger than your pinkie and flush it. Maybe that's not necessary but it's good practice. No one can trace the file back to me."

Cole nodded.

"Unless you plan to strangle him or knife him, the first time-consuming, the second messy, you'll need a gun. One with a silencer will be waiting for you in locker 719 in the Hauptbanhof, the railway station only a short walk from the Brahms, where you'll be staying. All of this is in the file I fixed up for you. Don't complain about the typing. I did it myself. Go to the Hauptbanhof between nine and twelve Monday night. Be careful that no one sees you take it out of the locker. Schade won't know about the gun. Get rid of it as soon as you can. *I mean rid of it.*"

Cole said, "I wish to hell I could get close enough to strangle the bastard. I'd go home happy if I knew I'd done it that way. Get my hands on his throat."

Wally shook his head. "You're a real case. I'm cutting off your drinks. Forget about satisfaction. Get him in sight, pull the trigger, make sure you've hit him good, then run for home. Above all, don't complicate it. Keep it simple. Quick and simple. You may have to take Noll out first. So be it. He deserves it, from what I've read. Just in case you find handcuffs on your wrist, there's a phone number of a Hamburg lawyer in that file. Copy it and put it in your wallet. That and Schade's number are the only things you'll copy. All the rest will be in your head. Okay?"

The martinis were taking hold. Cole's belly and bloodstream were feeling the spirits and juniper berries.

"My advice would be to shave off the beard, change clothes and get the hell out as soon as you know you got him. Most immigration officers compare mug shots when you enter, not when you leave, and leave as Cole Hickel, of course."

How wild, Cole thought, to be in fashionable Georgetown where the likes of Teddy Kennedy strolled around, and be talking about strangling and knifing and shooting. Or was that just the Whispers doing that?

They had what was left of the pot pie, a masterpiece as Wally had promised, and some fine Chileno chenin blanc, Wally rambling over everything from the fall of Saigon to the softshell crabs at Harvey's. Then he cleared the polished oak table and went about pulling drapes. Next he dug out a sixteen millimeter projector and unrolled a screen.

"Dirty movies?" Cole asked.

"Cross between 'Deep Throat' and that girl who looks like Marilyn Chambers but isn't in 'Penthouse Party.' Ever see it?"

"Bird colonels have to be careful about stags."

Wally put a bottle of Druro Brothers on the table edge with two snifters, clamped a reel on the projector, hit the lamps. The machine whirred, went through its 5-4-3-2-1 routine, passed the start mark and Cole saw an image in black and white, pretty grainy. A thirtyish man was walking down a narrow, quaint cobblestone street. Wally murmured, "Stefan Noll! To get to Klaus Hermann, you have to get past Noll. Take a good look. I'll run this three or four times."

"Where'd you get that film?"

Wally didn't answer.

The setting looked cold. The man was in a topcoat and wore a bob-cap. He moved with brisk, athletic steps.

"Interesting sidebar to young Herr Noll. His old man was SS. They were divided into five groups, you know. Pappy Noll was the SS Verfügungstruppe or Waffen SS. Not concentration camp guards. Special army corps. Anyway, in two separate *Stielhand-granate* attacks in one day he wiped out nineteen U.S. infantry-men. He got the Iron Cross First Class with oak leaves for that bit of work, and then had crossed swords added after the Malmedy Massacre. If Hitler had had a million soldiers like Gerhard Noll you might not have been born. Stefan has the right genes to be a security man and a killer."

"How old did you say he was?"

"Thirty-seven, supposedly. Before he went to work for Gerda Hermann he served in the West German army in the equivalent of our military police. Not too much is known about him but my guess is that he likes blood."

The lens zoomed in and held on the face, but it was not steady.

"Cameraman nervous?" Cole asked.

"Maybe. This was shot not long after Dr. Rensch was decapi-tated. Seven years ago. That little act endeared Stefan to old Gerda forever."

Conventional good-looking guy. Strong face. One that you might see on a 007 ski slope chasing Roger Moore. But it was the way he moved that impressed Cole. A confident walk. Cole had been watching men, and women, for a long time and could tell a lot from the way they walked. The camera panned with him, held on his back as he turned a corner, and then out.

"You got stills on him?" Cole asked.

"Nope. I could get them made but this is safer. Better. You'll know him when you see him."

Black leader spun by the lens and then lit up with a better image, either late spring or summer. Close-up: "Christamighty," said Cole, "he is perfect casting for one of those German guys who shoots at Roger Moore." There was an animal brutality in that high-boned face. His hair was light-colored, maybe blond, and styled.

"I don't see too many spy movies," said Wally. "And, dammit, they don't make many good detectives any more."

Noll came striding closer as the lens zoomed in again. There were two more short takes of film on Stefan Noll in different locales. One as he departed the gates of Hermann Werft; another as he shopped for fish at an outdoor seafood market.

"I'll run everything twice more. If need be, three or four more times. You tell me."

Suddenly Cole was aware he hadn't touched his brandy. He'd see that face in his sleep.

"You have nothing on Klaus Hermann?"

"No reason to put surveillance on him, at that time."

The spliced sixteen went through the sprockets another two times and Cole said, "That's enough. I won't forget him." At first glance it wasn't a frightening face, unless Noll's past was attached to it. Up close, the face took on a different dimension. The man had killed and not let it bother him too much, as Wally had said.

Taking a swig of his Druro, Wally shut down the projector, spun the film off the reel and went into the kitchen, standing by the sink. Cole saw a flare. "What are you doing?"

"Heat treatment. Don't ask me to run it again." He dropped the smoking twisted strip into the sink.

"All that trouble?"

"We do it all the time."

Then Wally came out again and went over to the stereo, lifting the black plastic lid to the turntable. It was a Fisher, with big speakers, linear tracking turntable and dual cassette deck for high speed dubbing. A record dropped, and Cole heard a violin begin to play. A solo. Like that voyage of the autumn leaf down the stream near Leesburg at noon. Dipping and gliding.

Cole frowned over at Wally. "What's the point?"

The CIA man was reflective, half-smiling; maybe a little drunk. Caught by the gliding leaf. "Paganini's Concerto No. 1 in D."

158

"So?" Cole knew little about music. He liked recent oldies. Herb Alpert, Hank Mancini, Ferrante and Teicher. "Jack Benny?"

Wally gave him a pained look and his steel-brake voice rose above the sweet strings. "Bah . . . bah . . . bahbahbahbahbah . . . bah . . . bah . . ."

"I give up," said Cole.

"That's Menuhin," Wally informed him.

"All right, but what's the point?"

"Klaus Hermann plays the violin, as I said before. Quite well, I'm told. He plays in amateur string quartets. Did it here in Washington at GW. He's done it in Germany, Denmark, Sweden . . ."

Cole shook his head.

Wally nodded. "Thought you'd like that."

"Christ, I can't believe I'm going over after a violin player."

Wally nodded. "Told you this was a creepy business."

"I ask you again—you sure you got the right guy?"

Above Paganini, Wally said, "Ho, ho! Sergey Gennadievich Nechayev played the violin and he was the greatest nihilist of them all. Greatest of 'em all, colonel."

"Never heard of him."

"He wrote, *The Revolutionary Catechism* when he was twenty-one. Lenin and Marx weren't even in kneepants when Nechayev was spreading terror. Those Russians go back a long way. He didn't invent the terrorist's bomb but did a lot to perfect the techniques. He died in Peter Paul Fortress in 1881 at the age of thirty-one. Don't let violin players fool you." Wally seemed to be enjoying himself.

"Whatever you say."

"What you're listening to, my friend, is one of Hermann's favorite pieces of music. If you hear Saint-Saens or Paganini coming from a house in Hamburg, Klaus may be near." Wally turned back to the Fisher, saying, "As a matter of fact, I like it myself."

One hard hand, trained in the UDTs, likely still a deadly hand if aroused, still capable of destruction, began to wave in the air and the steel-brake voice went back to "Bah . . . bah . . . bahbahbahbahbahbah . . . bah . . . babababababababa . . . bah . . ."

Eyes closed, he was conducting.

This son of a bitch is also half nuts, Cole thought, taking the rest of his brandy in one gulp.

Rondo Capriccioso, pronounced in elegant Italian by Wally, was next. "Saint-Saens, 1863, well before he wrote *Samson et Dalila.*"

"Where did you learn all this?"

"From a girlfriend, long time ago. She liked to play the classics while we screwed."

Soon, with the Hermann file tucked under his arm and with his new passport, complete with the color ID picture he had mailed from Tustin the past week, in his jacket pocket, Cole left Wally's apartment. The bearded man's name was now Charles Harvey, with all sorts of credit cards in that name. Visa, American Express, Health Plan, California driver's license, even a membership in the International Realtor's Association. As Hickel/Harvey closed the door, Wally Stonebridge was still listening to Saint-Saens.

The biographical data was not of too much interest—same items that Wally had read to him over the phone. But then it got better. Klaus was kicked out of Ruprecht-Karl-Universität in his second year of attendance because he had "allegedly assaulted a young fräulein on *Philosohenweg*—read Philosopher's Way—a path overlooking the 12th-century city"; there was another incident nine years later about a "forced friendship" (kidnapping) with a young actress who was working at the film studio in Wandsbek, almost under Gerda's umbrella. Finally, the twenty-two-year-old American university student from Indiana who was given thirty thousand in cash by a Washington lawyer. Precisely what Klaus had done to her was not known. She refused to talk. Cole got the idea there might be other cases unreported.

Cole stayed up with the file until almost three, then, as directed, tore the material into pieces no larger than his pinkie nail. The people in the room next door must have thought the occupant of 209 was stricken with the trots. The toilet flushed continuously for nearly a half hour.

* * *

"I'm going to be very honest with you, Gerda," said Dr. Hoger. "It is quite possible that Klaus did kill that girl in California, perhaps accidentally, one or two hard blows to the neck or head when he became so worked up that he could not control himself. The possibility is strong."

"I do not believe you," said Gerda angrily, knuckles getting white around the French phone in the suite's master bath, which was almost the size of a handball court. She was in pink-tinted suds up to her neck; hair tamped into a Sidi San Juan Sol shower cap.

"I said *possible*. I mean that under certain conditions he is quite capable of doing great harm. Though he may not look it, he is strong. Very strong. I have now talked to him many hours, as you know, and the preliminary conclusion is that he responds to certain sexual situations in an abnormal fashion. Compounding that now is cocaine usage. He has admitted he began sniffing the drug in Washington about a year ago, and these spells seem to coincide with the ingestion. However, we both know about the girl in Wandsbek. The drug had nothing to do with her broken shoulder."

"My son is not an addict," declared Gerda, glaring toward the north wall of the bathroom, a plastic-topped head and phone over the pink suds. No body.

"I did not say that he was. Not yet. But he has been using. Over four sessions the last week I questioned him about whether or not he had used on the day when he met the girl in California. Finally he acknowledged that he did. He also denied he ever touched her."

"And I believe him," said Gerda. "He is telling the truth. He might have frightened her, that's all."

Dr. Hoger tried not to sigh all the way from Hamburg to Alicante. "I cannot argue with the autopsy report in this case. The foreign office sent a copy when the panel examined him. But I am also equally convinced—"

Gerda interrupted sharply. "Franz, I'm not interested in these terrible accusations. You keep telling me all the bad things about Klaus and none of the good. Did you know he was given a commendation for his work in Washington?"

"No, I didn't know that," said Dr. Hoger wearily.

"He is so talented. Did you know he was painting a portrait of me? It is half finished and when I return we will find time to complete it."

"He hasn't told me he was painting you. I know he paints and plays the violin." So he's artistic! So was Adolf Hitler and his famous drawing of eight German soldiers in Flanders mud.

"All those letters he wrote at the embassy, and your panel had the nerve to say 'diminished capacity'..."

"You should be thankful we did. There was talk in Bonn of him facing extradition, as you know."

Gerda also ignored that. "As soon as you tell me he's cured he'll go back to his old position at the shipyard. He was doing quite well before he went to Washington. Or I've thought about trying to place him with Staatsoper and make use of his ability as an artist. He has such a good mind..."

Dr. Hoger nodded, closing his eyes, thankful she was not across from him. Speaking carefully, he said, "I am not sure there is a cure, Gerda. I am trying to find out what causes the abnormality, under what precise conditions..." At what point did the whip lashes...

Gerda snapped, interrupting again. "The *conditions* are that my poor son has been punished for looking strange. *And that is all.*"

Dr. Hoger said nothing, reaching for two antacid tablets while Gerda went on, and on, about Klaus and his overlooked good-nesses.

Dr. Hoger did keep a silent watch on the Japanese digital desk clock. He always charged double for these calls to Gerda.

22

COLE TOOK EASTERN to J.F. Kennedy, boarding Lufthansa 407 in early evening for Düsseldorf and Hamburg. On the flight up from Virginia, staring out the 727 window, trying to stay away from Ellen on the phone in the kitchen in a white terrycloth robe, towel piled up on her wet head, bare feet on the desktop, toes wriggling, Cole tried to recreate on the clouds the too handsome face of Stefan Noll, remember it clearly from the sixteen millimeter close-up. Now he was trying to do the same thing as the 747 climbed in twilight to cruising altitude while cocktail carts clattered down the aisles. Long after dinner and the movie he was still doing it as the moon moved around from laying a panel on the wing to casting its beam on the nose of the darkened, whistling Boeing. Noll was already unforgettable, a man off the alps.

Klaus Hermann remained frustratingly in shadow. From the descriptions, Cole was not able to get a good fix on the chubby violin player beyond the slick peach skin and his set of kinko tools. Inevitably, Ellen was soon there again in the long sleepless night. In stop frame, cheerleading at Cherry Point High School, at the top of a leap, her back a crescent. *Memory,* as the sergeant's daughter had sung at the memorial.

In the morning, after Düsseldorf and gliding down a long aerial hill through crumpling rain-laden clouds, vivid patches of green below kept jarring his eyes as the aircraft slid past puffs of white. Ellen rearing back to serve . . . he'd watched her play whenever he could . . . he should have taken more time to watch. Then the aircraft flattened out, finally slicking to a stop on a Hamburg Fuhlsbuttel runway.

Drizzly this day, as it was many days opposite England. Brolly weather. Even the customs and immigration man looked despairing as they okayed the entry of Charles F. Harvey, giving him only a glance. Real estate was the occupation written down on the entry form he had filled out on the jet. Unless Wally Stonebridge had told them, surely no German could have known that Ellen Hickel's father was walking out at Fuhlsbuttel. Yet Cole found himself jittery, already casting about for Stefan Noll.

It was that time of year in northern Europe when the days were long and nights only a few hours. Light at two-thirty or three in the morning. Even the darkness, setting in at eleven and growing shorter as the third week in June approached, was perverted, more chocolate than black. Gray morning had been around for hours.

Yawning, eyes stinging, joints stiff, Cole took himself into a diesel cab that looked just like the guide books said. The cab ground along past brown buildings, brick everywhere. The driver finally broke silence to announce, "Aussen Alster," pointing proudly. Big lake fit for sailboats and white ferries. What did Wally say? Outer Alster, where Klaus liked to tack around. Not today. Only the white ferries were playing in the light breezeless rain. The cab ground some more and finally Cole's half-drowse was shattered by the driver announcing the hotel, swinging up into a puny circle of driveway.

Fronting the busy thoroughfare by the big lake, Der Brahms stood as a small white citadel of European charm—Wally's choice. Cars parked precisely in front of it bore license plates of Switzerland, Holland, Belgium, France and Denmark. It looked exactly the way Wally said it would look. Flower boxes exploding red with geraniums were beneath all the windows. Little flags of a dozen non-Communist nations fanned over the entranceway. An American real estate man would fit right in.

_____

Behind the desk was a buxom, tawny woman in her forties blessed with an early suntan. This one was bursting with health. Sun club member at Sylt, was a good bet. Right place for birthday suits, said one of the guide books. The desk nameplate read "Frau Wegner." Cole smiled defensively at her and filled out the form, temporarily surrendering his "Harvey" passport and collecting the envelope marked Hold For Arrival in English. He felt for the Hauptbanhof key. It was safely there.

"Zehr gut," said Frau Wegner loudly, pounding the summons bell with a fist. "We hope your visit will be plessent," she added with a heavy accent. "We have the harbor and the Elba; also many beautiful *kirches* . . . then there is Planten und Blomen, the garden . . ."

Cole kept nodding tiredly, finally stopping the spiel with "Please tell me later."

"Yes, such a long long flight. Tch."

There was a big canvas portrait of Johannes on one wall of the lobby. The composer had fat cheeks, Cole noticed. Somber eyes.

He followed the Brahms' only porter, clad in a faded green smock, into the three-passenger elevator not much bigger than a phone both. Not wanting to appear unfriendly, Cole commented, "Rains a lot here, huh?"

Silver-haired, maybe an old Panzerman, maybe an old U-boat sailor, maybe just an old sore-footed bellboy. "No Englisch," he growled.

Cole shrugged. *Up yours, too.*

The elevator jiggled to an uncertain stop on the third floor and the Panzergrenadier made his way down a dark hall, finally stopping and opening a door. Cole looked in, pleasantly surprised. Three-Zero-Two was a combination bedroom-sitting room with brocaded chairs and delicate Dresden figurines on the coffee table. Crystal chandelier hanging in the center. No wonder Wally liked Der Brahms: huge bed, acres of it, with an eiderdown puffed out from beneath a lacy spread against one wall. The porter departed after a disappointed peek at his tip.

Cole took up the Greater Hamburg phone book and looked up

165

the Hermanns. There was no scarcity. They were like Smiths, all over the place, from Rotherbaum to Gross Flottbek. Sixteen were named Klaus Hermann. There were even von Hermanns listed. Chances were that *the* Klaus Hermann wasn't there. Gerda wasn't. Visit all sixteen?

He soon drew the drapes, locking out Hamburg mist, damping out the Alster road traffic, stripped down and disappeared under the eiderdown.

About four-thirty, after a cottony sleep so deep that he bottomed out, Cole awakened to see someone moving in the room. Coming out of bed, making knuckles on both hands, he drove the shape into a corner, taking it down. There was a girl's frightened scream, and he scrambled up, hitting the lights to reveal the milk-white face and cowering body of a maid in a uniform, scrunched down like she was about to be flayed.

Heart pounding, he said, "Goddamn, never do that again. Knock, turn the light on . . ."

The girl, no older than Ellen, crawled shakily to her feet, took a second look at the naked man with the slack penis, then shot out of Room 302, abandoning her water pitcher.

Grabbing pants, struggling into them, Cole followed and called for her to come back but she was already down two flights. He felt foolish. The old Nam hang-up. Anus doing circumnavigation if there was a loud noise outside the hootch. Shape in the shadows was dirty Charlie, reflexes went to work, still automatic. The old hang-up, but maybe good to have over here.

He called *privat detektiv* Gunther Schade, the other phone number Wally had given him. The answering female voice said Herr Schade would return shortly. "May I ask who is calling?" Only a trace of accent. He'd spent all that time with those lousy cassettes and now it seemed the world spoke English.

"Charles Harvey. I'm at the Brahms." *Harvey.*

He was afraid he'd blow it somewhere down the line, not respond. Sign something *Cole Hickel.* Maybe even *Colonel Cole Hickel.* He had said "Charles Harvey" to the mirror in Virginia;

166

said it in the immigration line; said it on the flight over. *Harvey, Harvey, Harvey.*

"Oh, yes," said the pleasant voice, "I shall have him call you."

Shaved, showered and down in the small lobby, where Frau Wegner was on the phone jabbering away in *"zeigen sies"* and *"wo zahles,"* Cole looked California casual. Blue slacks, light red sweater, white wash 'n wear shirt, soft shoes the color of doeskin. He had brought a sports jacket and tie along for night or going home. Wegner got off the phone and he smiled at her. "Any calls for me and I'll be in the bar."

"Ah, yes, Herr Harvey." She positively beamed at him.

A moment after sliding up to the Brahms' spirits dispensary, a comfy four-seater, Cole asked the British-sounding bartender which local tours he would recommend. Establish yourself, Wally had said. Name, occupation, where you're from, where you're going. Lie about all of them but do remember what you lied about.

"You're alone? No wife?"

"Afraid so."

"Go to the Reeperbahn and see all the girls you want. You don't need tours. Hamburg is not so much a tourist place, it's a business place. You're a businessman?"

"International real estate. Investment properties, mainly the Caribbean."

"Supah."

"You don't sound German."

"I'm not. Manchester. Married to a German girl."

Frau Wegner bore down on the bar. "You have a call, sir. Take it in the lobby."

Gunther Schade was on the other end saying he had been expecting Mr. Harvey. "I will see you." He, too, sounded efficient.

Cole went back to the bar and bought Frau Wegner a drink. Smiling widely, she said, "Thank you. You are some rested, Herr Harvey, but perhaps you need more sleep, coming all the way across the ocean . . ."

"I feel fine," said Cole.

She kept smiling. "There is much to see and do here, despite what the bartender told you. He always does that."

"Why?" Wally said to act like a visitor, be interested.

"He does not like it here, of course. But I suggest you go to Pöseldorf with its boutiques and galleries, my favorite place, or there is our main shopping street, Mönckebergstrasse. We call it 'Mö.' And for entertainment there is the Dom, our great carnival, and night clubs such as Onkel Pö or Fabrik . . ."

Cole kept the interested look on his face. "The bartender didn't mention those."

"Ah hah," Frau Wegner said, "And, of course, here we are on the historic Alster with the finest swans in all Europe. Our swan-keeper, a very famous man, takes them all to winter quarters in the fall and gives them back to us in the spring . . ."

"A regular swankeeper, eh?" said Cole.

"Oh, yes, so many things to see and do."

"Thank you for the information, Frau Wegner," Cole said, and meant it.

Her smile widened as she said it was her pleasure. She excused herself, taking the Scotch on the rocks back to the desk. Everyone in the informal friendly Brahms seemed friendly except the Panzer-man. And by sundown, everyone would know that casual Mr. Harvey sold expensive properties and was looking for investors: Mr. Harvey, the rich American from California with condos and hotels and beach frontage in St. Thomas, Virgin Gorda and Cancun and other assorted tropical paradises.

Schade arrived at a quarter to six, a smart, almost heel-popping, saluting arrival. Alert, sending off signals of energy, he was maybe forty, maybe fifty. Bad homemade dye job on his hair, but there wasn't a speck of gray. His face was a wedge with an unusually sharp nose. Casting around to see who else was in the Brahms, he took off driving gloves. A featherweight and wiry, he wore an impeccable black suit of hard worsted.

Frau Wegner nodded toward the tall bearded American at the bar and Schade came briskly over, introduced himself.

"I trust you had a good flight, Herr Harvey. We Germans pride ourselves on the cuisine of Lufthansa. First class is unequalled."

"I flew economy."

The hazel pick-eyes flickered. Herr Harvey had dropped a notch.

"Wally sends his regards," Cole said. Wally had sent no such thing.

"How is my old friend?"

Cole remembered Wally saying he had never met Schade. "Very well."

"*Zehr gut*. You speak German?"

"None at all."

"Well, I am at your service twenty-four hours a day. I just took three members of the Peruvian *vigilar* to the airport for their flight to Lima so I can devote my time entirely to your problems." Though slightly accented, his English was flawless. "You are here on business? Wally did not explain."

Cole nodded. "Real estate."

"Buy or sell?"

"Sell, mostly, in the Caribbean and Mexico. Beach frontage for investment. Hotels, villas, condos."

Schade waited.

"I need your help to locate a friend of a friend, Mr. Schade."

"Please call me Gunther."

The bartender's left ear was practically on Cole's shoulder. Cole had the choice of filling it or moving. He nodded toward a table against the wall. "We'll be more comfortable over there." Schade agreed and the Manchester man began doing busy work, pretending he had not been listening.

After they sat down Schade said that he was hired mostly by foreigners, spoke seven languages, including Russian. "My services are rather expensive. I have a select clientele, some of whom might be interested in Caribbean properties."

Wally had warned Cole about the prices. "I already have a select clientele . . ."

"Very good," Schade smiled back. "A thousand Deutschmarks a

day plus expenses. Double that for extra work away from Hamburg. I go anywhere on the continent."

Cole returned the radiance. "Five hundred Deutschmarks a day, Gunther. No extra work needed. I doubt you'll have to leave the city limits."

Schade shrugged, with only slight visible defeat. *"Alles in ordnung."*

"Zehr gut."

"Hah, you do speak Deutsch."

"Cassette overnight German."

They both laughed.

"Now, Mr. Harvey—"

"Charles . . ."

"Now, Charles, what can I do for you?"

"Locate a woman named Teddi Hagner."

"A wealthy woman? I have never heard of her."

"I've been told she's a whore."

"Ah, so you want her for business or pleasure."

"Not pleasure and not really business. I'm contacting her on behalf of a friend of mine, as I said." Several very close friends: Ellen, Katta, the kids, Phil Chiu . . .

"I was hoping it would be something more exciting, more challenging." Schade took a drink of Chivas.

You have no idea how exciting it might be before I'm through here, one way or the other, Cole thought. "Sorry," he said.

Schade laughed softly. "Hamburg is very large, the largest . . ." His voice drifted off. It was obvious that chasing whores was only a step above hunting lost dogs. "Is she a high-priced whore?"

"No idea."

"That makes it difficult. There are many girls here, over three thousand registered. God knows how many more unregistered." It appeared he was mentally checking off spots, rotating his Scotch glass as he did. "In the St. Georg? Oh, I don't know . . . we'll start in the St. Pauli, the largest redlight place, the Reeperbahn. On the Grösse Freiheit we have our famed temples of desire, the Colibri or Safari or Salambo or Tabu. But there are other places, too. Pick-up places like the Mon Amour or the Happy End. And then there are the very fancy places for the New York bankers and Texas oil men. It's all very legal here in Hamburg. We people on the Elbe long ago decided that this profession should be recognized for what it is. Morality is no factor. We are a legendary seaport town. Our opera singers sell their voices. Our whores sell their bodies."

A morality tale wasn't of much interest to Cole at the moment. "How long do you think it will take to find Teddi Hagner?"

Schade shrugged. "Six hours, ten hours, ten days . . . As I said, this is a big city. I will need to make many calls tonight and maybe again tomorrow after two o'clock. The night people don't wake up until then. If I don't call you during the day I'll pick you up tomorrow night about eight. Okay?"

"Okay."

In the lobby Cole said, "Nice painting of Johannes."

Schade corrected. "That isn't Johannes. That is Friedrich, burgomeister in the seventeen hundreds . . . *Auf weidersehen,*" Schade said, and departed, his stringy little body moving swiftly into the lobby, where he rattled some happy words at Frau Wegner, who seemed to be on duty day and night, and then was gone.

Back in the bar Cole asked the Brit's recommendation for a good place to eat close by. Walking distance.

"Dining room at the Atlantic. It's just up the street."

Cole downed his drink, went up to the room and placed a call to California. It was morning in Tustin.

"You okay, Cole?"

"I'm fine but I miss you already. Seems like I've been gone a week."

"Three days. It's hard for me to sleep."

"How's the weather?"

"Usual. Sunny, warm. How is it there?"

"Rain this morning, a little chilly. I slept for seven hours after I got off the plane."

My God, they didn't have anything to talk about, Cole thought. Anything they *could* talk about. And he knew that Katta was thinking the same thing five thousand miles away.

171

"How are the kids?"

"They're fine. In school, of course. Call tomorrow when they're home. It's nine here now."

"After six here."

"You're really okay?"

"Sure."

"How's the hotel?"

"Fine. You'd love the bed. Big as a football field. Eiderdown."

"Keep it solo, partner."

"On my honor."

He knew she didn't dare ask, Have you found out where *he* is? When will you do *it*? When will you come home? *Alive*?

"I'm going out to dinner soon. Right down the street. Town has great seafood, I hear."

"Eat heartily," Katta said, on the verge of tears.

"Yeh. Hey, I'll call at a better time tomorrow. Give my love to the kids. Take a lot for yourself."

"You take care. I love you. Goodbye."

If Frau Wegner was listening she had to feel let down.

Cole put on his jacket and tie and raincoat, then out into the misty night for the few blocks to the Atlantic, which looked like a lot of international businessman money, bankers from New York, Texas oil men. A considerable amount of their loot was taken in the dining room.

After dinner, checking his pocket guide, he went up the street and over to the Hauptbanhof, where the rush hour was history; trains idled for pre-midnight departures. The sandstone station smelled of diesel fumes. Nearly nine. He went around the blocks of lockers until he found 719. All was clear, so far as he could tell . . . no one watching to see who inserted the key. He quickly opened the door, extracting a worn leather suitcase. Scuffed hotel stickers on it were Canadian.

Walking leisurely, but feeling tingles, toward the only open newsstand, he bought a Paris *Herald-Tribune* and an overseas *Newsweek*, then strolled on out, returning to the Brahms, where a collegiate type was on the desk. He asked the boy for 302, gave his name and the big brass key slid across. Good-nights were exchanged. Cole looked in at the bar. A black man and a peroxide woman occupied two stools. The Brit from Manchester was still on duty. Cole waved to him and went on up in the phone-booth elevator carrying his suitcase.

He locked and chained the door, closed the drapes, then opened the leather bag to find big wads of the *Morgenpost*. Nestled deep inside the newsprint was a standard Smith and Wesson .38 and ammo. Cole was surprised that they had slipped him an American gun, but the silencer was Ludwigshafen. He stood there, looking at the pistol, thinking of Stefan Noll and Klaus Hermann. If he could keep Ellen in focus, that sickening sight of her as the coroner's assistant pulled the cloth back, the trigger would be easy to pull.

23

TAKING FRAU WEGNER'S ADVICE, not the Brit's, Cole spent the entire day sightseeing, just like any other tourist, taking a two-hour tour bus tour in the morning, and then doing two museums in the afternoon with a little left over for the Dom funfair. Just like any other tourist. A little sleep on top of that and then downstairs to the four-seater bar at about seven-thirty to hear the Brit say what was wrong with Hamburg.

He slid into the red VW at eight-thirty prompt, asking the driver, "You find her?"

Schade nodded. "Trinidad Club, Reeperbahn. But she also makes appointments. You know the kind I mean, eh?"

Cole had a notion. Whips and chains.

"First, pleasure. Where shall we eat?"

"Your territory," said Cole, looking over, studying the spic and span little detective.

Schade suggested, *"Erbensuppe mit Snuten und Poten."*

"What in hell is *that?*"

"Pea soup with pig's snout and knuckles. Fine local dish." There was laughter.

It wasn't what Cole had in mind.

The *detektiv,* smiling, moved his VW skillfully through auto and motorscooter traffic along the Binnen Alster, the smaller lake of the twins, then across a bridge and by frowning government buildings and parks full of old people. Up a low hill, then the VW descended to the mottled brown Elbe. Schade had not shut up since pulling away from the Brahms. Nor had he said anything useful. Volunteered facts of Schade's life, or facts that Schade said were of his life, were not of interest to Cole. At one point Gunther said he had been in counterintelligence, the Federal Office for Protection of the Constitution in Cologne. Maybe out of that past Wally had dredged him up . . .

There were fresh red carnations in a small vase attached to the dash with a suction cup. Not in keeping with the Federal Office.

"What else did you learn about Teddi Hagner?" Cole pressed.

"Later," said Schade.

Annoyed, Cole let it go. What choice did he have?

Speeding for five or six blocks, Schade then turned in a tight circle in front of a restaurant tucked into warehouses and fishing industry sheds fronting the river. Inside they passed an elaborate glass tank in which eels water-danced on their tails as if receiving jolts of electricity.

"Select your own," Schade observed. "Look at that fat strong one. *Wunderbar.*"

After he snapped fingers at a beefy waiter they went toward large windows that looked out on the river. Looming almost directly across was a large, lighted Hermann Werft sign. Startled, Cole stared at it. Had Wally lied? Did Gunther Schade know all along why he'd come here? Or was this some crazy coincidence? Whatever, it was unnerving.

The Elbe was choppy. Big ships paraded by. Small, high-stacked tugs darted under sleek prows. Work boats plied along, even at this dining drinking hour, slithering through jammed ferries and squat power barges. Mooring boats scooted about.

Chivas Regal for Herr Schade, vodka straight-up for Herr Harvey. Send over the wine list. *"Ah, ein Rothandels, bitte."* Schade ate, drank and smoked well, on his clients, smiling all the while.

Cole nodded casually at the river and beyond. "Big shipyard, huh?" He watched Schade's reaction. Nothing. Coincidence? Probably.

"Almost as big as Blohm and Voss. Container ships mostly but now and then a cruise ship for the Scandinavians. Thousands of barges, they build at Hermann Werft."

"Who runs it?"

"Female shark. An old lady named Gerda. Worth millions of Deutchmarks."

"Be dammed. A woman runs it?"

"Had you seen this in 1945, Charles, you would not believe today. Three thousand wrecks in the river and harbor. Forty million cubic meters of debris. The British started a firestorm they named Gomorrah and charred seventy thousand of us in one night. In the Borstelmannsweg section the temperature reached 1,472 degrees Fahrenheit . . ."

"You were here?"

"No, no, no. I was only eight years old on our farm near Neustadt. We saw the red sky, then smelled burnt bodies for days until the wind shifted. We visited here about three months after Gomorrah. I couldn't believe the destruction."

"Is that right?" Old Ernst had helped clean it up and that's why Gerda was now so rich.

Plates vanquished, Schade ordered rhum-babas, Remy-Martin, a cigar for himself, and talked on about the city. Cole was not listening. He was thinking about Klaus Hermann.

While Schade scanned the bill, rubbing Charles Harvey's Visa between his fingers, mumbling to himself in German, Cole kept his eyes on the shipyard. No matter how many millions Gerda had, she could not buy Ellen's life.

Soon they were moving up the Reeperbahn. *Würsts* frying in stale grease sent up acrid smoke. Uniformed doormen hawked a mixture of German and English in front of gaudy facades covered with fading nude photos.

Schade grinned. "You like?"

Cole shrugged. "Every town should have one, I guess."

Rhumbas and California rock collided mid-street with brass oom-pah from the beer gardens.

"You could go deaf here," said Cole.

"You also can get anything you want—anything—from hashish oil and coke to speed and acid, heroin, PCB . . ."

"Just ask?"

"Just ask. Anything. You like the unique? Whip girls in purple leather overalls? We have them," said Schade with a bit of tour guide pride. "You like beatings with birch branches? We have them. Girl with donkey. Boy with sheep. Naked mud wrestlers. You want to make love in the mud? Name what you want." Schade seemed amused. A thin smile was sitting on the wedge face, hazel eyes ranging far out, scanning for the bizarre.

It was indeed all there. Punk rockers with green spike hair, pimps and pickpockets and snow peddlers. Suddenly Cole saw two U.S. Marines in full bemedaled dress walking toward them, sticking out like crown jewels in a garbage scow. Half-bagged, they were laughing and talking loud and having a big old time. Fine uniformed salesmen, they were just what Uncle Sam needed overseas, what the Marine Corps needed.

"For Chrissakes," Cole muttered, they looked like they'd just come off presidential review. "What the hell," he said, as they kept coming on, hooting it up. One was a good six-two and bulky; the other a head shorter. Mutt and Jeff. Those full-dress uniforms weren't allowed out on the street this time of night. Breaking away from Schade, Cole angled across the sidewalk, Schade asking, "Where are you going?"

Cole didn't hear him. "You Marines," he barked, coming up chest to chest with the big redneck sergeant. "Get off this goddamn street in those uniforms or I'll call the military police."

The big one formed a fat O in surprise, then said, "Ol' man turdface, who you tellin' what to do?"

Cole said, "Listen to me, sergeant, get your ass off this street and get back to your unit pronto. That goes for you, too, private. You're both disgraces to your uniform—"

"Lissen, fuckhead," said the sergeant, "get outta my way or I'll clean your fuckin' stack." One big hand came up from below his hip and started in a round-house when Cole sank a right into his belly.

A suction sound like a sink drain being cleared came out of the sergeant as he bent in the middle. Cole karate-chopped him on the back of his neck and he went down in a pile of Marine dress blues. Rolling over, he fought to get air to his lungs.

The other shook off his schnapps and pawed out toward Cole just in time to take a shot on the bridge of his nose. He ran off.

As a crowd gathered Schade had Cole by the arm. "What's wrong with you? Have you gone crazy?"

Now that it was over, Cole found himself trembling, adrenalin pumping. Taking in deep breaths, he stood there watching the sergeant get to his knees and throw up in the gutter.

Two green and white polizei cars came zipping up out of nowhere, angling to the curb.

Shaking his head, Schade asked, "Why did you do that? They weren't hurting you—"

"They were hurting me and every other American, disgracing those uniforms—"

"They aren't Marines," Schade seethed. "They are doing dress-up."

"Doing what?"

"Later," Schade snapped. "Say nothing."

Three of the polizei confronted Cole while the other bent over the sarge. Schade began volleying German at them, motioning to the sergeant and then to Cole.

They listened, then one said something in an angry voice to Cole and pointed his finger.

Schade translated. "He said for you to get off the street. They want no trouble here tonight. We go."

"How about him?" Cole asked, nodding toward the man who was still down.

"We *go*," snapped Schade.

Cole was still shaking slightly as they walked away, polizei and the silent small crowd staring after them.

"What the hell do you mean they weren't Marines?"

"Places here rent costumes. People cruise, as you say."

Phonies. "Holy shit," said Cole, knowing immediately he almost blew everything. Maybe did. They were walking rapidly.

"You could have been arrested for assault. I told him the sergeant hit you first, you were defending yourself. One of the police knew me. I'm a friend of the chief of Davidwache, the station here. I told him I was your private tour guide tonight, escorting you. They just don't want trouble here in the St. Pauli. There is enough already."

What a dumb-ass thing to do, Cole thought, suddenly realizing the knuckles on his right hand were stinging. The boy's nose was hard. Beyond embarrassing—stupid, and dangerous.

"Forget it," said Schade. "But *ask* me before you act. Ask me."

Cole nodded, ears red with embarrassment.

Schade looked at him now, curiously. "What you did back there was professional. Are you professional?"

"I'm in real estate," Cole said, winding down. "But I've done some boxing in college, studied a little karate . . ."

Fight on a German street! Blow everything! Pure dumb luck I didn't have the gun on me. It would have dropped out, right in front of that crowd.

Schade kept looking at him. "Don't go asking for trouble in the St. Pauli. You'll always find it."

"Who were those jerks?"

"Probably American merchant seamen having some fun. Look, Charles, this is the St. Pauli, not Los Angeles. Two weeks ago I saw a Colonel Quaddafi. You want to wear a Russian general's uniform? Vatican guard? Foreign legion? There is a rental place. You want to dress up like Marilyn Monroe? They've got strap-around tits. This is one big party."

Shaking had stopped, the heart had begun to flatten . . . Cole thought of how he hadn't had a fistfight since Nam, and even then hadn't picked it.

They went on. Dujardin's red emblem stuttered in neon, and Gunther Schade took up the lecture once again. Zillertal was for peasants to beer-up and polka; Ebony and Top Ten were discos. "But you should see it again when the lights go out and the girls go home. It is suddenly very sad," Schade said, touching Cole's elbow.

They turned into a door under a sky-rising marquee that proclaimed La Trinidad. Above it, climbing into twilight, was a dis-

180

membered nude, torso becoming whole as red and blue neons painted her in. They went down a stairway into a large room smelling of stale drinks and penny-perfume squirts. Fluorescent wall paint burned exotic colors into thighs and mammaries and pubic patches.

"Guten abend, guten abend, minen herren," fell upon them from an anxious maitre d'. Business was bad. Schade ignored him, peering about in the gloom.

On a match-box stage a middle-aged stripper was getting down to her final patch. Her eyes were at half-mast. She had massive nipples on drooping breasts. A combo was doing "Born Free." Schade looked at her, then back at Cole. He spoke to the maitre d', and Cole heard Teddi's name mentioned. The Trinidad man checked his watch, shook his head.

"Take a table," Schade directed.

Wide choice. Eight or ten girls were haphazardly staked out. Blue light didn't do too much for them. They signaled to each other, almost imperceptibly, and then two split off.

The maitre d' went to the office and made a call to Blankenese, a village not far down the Elbe. He said, 'Herr Stern, someone has finally come in asking for Teddi. An American and a man I've seen before. He is a private investigator, Gunther Schade."

"How does the American look?"

"Tall. Has a gray with brown beard. About forty, I would say."

"Thank you," said "Stern," and hung up.

The maitre d' put the phone down, thinking it was the easiest two hundred deutschmarks he had ever earned. The man who said his name was Stern had asked to be notified if anyone inquired about Teddi Hagner. That was more than a month ago. Teddi did not operate out of the Trinidad, she dropped in now and then to see the man who played piano in the combo.

A half hour later "Herr Stern" moved quickly down the steps of the Trinidad, stayed in the shadows by the *damen* and *herren,* took a long look at Gunther Schade and the *Amerikanischer* with the beard and departed.

* * *

181

A tall blonde in a filmy white evening gown that became azure in the psychedelic lighting swung her hips into the chair beside Cole, stroking his sleeve. *"Geben zie mir etwas zu trinken?"*

Cole put on a helpless look.

Schade nodded toward him. *"Amerikanischer."*

The blonde's eyes brightened. "Honey, some champagne for me, please."

Schade snapped his fingers at the waiter. The girl who had come to roost by the detective rattled away at him in German, frequently glancing at Cole, figuring he had the money. Schade was obviously known at the Trinidad. He ordered champagne in the fashion of a millionaire, grinning at Cole.

"My name is Hilda," said the blonde.

"I'm Lee Iacocca," Cole replied.

"Lee, vill you buy some cigarettes?" asked the blonde. "Be a good boy *und* buy some."

Cole nodded. You pay for information, Wally had said. Don't quibble, just pay. Time is too short. He massaged his reddened knuckles.

Hilda popped her fingers at a tired old woman, a hooker long past her prime, standing at the foot of the stairs, trapped in the Trinidad, tending the *damen* and *herren* and selling Rothandels and "Looky Strikes" and Camels. She looked at least sixty. She wore cloth bedroom slippers.

Hilda selected two packs of Winston-Salems, five times the cost of German filters, gave off a little-girl smile, squeezing Cole's hand. Hilda, about twenty-five with a nice body, playfully checked Cole's fingers and spun his wedding ring; examined his palm and murmured that he had a good love-line and that she liked his beard. Then she leaned close to whisper, "You vill go wiss me tonight, eh? I'm very goot in bed."

Cole whispered back, "Maybe."

She gave him a wide smile, rubbed her palm over his scuffed knuckles, then winked and let her other hand drop to his crotch. Champagne arrived and Hilda filled his glass; then her colored water was deposited. She swilled it in a gulp and called for the waiter.

"You know Teddi Hagner? She comes here?"

Hilda looked at him. "You would not like her. She iss older. She does bad things."

"What bad things?"

"Bad things. Not nice things like I do."

"Tell me, Hilda."

"No." She swilled the second one down and then said nervously, "Vee go now. My place is near. You vill like my place. Very clean."

Schade spoke to her sharply and she stuck out an impish tongue. "Focking German mens, ach," she said to Cole. "I like zee Americans, *und* zee Australian, not zee Italian, *ider . . .*"

Another stripper did her last grind and then scooped up her leopard suit to dart off into the shadows. The combo segued into dance music and Hilda demanded, "Come," leading Cole to the dance floor, doing her best to attach her pelvic bone to his. "Tell me about Teddi," he said.

"No. She iss not nice."

"And you are?"

"Yiss," she grinned, undulating expertly, slowly and expertly, waiting for Cole to undulate back. "I'm very goot," she whispered. "I do everything."

"I'm sure," he said.

Another half hour of Hilda; another two bottles of five deutschmark champagne for which he was charged fifty-five, and Teddi Hagner still had not shown. Schade broke away from his girl to make phone calls. After the last one he returned to say, "She will be home about twelve-thirty."

Hilda spat on the table and walked away while Schade shouted curses at her in his best St. Pauli.

They left La Trinidad at 12:15 but not before the old cigarette girl tried to peddle a batch of hardcore photos. Grinning, she flipped through them, nominating choice ones as she went.

183

24

TEDDI HAGNER lived in the Ottensen district northwest of Altona station, where factories once thrived before Gomorrah. Cole watched for signs. They went up Behrenfelder, then on to Daimlerstrasse, going roundabout, it seemed, as if shaking someone. Then Schade dodged the VW back into narrow, darker streets, and Cole saw Planckstrasse flash by. Remember them, he told himself, in case he had to come back alone. It all looked rebuilt from another time. Cobblestones and gas lights, like Wally's apartment building. Now the car took another sharp turn and stopped abruptly in front of a building that Gomorrah apparently had not fried. Old brick, four or five stories up, it looked turn-of-century.

Schade's head bobbed toward 152. "In there, apartment thirty-six. This is Langhanstrasse. Take a cab home. Good luck. *Guten abend.*" He seemed anxious and sped off.

For a few moments Cole felt he was being watched, yet no one was visible in either direction in the ersatz night. Cars were parked all along Langhanstrasse, but he was not about to check them for Stefan Noll.

Going up, Cole wondered when Klaus Hermann had last climbed these creaking stairs, if ever. They were washed with onion odors soaked in the steam of boiled potatoes and cabbage. Carpeting was shredded at the riser edges.

Cole pushed the bell of 36 and a moment later got his first look at bare-shouldered Teddi Hagner. A white leather miniskirt didn't go ten inches below her navel. Black full length patent-leather boots rode high up on her thighs. A shiny red leather vest barely covered the swell of her breasts. This girl hadn't been in the sun since kindergarten.

Her voice was surprisingly deep. *"Kommen sie herein, bitte."*

"I'm American," Cole said.

"Ah, so," she said, "come in, please, Amerikan."

A pretty thing at one time, not bad now. Short cut red hair, the space between her vee-neck and her hairline, which included a full mouth and pert nose, was milk-white. Actually she looked a little like Shirley MacLaine, though not so leggy. The red hair set off the milk whiteness and greenish eyes.

Cole went on in. Everything was pink and flowery. Swaying toward the pink-flowered couch, she had a little trouble walking in the spike-heeled boots almost the length of waders. She motioned and Cole sat down beside her.

"Brandy? Beer? No charge."

The voice was so deep that Cole thought she might be a female impersonator. But the breasts didn't look false . . . still, with sex-changes nowadays, who knew?

His mouth was dry. "Beer, please."

She swayed on out to the small kitchen, calling from it, "You are a tourist?"

"On business. Real estate."

"Ah, Amerikan businessman. Who told you about me?" The English was accented but easy to understand.

"A friend, Herr Schade."

"Herr Schade, eh? Yes, he called me."

A photo sat on the lamp table by the couch. A boy. Maybe her kid brother? Late teens, early twenties. Cole was looking at him when Teddi came back, poured the beer and sat down as demurely as she could manage on the couch four feet away.

"You do not act like my usual clients. Sometimes I have Amerikan tourists."

"How do your usual clients act?"

"Their lips are always wet when they come here. But maybe your face hides something beneath the beard."

"I doubt that," Cole said, angling his head toward the photo. "Your brother?"

"No, my son," said Teddi, suddenly smiling. "My only son, my pride, my joy..."

"Handsome boy," said Cole. My dear sweet mother, the whip girl.

"Thank you. That is my Christian. He is in our air force, the new Luftwaffe."

Cole was beginning to feel a little more comfortable with her. Motherhood worked wonders... "You surprise me, having a son that old."

"I'm thirty-six."

"You sure don't look it."

She got up. "You can take your beer in. Follow me, please."

Cole got up, wondering where "in" was.

Teddi did not go into the room that afforded a peek at a bed that kept up the pink flower motif and where a huge goggle-eyed pink doll sat on a pillow. She opened up the door to a smaller room and said impatiently, "Come, come."

Cole stood by the door, peering in. A fine little pain chamber. White rubber sheeting on a single bed. Hanging on the walls were whips of a dozen kinds. Bullwhips. Braided cat-o'-nine-tails. Riding crops. Keen little Spanish jobs about three feet long. A ping-pong paddle. Chains, all sizes, all kinds. In one corner of Teddi's workshop was a big brass Indian pot filled with fresh pussy willow branches. On a table were handcuffs and rope coils. Prominently on a clothes rack were uniforms: nun's habit, cowgirl suit, nurse's outfit with a little cap; police lady shirt, skirt and hat. He stared at the nurse outfit.

"Take your clothes off. Is what I have on all right or would you like the cowgirl, Amerikan?"

Cole laughed nervously, hearing his own high-pitched echo; he'd never heard himself laugh that way before. "You got the wrong boy."

She was puzzled. "Then why are you here?"

Her usual wet-lipped johns came in, stripped down, stretched out on her sheet and got their kicks looking at her costumes while loving the whips and chains.

"Teddi, if I'm going to shed some blood it won't be in there."

She repeated, "Why are you here?"

Standing by the sheeting, suddenly there was wariness in the greenish eyes, tenseness in the creamy body.

"I'm here to talk about a man who might be a client of yours."

She tightened even more. "I do not talk about my clients."

"At this hour of night, isn't it easier to earn two hundred deutschmarks talking? Easier than the whips."

"Whips are easy."

"Two-fifty." He was spending money like he had it.

She looked at him, then said, scarcely above a whisper, "Just a moment, please." She passed by him, closing the door to the whip room.

When she returned she had taken off the leather suit and was wearing a blue negligee and scuffs, looking older, more worn, but softer too. She now looked, for example, like she could be Christian Hagner's mother. Going back into the kitchen, she stayed long enough to pour a glass of milk, then returned to the couch. After lighting a cigarette, offering him one, she asked, "Who is this client?"

Cole deliberated. Should he name names? Why not? He didn't have that long to hang around. "I'm Charles Harvey. I represent a family back in the United States who recently lost a daughter. Abused, then murdered. Then there was another girl in Washington, D.C., who was kidnapped and abused. And I'm told there was one over here in Heidelberg a long time ago who was unlucky enough to tangle with this creep. All students. All pretty. All about the age of your Christian . . ." He let that thought hang over Teddi, sink in.

Sucking in smoke, blowing it out nervously, she said, "Describe this man to me."

Cole described Klaus Hermann as best he could and saw a slight change in Teddi's eyes when he mentioned the grotesque skin condition. Yellowy-red, no hair. "Who are you?"

188

Cole studied the mother of the Luftwaffe boy and decided to gamble. "The father of that daughter who was kidnapped, raped and murdered recently in California. I'm told the man who did it lives in Hamburg and I think he comes here to you from time to time." Big gamble, telling all. But could pay off. And time was money. Wally, though, would say, Are you crazy, man? She'll call Hermann the minute you walk out . . .

"Who told you that?"

"A friend who has many contacts."

Teddi snuffed her cigarette and lit another. "What do you want of me?" She *was* nervous.

"Could I have some more beer, please?"

As she walked back toward the kitchen he said after her, "Confirm that you know such a man. Tell me where I can find him—"

"Then what?" She was back, standing over him, holding the bottle.

"I just want to talk to him."

"Just talk?" She gazed down. "Herr Schade should not have sent you. When he called he only said—"

"He doesn't know why I came."

She was still standing, looking down at Cole. "I have several clients who wear party masks, putting them on just before they enter. It is part of the costume game we play but it also hides identity. I have two of those. Government officials, I think. They both pay well, one in particular. He brings a symphonic cassette to play while we are in there." She nodded toward her chamber of horrors. "He would never rape anyone. When he wants normal sex he goes to young girls, I know. College students. Picks them up in the dating clubs. Pays them well. He has told me . . ."

"Don't stop now," Cole said.

"I have to tell you this. The men who come to me have many strange things inside them. The beatings seem to let them out. It is like devils being caged up. They hate themselves and the whip lets it all out. I even have a priest who comes here. You see? I half pity them and half hate them. But I know that none of them would ever rape any woman."

"I'd like to judge for myself."

"Maybe it is better you don't know."

Cole said, "Who is he? Put a name on this man who likes symphonic music while you're cutting up his back."

"I think not," she said. "I think you want to harm him. I think you want to kill him."

Wally would have jumped out the window, Cole knew. "Do you have any idea what it would be like to lose Christian? To have him murdered?" He said it slowly.

She answered very quietly. "I think it would probably kill me."

"That's how my wife and I feel about Ellen. We're robbed of her life. She was robbed of her life. I'll pay you well to tell me where he is."

Teddi got up. "I will think about it. Where are you staying?"

"The Brahms. Room 302."

She nodded as Cole got to his feet and began counting off deutschmarks. She stopped him at a hundred. "We have only talked."

At the door, she said, "I never get men like you. Normal men. I miss them. Would you like to make love tonight? The usual way. I can do that, too. I think I am good."

"I'm sure you are," Cole said, half meaning it, "but I'm really bushed, lady. I wouldn't do *you* much good right now."

Outside, he again felt eyes from somewhere along the street, but not even the alley cats were out that he could see. He walked quickly toward Bahrenfelder, winding around the narrow streets, retracing Schade's navigation, and then had to wait twenty minutes in mist and chill before a cab came by.

The old Panzerman was on night duty, and after keeping him waiting ten minutes opened the door of the Brahms for him, dour face, saying that management shouldn't permit American dogs after midnight.

About 1:20 Stefan Noll rapped on Teddi Hagner's door. Unannounced and unexpected banging on her door was not unusual at any hour ... it was the miserable human services business that she was in.

"Who is it?"

"Stern. Open the door."

This Bavarian she knew as "Stern" had brought the client who doubled the usual fee every other week for the past six weeks. The first two times she had been taken to the large house in Blankenese, where the client lived. Frightened at the harsh tone of "Stern's" voice, she nonetheless undid the door chain. If she had refused she could also have risked the income from his client.

He stepped inside and closed the door. "What did you tell the American with the beard?"

"Nothing. I swear to you, *nothing.*"

His gloved fist closed over her right hand. "I will kill you if you lie to me." The first time she had seen him she had decided he was a bodyguard to the wealthy customer, not just a friend or driver. The outline of a gun under his jacket was telltale.

"Please," Teddi said, wincing as her hand was squeezed. "You're hurting me—"

"What did he ask?"

"He asked about my clients."

"And?"

"I told him I never talk about my clients. Please . . . please let go my hand."

"Did he tell you who he was?"

"Not his name."

"What did he tell you?"

Her lips closed.

"What?"

The pain from his hand was excruciating, and now she went down to her knees. "Please don't . . . please don't . . ."

"What did he tell you?"

Pressure increased, squeezing bone against bone.

"Ah . . . that his daughter had been murdered by someone who lives here. He wanted to know where that man lives."

"And you told him?"

"I did not. I swear to it, I did not. Oh, don't please . . ."

"But you talked about your client?"

"I just said he was a . . . a nice man. I said he was . . . ah . . . special but would harm no one . . ."

"Liar." Stern was looking down at her, a figure in judgment; she the supplicant penitent.

He increased the pressure on her hand, crushing it. "Where is he staying?"

She was silent until the pain became unbearable. ". . . The Brahms." The crushing stopped.

"Now, what is his name?"

She tried silence again, but the pain became so severe that she said it. "Har-vee . . . now please go," she whimpered. Her hand felt broken.

He nodded. Still holding her left hand, he began to beat her about the nose and mouth. She screamed only once, then passed out as the gloved right hand smashed into her face and neck, again and again . . .

Finally he let go her hand and the arm fell limp. He kicked her in the ribs, at the point where her heart had been beating; then walked to the door, reset the lock and shut it tightly.

One beaten up whore mattered little in Hamburg. Happened all the time in the St. Pauli; even in upscale Ottensen.

25

THE PHONE RANG.

For a moment there was only breathing, labored stopped-up breathing like an ill person's. Then a female voice managed to get out, "Harvee . . ."

"Who is it?"

"Ted . . . di . . ." It sounded as though she was talking with something in her mouth. A gag?

"What's wrong, what is it?"

"Klaus Hermann is who . . . you want . . ."

"I know that, Teddi, I know that. Where is he?"

There was pain-wracked "ahh . . ." Somebody had worked her over, brutally, Cole guessed.

"Where is he, Teddi? That's what I need to know. *Where is he?*"

"Oh, Blanke . . ." The jabs of pain took her away.

Trying to cut through, Cole said harshly, "What? Say again, Teddi."

No answer. Just the congested breathing. But at least she was still hanging onto the phone.

"I'm coming over . . ."

"No, no . . . beat me, Stern beat me . . ."

"I'm coming over, Teddi. I'll get help . . ."

"No, no...he'll kill you..." Then the phone fell away, he heard it hit something.

Cole dressed and ran down the steps, stopping at the desk. The Panzerman regarded him with the same hostile glare as when he had entered.

Cole said quietly, "I'm going out and when I come back I'll break the goddamn door down if you don't open it in a hurry."

The Panzerman moved slowly from behind the desk with his ring of keys, never taking his eyes off the American.

Outside, Cole ran up deserted An der Alster and into the Atlantic. Two night clerks were on duty, formally dressed in frock coats and striped pants as if it were high noon in Geneva. They looked like royal attendants, even to lapel carnations. They belonged in an antechamber.

"I need help," Cole said. "I can't speak German and a woman has been badly beaten at Langhanstrasse 152..."

"Number again, please," said the oldest of the two clerks in excellent English, dark eyes narrowing. He looked Vietnamese, and Cole thought, Oh, boy, Da Nang, An Trach...another Charlie. We can't escape...

Cole repeated the number, adding, "Apartment thirty-six."

It had been a spur-of-the-moment notion, this going into the Atlantic for help. It seemed smarter than calling the police direct. But maybe it wasn't too late to try that.

"Ah," said the Vietnamese, "you are a guest here, sir?"

Now Wally would really like this little scene, Cole thought. "No, I'm not, but I'd like you to call an ambulance and the police."

"Could I please have your name, sir?" the Saigon clerk's pen was poised to write it down.

Oh, Christ, Cole thought, in deep shit already. He grabbed a name from the air group. Novak. "Novak. John Novak." He spelled it out. CH-53 pilot. "Thank you, thank you very much," Cole blurted, moving quickly away from the desk, betting that the man from Da Nang or Saigon or wherever he was from would not only call the police but describe in detail the American informer.

Wally would have said, Forget the hooker, for Chrissakes. Your butt is on the line. Stay in the Brahms; stay *alive*.

With the curious looks of the night clerks following him, he went out of the Atlantic and walked rapidly toward the Hauptbanhof. It was already a dampish daylight at three a.m., gray tinted. The train station was beginning to show signs of waking up. Supplies were being unloaded at the snack bars. Bunches of flowers were going into the *blomen* stalls. Newspapers were being racked. By the bank of phones Cole searched his palm for the right coin, then dialed Schade's home number. No answer. A dozen rings and no answer. Cole was worried about Schade. He deserved the truth if "Stern" was out beating up people. Maybe Schade had gone back to that last girl at La Trinidad? Was Stern Stefan Noll?

Cole stood for a few indecisive moments at the Hauptbanhof taxi stand, where three cabs were waiting, and then climbed into the front one, checking Schade's business card, looking at the scribbled home address. "Falkendamn 41, *bitte*." He thought he needed to warn Schade, come clean on why he was there. The cab raced along in the gray dampness, little or no traffic rolling at this hour.

Again, Wally would be saying, Gunther Schade is a big boy. He can take care of himself. Damn well not if he didn't know what Klaus Hermann was all about; or Stefan Noll . . . "Stern"?

The unmistakable red VW was not to be seen in the vicinity of Falkendamn 41, block brown ugliness that looked like it had been built in haste just after the war. "Wait here," said Cole, not getting out, trying to be smart about that. The meter ticked away for almost an hour and the cabbie dozed. So did Cole, waiting for Schade to come home from wherever he was. Finally Cole tapped the driver's shoulder. "Brahms." And off they went.

This time Cole had only to rap twice to get the Panzerman away from the desk to open up. Not bothering to say thanks, he felt daggers in his back as he climbed the steps.

He opened the door, stopped abruptly. *Room 302 was torn apart.* Luggage opened, shaving kit dumped, cushions on the floor. Bed torn apart. He looked about frantically, knowing already that the gun was gone. Under the bed? He'd put it under the mattress. Gone all right. He flipped the mattress in a rage, directed as much at himself as at whomever had taken it. Fly an ocean and then blow it. Feeling sick, feeling stupid, he sat down on the edge of the ruptured bed and tried to think. What to do? *What in hell to do now?* Suddenly he lunged up and took the steps down to the lobby and the Panzerman two at a time.

"Who got into my room while I was gone?"

The black-jacketed porter, flecks of dandruff on his lapels, just stared back at the bearded man, saying nothing.

"You hear me? Who got into my room? You let anybody in? Who else has the keys beside you and the maid?"

The Panzerman just stared back, and Cole was tempted to jerk him out from behind the desk and beat the answers out of him.

"Answer me, goddammit."

The Panzerman shook his head and waved Cole away with one splotched hand, placing the other on the switchboard telephone.

"Who got into my room?" Cole again demanded, this time trying to keep his voice down at four-thirty a.m.

Glaring back, the old man said, *"Polizei,"* which Cole understood as a threat, not an identification.

"Frau Wegner, does she live here?"

"Nein, nein . . . polizei," the Panzerman said again, and began to dial the number.

Cole backed off. If Noll or Stern or whoever hadn't taken it, maybe the old man himself? He'd let someone in, that was certain, during that hour on Falkendamn.

Cole turned away from the desk and began to climb the stairs, slowly, wearily, not able to believe his own carelessness. He knew enough not to hide even a wallet under a mattress, and yet he'd put the gun there. He didn't deserve to command cub scouts.

He spotted the sheet of Der Brahms stationery on the desk top. A single word had been printed on it in block letters: AUSGANG. He knew the word: *Exit.* Get out. He stood looking down at it for a moment, then muttered tiredly at the paper, "You didn't have the guts to sign your name, asshole," but the brave, lonesome talk didn't make him feel any better.

After washing his face in cold water he slumped down in one of the brocaded chairs by the coffee table, staring at the Dresden figurine. Four-forty Hamburg time; eleven-forty in Washington. Wally should be home, but Cole knew he was out of luck if the Panzerman had to work that joke of a switchboard. If Wally had put him into the Atlantic instead of this jerk hotel—

Cut it out. Wally wasn't to blame.

Cole sprawled out on the ripped-up bed, mind groping, thinking of a destroyed Teddi Hagner and the missing gun, and fell asleep, though not meaning to.

Exhaustion took him out.

He woke up a few minutes after seven, stiff-necked and tasting acids of a long night. Toothpaste and a cold shower helped, then he called down to the desk and Frau Wegner, having relieved the Panzerman, answered with a cheerful *"guten morgen."*

He decided not to tell her about the robbery, told her instead that he wanted to place a call to Washington, D.C., and gave her Wally's home phone.

"It is still very early back there—"

"I know that," Cole said, trying to be indulgent, thankful he had had at least two hours sleep. "Please place the call."

"As you say, sir."

Five minutes later the Georgetown phone began ringing and Wally finally answered. "Who the hell is this?"

"Charles Harvey. I had to call."

It took Wally a moment to adjust. *Charles who?* "Yeh, sure . . . are you all right?"

Wally sounded faintly pissed off. Who could blame him . . . "Not quite. Someone helped themselves to that object I got at the Hauptbanhof."

Wally said "Good God" with a disgust that clearly spanned an ocean.

"I was afraid to take it out with me. Hid it in the room."

There was a long pause, then Wally said, "Come on home. You've made your try."

Jerk, Wally was likely thinking. True. Idiot. Harebrain. "I talked with the girl, then someone beat her up. They must know I'm here."

"All the more reason to come home. I repeat, come home, *now.*"

"I can't do that. Not yet."

"Christamighty, you don't know what you're doing over there. You'll get yourself killed. You've got a wife and kids—"

"Listen, Wally, I've come this far—"

"You're crazy, what's wrong with you? You're an amateur and you're dangerous. I'm sorry I ever helped you. If they beat that girl you're already getting other people hurt. I'll call your wife and tell her you're on your way—"

"Don't do that, Wally."

Wally hung up.

So did Frau Wegner down at the little switchboard. She was frowning. If she wasn't too busy she liked to listen to the overseas calls, especially the ones to England and America. It improved her skills. She looked at the phone again, still frowning. Talk of someone getting beaten, someone getting killed? *You've got a wife and kids. Come home.* Who was this real estate man, Charles Harvey? And who was the man in America?

Cole sat on the edge of the bed for a few minutes collecting his thoughts, not wanting to accept that Wally was right, yet suspecting he was. Noll and Klaus Hermann now knew he was in town. Teddi Hagner beaten; Schade probably in danger. So far he'd been an ace bungler. The colonel was out of his element. All right, then try to get with it.

He dressed in slacks, white shirt, and the light red sweater. Another American tourist visiting Hamburg. He looked out the window to see if Noll was anywhere in view. Cars were parked precisely in front of the Brahms. The West German flag quivered in the stiff breeze of the Alster. Down on the avenue VWs, BMWs, Mercedes, Opels and motorbikes scooted toward work. The bicycle path was full of men with briefcases and secretaries with lunches pumping from Bramfeld and Barmbek and Dulsberg and Winterhude for a hard day in the buildings along the Zollcanal.

Cole went down to the lobby, waved unsmiling at Frau Wegner and went on out to get a cab.

"Mrs. Hickel, I'd like to take to your husband," said Detective Sergeant Louderholt, calling from UCI.

"I'm sorry. Cole isn't here. He's off on a business trip. Is there anything I can do?"

"Will you be talking to him?"

"Yes."

"May I come over there?"

"Surely. You know how?"

"Yes, I remember how. I came over to get Ellen's picture. Remember?"

"Oh, yes."

Thirty minutes later Louderholt was in the living room, sitting on the edge of the couch, anxious and fidgety. "I haven't let this case go for an hour since it happened. I've been thinking that certain things didn't match up."

"What do you mean?" asked Katta.

"Well, I'm sure that Ellen was in that vehicle, the Mercedes. No doubt about that. But I'm not sure that Klaus Hermann killed her."

"I don't follow you," said Katta, head tilting over, frown beginning to widen. Good Lord, now what?

"It's possible that somebody else is responsible for her death. The sheriff's crime lab can't match any tire track found on that road near Ellen's body with the tires of that Mercedes. And it's always bothered me that Hermann could have found that dirt road. I had a hard time finding it. The lab people say that the freshest track that day belonged to another vehicle. Those tires were worn about forty percent. Winstons. The tires on the Mercedes were about twenty percent. Pirellis."

Katta's frown stayed. They had never, of course, thought beyond the German. Why should they? "Can you find the other vehicle?"

"Only if miracles still happen. It would have to be involved in something else, maybe another felony where it would be important to make a mold. Winston sells a lot of tires to a lot of people out here. It'd be pure luck for us to find the other car."

Thinking of Cole stalking around in Hamburg, Katta said, "This doesn't let Klaus Hermann off the hook?"

"Not at all, and maybe I shouldn't have told you—"

"Oh, yes. I want you to tell us everything. Please."

"All right . . . well, for example, there was this case in Maryland, one that I know about personally, where a girl was raped and got away from that man but then had the bad luck to be in a part of town where life isn't worth very much. It took the first man to reach death row before the second one confessed to murder."

"You mean that could have happened to Ellen?"

"It's just a guess, a maybe, because as I said, some of the other parts don't fit."

"Could this change the extradition business?"

Louderholt shook her head. "It would be all the more reason for the Germans not to send him back here. They'd say, See, he didn't do it. Any government is always worried about what might happen to a citizen on trial in another country. Different laws, different trial procedures. That's why they usually turn us down. Even friendly countries."

Katta studied the detective a moment, then asked, slowly, "In your mind is there any big difference between rape and murder?"

Louderholt shook her head. "That's a tough one for me. Real tough. You always have to ask yourself, sympathetic or not, did she bring it on herself? If she didn't then in my mind there's not a lot of difference in the punishment it rates. I've always thought that the penalty for proven rape should be a pair of testicles. But then that's a female point of view. If you can prove that no come-on was involved, no frame job, then just cut them off. That's almost as good as a death penalty, don't you think?"

"I don't know," said Katta, thinking more about what to tell Cole when he called. Tell him he might be going after the wrong person? Or not the only person?

They sat there a moment in silence, and then Katta asked, "Suppose . . . like the Baltimore case . . . that Klaus Hermann kidnapped and raped Ellen but didn't kill her, what are those consequences?"

Louderholt said, "Oh, boy, I'm not a lawyer or a judge or a jury, but I'd say those two add up as bad as murder. Kidnapping and rape. But there's also a problem. How do we prove kidnapping? We know she was in the car because of the fingerprints, but then you'd have to prove kidnapping, I guess. How to do that when Ellen isn't alive, I don't know. The least that you could say is that he placed her in terrible jeopardy sometime that night. You should talk to a prosecutor, it's a tough one."

Katta sighed deeply, knowing that Cole Hickel would not accept any nonsense about "jeopardy."

26

STILL NO RED VW outside that blocky brown eyesore as Cole went up Schade's steps as if treading on razor blades, now convinced that Stefan Noll had discovered that Gunther Schade was the connection to Teddi Hagner, that the "Stern" who had beaten her and Stefan Noll were likely one and the same. He had been thinking about that all the way over to Falkendamn.

On the third door along the dark hallway Cole found Gunther's nameplate. He tapped first, then rapped hard, calling out the detective's name. Nothing. He rattled the knob, knocked again. A night of no answers had tracked into full day. He banged and called out again, and then quickly departed when a woman next door stuck her head out and sprayed German. He had not the faintest idea what she was saying and retreated back to the street.

Ahead he saw traffic moving steadily on what appeared to be a main avenue and walked toward it, trying to hope that Schade was only sleeping late with the La Trinidad girl or having his *Eier mit Speck* and hot milk somewhere else. Well, Wally might think he was nuts for being so concerned about Schade, but the dapper man was also the key to getting another gun. He stopped at a pay booth and called the detective's office. It was 8:35. A machine answered. In German, of course. He walked three blocks and was beginning to sweat.

He flagged a cab and struggled with directions until the driver finally said, "Ah, so. Ah, so." What did the Germans and Japanese have in common beside a trade surplus? *Ah, so*. Somebody has just dropped a nuke. "Ah, so."

As he went on toward Ottensen, Cole persuaded himself that too much pain and love of Ellen had been invested to turn back now just because he'd lost the gun. Like flying past the point of no return over water; not enough fuel to get you back so you had to fly on and hope someone was watching out for you. Wally just didn't understand . . . he'd call Katta later in the day, say it might take longer than he thought. Just that, nothing else. Get off the phone quick. Talk too long and be trapped, give in, go home . . .

As Behrenfelder came up he directed the cabbie on to Daimler-strasse, then finally saw the sign of Planckstrasse. Using his cassette German, he said, *"Mehr, mehr."* Here, here. A big Agfa billboard came up to the left that Cole remembered. *"Halt, bitte, halt,"* he said, paying off the cab.

Everything looked different in daylight. Harsher and brooding. It took several block circlings to find the old building. Then when he found it he decided he didn't want to go in, after all. Three green-and-white polizei vehicles and an ambulance were wedged around the front. It could be some ancient bookbinder with an after-breakfast heart attack, but Cole knew it was more likely Christian Hagner's battered mother.

Cole shook his head, thinking as much about the son as about Teddi. God knew he hadn't meant for this to happen, hadn't meant to trigger it. He stood looking at the cop cars. God knows he hadn't, but goddamn it, he had . . .

Fingerprints were being lifted in the apartment from the door-knobs and then the glasses that had held beer and milk as the medical examiner finished his work. The ashtrays had been emptied and the couch and floor had already been vacuumed. There was no question that Teddi had been murdered. One of the worst beatings he had seen lately, said the medical examiner. Vicious.

The chief investigator, Ulrich Karh, barely thirty, was studying a single name on a notepad—"Harvee." It was beside the telephone, blood-stained; handwriting seemed to be the same as that on the half-written letter addressed to "My dearest Christian" dated two days earlier.

Although "Harvee" could be a German name it was certainly not a common one like Heinz or Hans or Helmuth. Karh repeated to himself, "Harvee, Harvee," and carefully, using his fingers as a tweezer, dropped the notesheet into a glassine bag. English name? American name?

Cole stayed across the street, tucked into a small crowd of busy-body neighbors and red-cheeked mothers with babies in strollers. Teddi's flat was to the rear of the building so there was no chance to see whether or not there was activity inside 36. Cole stayed, feeling guilt, grief and rage all at the same time, until they carried the cart down the last steps and rolled it to the ambulance. There was a dingy blanket covering the motionless form, head to feet. A TV crew was on hand to put it all on film. Teddi was a star, finally.

Then a man in civilian clothes came out of 152 Langhanstrasse followed by a young man in a Luftwaffe uniform. Cole swallowed. Christian. My pride, my joy, Teddi had said. Cole asked a mother of twins, *"Entschuldigen sie, was gibt das?"* The cassettes had finally paid off.

She gave a little speech and out of it he picked *"frau"* and *"shrecklich,"* her pretty face showing anguish when she said the latter word. That was enough. No old *buchbinder* was dead. No incentive to stay longer in Ottensen.

He hailed an Opel cab, swayed with the motion, face blank, washed out. Even good old Mike Goody had never seen him this way in Nam or anywhere else. The colonel was hurting. He hadn't eaten anything but wasn't hungry. Having the cabbie stop at the Atlantic, he crossed An der Alster, beginning to walk slowly through the small parkland by lake's edge, by swans, toward the Brahms. It was a little after ten, a rare balmy late spring Wednesday. Strong breeze had chased away mist and smog. The steeples of St. Michaels and the bombed St. Nikolai monument were sharp against the horizon. Lovely sunny morning.

Under shade trees he moved along through the pensioners with canes, by old ladies in boxy hats with big rumps. Baby buggy and tricycle traffic was out there too. Not many days like this by the Alsters. The big lake was spotted with sails and the white ferries; shoreside cafes were already beginning to seat customers. As he walked along, thinking now about Teddi, he knew she would have been alive if he hadn't come to Hamburg. There was no other way but to go on. Find Schade, find out what Teddi meant by "blanke," get another gun.

There was a flash of red through the trees coming slowly west along the stroll path. Stefan Noll straightened up, wishing he had brought binoculars. If the colonel was still wearing that bright red sweater of last night, and if he crossed directly to the hotel, it would be like target practice. And Noll was a good shot.

Quickly he opened the back doors of the unmarked black panel truck and crawled inside, pulling his knees up to brace his elbows. He closed the two doors to a crack about four inches wide, knowing he could widen them with a nudge of his foot, then held the silenced parabellum Luger steady, clasping his right wrist with his left hand. And waited.

In a moment the American in the red sweater turned off the path toward the hotel and began walking dead ahead. Noll had thought the angle would be to the left. In a few seconds the tall man would walk right into the back of the truck. Traffic was spasmodic and he would surely cross in a lull. Then, suddenly, the colonel stopped dead-still and froze, looking up at the Brahms, looking over the truck. What was he doing? What was he doing?

Cole was watching a green smocked figure in an open window three across from his own 302, framed over the geranium box. Not good-looking Stefan Noll up there but a meaty Holstein face. The man was peering down toward the Atlantic; looked like he was watching the sidewalk, not expecting his target, if there was a target, to come from under the shade trees.

Cole wondered if he was beginning to imagine things. Was that an odd-looking window washer-handle or was that a rifle with a sniperscope on top and a silencer tube on the spitting end? Was the man maintaining a surveillance with intent to kill, or was he merely taking a breath of midmorning Alster air? Now the man in the green smock and beret was fiddling with the end of the short black rod, twisted something so that it lined up horizontally, turned, and began briskly washing the upper part of the French windows.

Cole let out a breath and felt foolish once again, pulse rate slacking off. He stood watching the window activity on the third floor a moment longer, shaking his head. The outside of the hotel was about as sinister as a candy shoppe. He started to cross the street. He hadn't been this jumpy, this scared, since An Trach. Traffic momentarily cleared and Cole stepped off to begin his jay-walk home.

Just as he completed the second step a big white Yamaha thundered out of nowhere not six feet from his toes, white-helmeted rider looking like he had been shot out of a circus cannon, bike skidding on its side, screeching and throwing sparks, wheels spinning.

Cole impulsively started for the rider, who had landed on his shoulder and head, then woke up to the fact that a bullet had just whined off into the trees. He twisted away from being a good Samaritan and started running for the stroll path as another chipped a tree at arm's length sending a shower of slivers. He felt a bee-sting on the back of his neck but kept running until he again reached mid-path, where people were stopping and looking over at the commotion in the street—bike and rider down, black panel truck pulling away from the Brahms. Yells and shouts: *"Kranken-wagen, krankenwagen . . ."* Whatever that was.

Cole ran on for a short distance, then slowed to a rapid walk in the thick of bodies, baby buggy and pensioner traffic, now and then looking back to see if anyone was following.

What was it that Wally had said over pot pie that night in Georgetown? *Don't be a hero, chum. Get away and fight another day. The first inclination is to get lonely. Don't do it. The smart ones, the survivors, have learned to wade into the thick pedestrian tides. People on all sides. Move right into the middle. That's basic.*

Keep a steady pace. Keep moving. If a car exhaust goes bang, jump like everybody else. But don't break out and run.

Keep moving . . .

Going steadily toward the Kennedy Bridge and little Alster, feeling somehow settled down for the first time in six hours—the bullets had done that—he glanced back and said aloud to Stefan Noll, or whoever had pulled the trigger, "I've been shot at before, you son of a bitch. I know the territory. . ." And he was all but certain it was Noll, doing exactly what Wally had said he would do.

In the distance, and growing, was the shrilling "hee-haw" of the *krankenwagen,* coming to scoop up the rider. Cole guessed that his neck had been snapped from the way he hit. In the split-seconds he had only seen the motorcycle and rider, not where the shots came from.

Now he began to sort it out: the poor bastard on the Yamaha had the bad luck to come along as the trigger was pulled and took the first bullet. The next two were off because the shooter was surprised by that helmeted body doing a double-gainer and all those sparks flashing.

Cole kept moving.

Now that the Smith & Wesson was gone, nothing of value had been left at the Brahms, and he'd already signed the American Express chit for room rental. The Panzerman might end up with a raincoat, sports jacket and pants, some socks, the Lacoste red cotton, three white shirts and a Tourist's Atlas of Germany. Not exactly a major haul.

Coming away from the lakes, Cole moved onto Ballindamm and then into the thick of the shopping arcades, stopping twice to try Schade's office phone. The girl kept saying sorry she hadn't heard from Herr Schade this morning, could Herr Harvey please leave a number?

He kept on walking, feeling conspicuous, vulnerable. Tall foreigner, head six inches higher than the Frauen and pretty Frauleins on the sidewalks with their purchases. Who but a dunce on the run would wear a red sweater? Without losing stride he took it off, holding it until the next trash receptacle.

He walked the area—Jungfernsteig, Mönckebergstrasse—finally having an omelet with fries at a little place where he could sit with his back to the wall. A TV set was high up in a far corner and the noon news came up on ARD-Aktuell with a female commentator. She was speaking so rapidly that he couldn't follow her but stopped in the middle of a bite when Langhanstrasse 152 came up on the screen, with police cars and the ambulance; Christian Hagner and the man in civvies. Then the camera panned to the spectators, and there was bearded "Charles Harvey" twice as big as life in a red sweater talking to a mother of twins.

Cole almost turned the small table over getting up. He paid the bill and was out of the little cafe in less than three minutes, walked another five or six blocks before buying a brown leather jacket, a Swissair flight bag, a shaving kit and a Dutch maritime cap. At least he didn't look too much like the red-sweatered man on TV.

In the afternoon, he went to Planten un Blomen, the gardens between Rötherbaum and the St. Pauli, where large numbers of people strolled about in the warm sunshine. He called Schade every hour. Stay with the crowds, Wally had said. He finally dozed a short while on a bench near the fountains, waking with a start from a dream in which he was falling. One of those dreams where the territory was totally new . . . a mountain he'd never seen before. Not in Nam. Maybe from childhood.

Then about five he found a sailor's bar in the St. Pauli and sat down by a broken-English talking big Finn who was drinking something called a "Brazil"—chew a half dozen roasted coffee beans, suck a sugar cube, quaff down a shot of Cuban rum. Cole discovered it was a desperately fast way to get drunk, which was what he wanted to do. Teddi Hagner and Ellen were competing for his thoughts. Soon he was trying to tell the Finn, who listened raptly and understood little, about his daughter Ellen . . . as though she were still alive.

He stayed at the bar until about 7:30, when he staggered out and checked into a grungy hotel a block away, enough caution remaining in unfried brain cells to make him lock the door and pull the dresser up in front of it.

Then he collapsed on the bed.

* * *

Katta found Wally Stonebridge's number in the black looseleaf that had all the numbers not connected with the air group or the station—Cole's brother in Omaha, the Austin-Healey Club of Southern California, Antique Car Auto Parts, Dana Point Sports Fishing and so forth. There was a notation by Wally's name not to call before five p.m. Tustin time.

She waited until five-thirty and then dialed the 202 area code and was connected within seconds.

He asked how she was.

"All right, I guess." A lie. "I'm terribly worried about Cole, though."

"Well, you know better than I do that Cole is capable of taking care of himself in most situations. Hasn't he called you?"

He sounded wary to Katta. Maybe he sounded that way all the time in Washington on account of his job. "Three days ago, just after he got to Hamburg was the only time. Has he talked to you since?"

"Last night . . . I tried to get him to come home."

"And he didn't listen?"

"No."

Katta sighed. "He's always been stubborn. Once he makes up his mind to do something, that's it . . . Wally, I must talk to him. A detective who has been following the case came to see me yesterday. She said that someone else may be involved in Ellen's death. So it's very important that I talk to Cole—"

"Katta, frankly, I'm afraid he's a sort of loose cannon now. Anyway, try to get him to drop the whole thing and take the next flight out. For his sake and yours."

"Wally, I don't even know what name he's using. This was all a crazy game we played. He said he was going there to consult with a helicopter company. We both knew he wasn't but we couldn't say it to each other. We couldn't talk openly about what he was going to do . . ."

Wally's voice turned remote. "I know very little about it."

"Do you know what name he's using?"

210

"No..."

"Do you know what hotel he's in?"

"No, I'm afraid I don't, Katta."

Katta said thanks and hung up, unable to give in to her feelings
... the kids were home ...

Wally put the phone down. When things went too wrong he'd
learned to cut losses, control damage. Now was such a time. He'd
paid his Vietnam debt to the colonel. No more. No more involvement. Sorry chum ... sorry Katta.

The hangover from Brazil was almost as big as the hangover
from the Snowshoes of Marble Mountain, but Cole had needed to
be knocked out, needed to be cold-cocked, needed that anesthesia.
It was all medicinal, all mind-healing. But he didn't know until
morning that the collar of his shirt was bloody and that the splinter
of wood from the near-miss was still in the back of his neck. He
pulled it out and compressed the wound with wads of toilet paper.

Checking out of Haus Elbe, eating heartily on a side street, buying a couple of work shirts and stuffing them into the Swissair bag,
Cole went back to the Hauptbanhof because it was central. He
called Schade every half hour and bought the *Morgenpost,* seeing a
large picture of a white Yamaha down on the An der Alster, helmeted body beside it. He figured out the text—motorcyclist mys-
teriously shot and in critical condition. Then there was a shorter
item two pages over about Teddi Hagner. Plus a picture.

He finally got Schade about ten. "Where the hell have you
been?" he asked as if he owned the *privat detektiv.*

Schade was startled. "Bremerhaven. Why?"

"I need you."

"Teddi Hagner did not provide the information?"

"She's dead."

A long pause, a change in voice; a lowering, a sudden wariness.
"When? I haven't read the papers. There was something on the
radio about a prostitute dead in Ottensen. Beaten up. That happens
all the time. I paid no attention—"

"The same man is trying to get me. Tried after he worked Teddi
Hagner over."

Silence from Schade, the silence of graveyards and empty churches. "You should go to the police."

"I can't. Gunther, we need to talk."

Another pause. "All right, I'm seeing a client in twenty minutes but I'll pick you up at noon. Where are you? At the Brahms?"

"No. Hauptbanhof."

"Okay. Go out that exit nearest the Atlantic. Noon."

Cole sat down to look at the paper again, turning to the picture of Christian Hagner's mother. The kid might never know why. Cole kept seeing her as she sat on the couch in the proper blue negligee, not the shiny red leather vest and black waders, talking about Christian. "My pride, my joy. . . ."

A few minutes after noon Schade's VW pulled away from the train station with Cole inside. "I tried to call you all day yesterday," Cole said.

Schade glanced over. "Who's after you—and why?"

"Man named Stefan Noll. He's local."

Schade nodded. "No wonder you don't look well. Stefan Noll."

"He's head of security at the Hermann Werft. I'm told he can be very dangerous."

"Yes, he can. Why is he after you? Or why do you think he's after you?"

"Long story," Cole said.

"So we're going to take a nice ride out in the country and you can tell me. I may decide to say goodbye to you. Wally didn't tell me much. Now I see why."

They finally got on to Segeberger Chausee, heading for cow pasture country and the upper reaches of the Alster. Soon the city was left behind as the VW coursed by farmland greenery, quickset hedges and ancient estates now mostly public reserves. Except for a few mistakes by RAF bombadiers war never touched Duvenstedt and Tangstedt. Open heath and moorland was almost the same as it was when Charlemagne held the area in 810.

"Why are we coming all the way out here?" Cole asked.

"So I'm not seen with you."

"I suddenly have a disease?"

"I think so," said Schade.

Cole finished his story opposite Jersbeker Forest, home to the fox, and Schade said, "Hah, I wish that Wally had not called me, and I will tell anyone I have not heard anything you just told me. If anyone asks, I don't know who you are and I have never met you before—"

"Is this the way you people usually operate? You and Wally?"

Schade nodded. "It's the way I operate when an assassin is mistakenly sent to me, no matter his story. I am not in that business, Herr Harvey or whatever your name is. I have only had one such case in my whole career and I called the police. Two minutes it took me to do that. Wally should know better."

"You plan to do that with me?"

Schade's eyes pulled away from the road and met Cole's. "You pay me triple and I will try to find out where Klaus Hermann is. I have a contact in the shipyard. One-third is for her. I'll tell you, then I bow out."

"Okay, you've got a deal. But I need a gun."

Schade's quick burst of laughter had vinegar in it. "Hah, no guns from me."

"Any suggestions?"

"None. Strangle him, drown him, knife him. You can buy hunting knives in Hamburg. They're silent, at least."

"Thanks." Schade was coming through in spite of his understandable sentiments.

"Where did you stay last night?"

"Haus Elbe. Terrible place. Cockroaches. Drunks. Lice. You name it."

"But probably safe. I'd advise you to stay around the St. Pauli. People take you for an officer off an American ship. That's good."

"When do I call you?"

"Noon tomorrow?"

Schade went off to the right near a farm. "The mentally handicapped live there," he said, as if Cole should join them, and did a U-turn, heading back for Hamburg.

"When Teddi called me she said that Klaus Hermann was at a place called 'blanke'—"

"Likely she meant Blankenese, on the Elbe above Wedel. Those are many nice houses out there, two or three stories. Klaus Hermann could well live in one of them. I'll check for you."

Once back in town, Schade asked, "Where do you want to go now?"

"Hauptbanhof. I'm getting to like it there. World's greatest phone booth."

27

FRIDAY.

Stefan Noll's secretary, who had hated her boss for a long time
—promises made, promises not kept, in and out of European beds
—said, "They're now in Denmark, staying at Klaus' apartment at
Gunsloggade 12, Copenhagen. Left about three hours ago. If they
do as usual, and the weather is good, they will rent a boat on
Sunday and go for a sail out of Tarbaek-Strandvej. Klaus likes to
sail. Maybe you have heard? Then on Monday night he will play
the violin in a chamber group at Humlebaek. On Tuesday they will
go to the cottage in Sweden, the place in Karlstrand, near Göteburg. Mr. Noll did not tell me for how long."

Schade asked her to spell the apartment street and the place
where they would take a sail. After she did that, he asked, "Will
someone else be with them? Someone from shipyard security?"

"No. Just the two."

Schade told the farmer's daughter from Husum where she could
pick up her three hundred deutschmarks, an envelope at his office,
and reminded her for both their sakes to forget he had ever called.
Promise.

Feeling better than she had in a long time, she laughed and told
him not to worry.

An hour later, noon, the red VW made the Hauptbanhof exit and Gunther leaned out to say, "Wait here. I'll park."

Cole waited.

Smelling of musk cologne, white carnation in his lapel, dapper as a jaybird on an April morn, in a few minutes Schade's heels were tapping up and they entered the station together. Weekend travelers had already descended, the place was thumping and bumping, P.A. system chiming and calling off trains to München and Rotterdam and beyond.

"There," said Schade, guiding Cole's arm, two old friends to occupy a bench while waiting for the 12:40 express to Hannover.

Cole said, "After a while this place gets to you. I even know what the station master had for breakfast. Eel and eggs."

Looking about, Schade said, "I was here once when I was a small boy, just before the war, before all the diesels. A train was a train then. Smell was better then. Real train smell. Coal smoke. Left a bad taste in your mouth but opened your nostrils."

Not much had changed, Cole thought, even without the coal smoke. Until the Hauptbanhof he had not spent twenty minutes in train stations. He would have trouble recommending this one.

Schade passed over a sheet of plain paper, not removing his gloves so there would be no fingerprints. At least, not his. The information was hand-printed in blocky letters to avoid typewriter identification. Speaking very quietly, close to Cole's ear, like two old friends talking earnest business . . . "It is all here for you. Written down. Klaus Hermann has left Deutschland—"

Cole pushed out a "What?"

"Just keep listening to me and read the message. Put it into your pocket and nod and smile, okay?"

Were they being watched? Who? Where? Or was Schade just earning his spook money? Cole played along, nodding and smiling stiffly. Both of them out of Germany?

Schade went on, "They're in Denmark now, next door. You will see where they'll be and when. Now, I will give you a name to remember. I did not write it down, *for his safety.* Rolf Halvorsen, with an 'e,' in Copenhagen, on Nyhavn. N-y-h-a-v-n."

Cole repeated the words.

"Again."

"Rolf Halvorsen. Nyhavn."

"I talked to him a half hour ago. He suggested you stay at the Broen, not too far from his place of business."

"Brawn?"

"B-r-o-e-n. He made a reservation."

"Is Rolf another detective?"

"Friend," said Schade, dismissing specifics, glancing behind them.

Cole looked around, too, to see if anybody was on the other side of the back-to-back benches. No one. The noontime chiming din kept up, along with babble and announcements, all sounding hollow in the acrid cavern off Steintorwall. "Your friend can get me a gun?"

Schade shrugged.

"How much will he cost?"

"That depends on what you want him to do."

"I don't have all that much left." Cole had counted his money before he checked out of the cockroach hotel in the St. Pauli. Two thousand odd in travelers checks and another two hundred or so in deutschmarkes.

"Explain to Rolf," Schade suggested, "and now you can come with me to the car and pay me. I must give someone else five hundred deutschmarkes."

"Someone else?"

"The girl in the shipyard. And, of course, there is another five hundred for me."

"I have to cash in my money," said Cole, rising, feeling the price was going up. He'd already given Schade twelve hundred, but what the hell. Going to the nearest *wechsel* several hundred feet away he made the exchange for a thousand more deutschmarks and then walked with Schade out to the VW. Paying him, Cole asked, an edge in his voice, "How do you suggest I go to Denmark?" Directing ought to be part of the deal, he felt.

"Take the bus to Kiel, stay at the Griffon there tonight, then ferry to Korsør on Zealand, then bus to Copenhagen." Schade spelled out Griffon and Korsør for him. "It's better not to fly, just in case there is a problem with what happened in Ottensen. Immigration people at the ferries aren't as strict as at the airport. Usually they just glance at your passport picture and wave you through."

Cole nodded. He did not want to get involved with Ottensen.

"Good luck," said Schade.

"You, too," said Cole, thinking Schade had really not done much more. Well, forget it. Get back on the track for the major event. Cole shook his hand perfunctorily, just gave him a nod and moved away from the VW as Schade climbed in and took off, grinning.

As the VW disappeared, Cole reached into his pocket and fished out Schade's hand-printed message. Sailing. Violin concert! Karlstrand, Sweden. Hermann was acting like nothing had happened. Cole felt an upsurge of rage.

Back in the station he bought a small pair of scissors, a razor, a can of squirt shave cream and a small bottle of lotion, then went into the men's room. The usual stop-and-pee traffic was in there along with a few like Cole who wanted to shave or wash up.

Stripping to the waist, he began hacking away at the beard, bringing a laugh from a beer-belly two basins over. The man unleashed German and the only word that even sounded close was "sheer."

"Ya, ya," Cole laughed back, snipping away, grunting as the scissors pulled. What seemed like so long ago, Wally had said to get rid of the beard when it was time to leave Germany; go back to being Cole Hickel. Use the authentic passport. In fifteen minutes Cole saw the old Cole, the one he knew best, was most at ease with—Hickel, C.L., USMC (Ret.). Well that last, "Ret.," wasn't something easy to live with, but it had been necessary.

There were a few chin nicks, one raw red scrape down under the right earlobe. Otherwise, he was back. Just taking off the whiskers, getting rid of the itch, made him feel better. Why anybody grew a beard, except to hide, was beyond him. Dropping the shaving stuff into the Swissair flight bag, pulling on his work shirt and the jacket, he went into the john, shutting the door tightly.

218

Tearing the passport that Wally had prepared into tiny pieces, Cole watched the last of "Charles Harvey" wash down the porcelain chute. No regrets. Maybe as just plain Cole Hickel he would make out better. At 1:30 he left the Hauptbanhof in his Greek-Dutch sailor's hat and took a bus to Kiel, checking into the Griffon.

Dearest Kot:

I knew that if I called you, if I heard your voice, I'd start home. I'm in a small hotel in Kiel, not too far from where I'll take a ferry to Denmark in the morning. I have thought of you and the children so many times in the past few days, so tempted to give this up. But each time Ellen comes back and I have the same feeling—that I haven't made all this right. And that I have to. At least try.

The man I'm after seems to be going about life as if nothing ever happened. Sailing a boat this weekend, I'm told. Playing his violin Monday night at a place in Denmark. I'm sorry, I can't let him get away with it. Please try to understand.

I hope that I can call you in a day or two to say that everything is all right, to say I'm catching the next flight home. If so I'll be home and you'll be in my arms by the time this letter arrives.

Tell the children how much I love them. Just thinking of you I gather the strength for what needs to be done.

All my love,
Cole

Cole watched the flag popping at the stern of the fast ferry to Denmark. Beyond the whipping flag, sour smoke from the raked twin stacks spun down to dust whitecaps. At first no one else was on deck in the early morning chill. Then a dark-skinned little man, maybe a Malaysian, wearing a white jacket and greasy pants and greasy shoes, came past with a big dishpan full of garbage. Gulls came squawking in as the slop was flung into the air on the lee side. The setting matched the mood. Gray skies and a cold summer wind out of the Arctic. One dead, the cyclist maybe dead by now, and Cole hadn't even seen the back of Klaus Hermann's head or the Bavarian ski-slope profile of Stefan Noll.

He went inside for breakfast. Ham and egg sandwich on brown

bread, with butter that looked and tasted like cheese. He tried to occupy himself watching two grandmother types in felt hats smoke long black cigars.

The big problem had been he hadn't had any plan, like Mike Goody had suggested he have. Just some vague idea of going to Germany, finding out where Hermann lived, going there, pulling the trigger and getting out. No wonder Wally Stonebridge, though cooperative, thought he was a dangerous idiot. Here he'd spent his whole life, Annapolis on, planning things, from lifting a gunship off and coming back alive to ferrying the president to Camp David to running an air group, yet for *this* one he hadn't any notion how to do it right. On the other hand, to give himself his due, in a deal like this, there were no precedents, no book to go by. In a way it was like a guerrilla action where you didn't and couldn't know what was going to happen. Where the enemy would be and when. Except that now, finally, he had dates and places for Klaus Hermann . . .

The ferry sped on north toward Langeland, and he went back to the stern rail and watched the wake. The best place would be out on the water. Rent a boat, come alongside, say hello to them and shoot to kill. Fly home. At least keep it simple, as Wally had said.

After hours of calling from the Ottensen district police headquarters, Ulrich Karh had finally located someone named "Harvey," not "Harvee," a tall, bearded American who had stayed at the Brahms for two nights, then departed the hotel hurriedly, according to Frau Wegner. He had left clothing behind, she said. Had not signed out.

Karh went to the Brahms to discuss further this man "Harvey" with Frau Wegner and anyone else who had talked to him. The bartender from Manchester said he had talked about real estate in the Caribbean; both Wegner and the bartender said he had a meeting with Gunther Schade, the *privat detektiv.* The old porter and night clerk, on from twelve to six that night, remembered that "Herr Harvey" seemed very agitated at the time that Teddi Hagner was murdered.

Did the hotel have the registration the American had signed?

Oh, yes, said Frau Wegner.

Would it be possible to borrow that form for the purpose of obtaining fingerprints?

Oh, yes,said Frau Wegner, surprised that the tall guest would be involved in crime. He seemed such a nice man. She had decided not to tell Ulrich Karh what she had heard while eavesdropping. But gentlemen who went to prostitutes sometimes deserved what they got, as, of course, did the prostitutes.

Within a few hours, after the prints found in Apartment 36 on Langhanstrasse were matched up with those of the "Charles Harvey" on the Brahms registration, Karh issued a bulletin for the apprehension of a suspect in the homicide death of Theodora ("Teddi") Hagner—suspect believed to be an American, slender, about six-feet-two; in his early forties, gray and brown beard; representing himself as an international real estate broker. The bulletin was issued to all German law enforcement agencies as well as Interpol.

Ulrich Karh then phoned Gunther Schade.

Schade swore he knew nothing about Charles Harvey except that he was a California real estate man who needed help in locating a lady who held deed to some property in the American Virgin Islands. What was her name? Karh asked. Schade, looking out his window at a dress shop sign that said von Kluyver, said to Karh, "Lilli von Kluyver. I haven't found her as yet."

The name of Charles Harvey, U.S. citizen, suspect in the murder of Theodora Hagner, went out on the teletype to all law enforcement, customs and immigration agencies in West Germany.

As yet, Karh had not linked the accidental shooting of the Yamaha rider with the former guest of Hotel Brahms.

28

COLE CHECKED INTO THE BROEN near the waterfront. Fodor's probably listed it as budget. The small lobby was neat, done in chrome and mellow woods like the exported furniture. Like, in fact, Denmark itself, there was a tidy brightness to the Broen.

Up in the room he told the operator to dial his home collect, then canceled the call before Katta could come on. The letter would not arrive in Tustin for days and was useless anyway. But he thought he needed more time to rehearse what he was going to say about leaving Germany. In the bathroom he admitted to the mirror that he was afraid to call her. Maybe tonight. Checking the phone book for Rolf Halvorsen, the only Halvorsen doing business on Nyhavn was a Jorgen. Down at the desk he was told that Nyhavn was only five blocks from the hotel, and was then pointed in the right direction.

Nyhavn was an old seafarer's alley on a canal where the clock had been turned back. Here were echoes of days under sail when Denmark was a global somebody. Cole inspected each door, until he saw "Tatover Jorgen." The address was right, if not the name.

A cellar shop, down a flight of shallowing brick stairs, it looked like a movie set from the thirties. In the dusty window were large red, white and black drawings of tattoo designs. Usual sailing

223

ships, twined serpents, bleeding hearts with dagger; bashful nudes. Somehow the nudes never kept up with the calendar, always looking 1895 on 1985 biceps. Another sign said, "English spoken."

He had been passed to a dye artist. A needle squirter! He went on down the brick-well, finally pulling a bellrope on a green door that was further inscribed in sailing ship scroll—"Jorgen Halvorsen." There was a shout from inside and Cole pushed on the brass knob. A big, ruddy-skinned, shaggy-haired man with a warlike British Tommy mustache stood over a youth who was naked to the waist. The zizzing needle in the *tatover's* right hand was assigned to the boy's upper right arm, where a red heart was inking in. Another sailor stood entranced, eyes dull with whiskey. The big man with the Tommy mustache, his upper bulk compressed into a brown corduroy jacket, thick legs stuffed into faded jeans, looked up.

"God aften," he said in Danish.

"I'm American."

"Amer-i-kan," the *tatover* repeated. His voice was gravelly and smoky hoarse. Much worse than Wally's. "You must wait until I've finished with these two drunken Danes." All the while carefully guiding the hummingbird peck of the needle, he continued, "But this child should be in school. He's trembling like a newborn lamb and it isn't that cold down here. He should be smoking his first pipe in secret instead of getting his first art."

The boy wasn't more than sixteen.

"But the new sailors in the dying fishing fleet, the cousins and sons of someone, get drunk, tattooed and get a girl—just like the old sailors did—after their first trip. Nothing has changed and everything has changed."

He stopped talking to squeeze the boy's arm. "This one couldn't lift a shackle," he bellowed. The boy almost fainted.

Cole wondered if he was Jorgen or Rolf. Maybe a retired cop, maybe an old intelligence man. His face was paved with thin surface blood vessels. Tiny threads of purple flowered especially around the curve of his cheekbones. His brows were bushy, hairs curled from his nostrils, and he'd likely threatened any barber at the mere mention of trimming. His nose was large, again with tributaries. He appeared to be fifty or so, a powerful man. Things were maybe looking up, Cole thought.

The *tatover* finished the bleeding heart, stood back to survey his work, then slapped the youngster on the back, murmuring, *"Den er fine,"* or some such . . . it sounded to Cole like a waterless gargle.

After fifteen minutes Jorgen or Rolf or whoever he was finished the other sailor and when the door closed with a tinkle of bell, brown eyes probing, said, "Now, sir, what would you like? Something on the bicep? You are suited for that, I think."

"Thanks, I guess, but no thanks. My name is Hickel and I'm looking for Rolf Halvorsen."

"I'm Rolf," he said, eyes still squinting, probing, weighing.

"I was told to contact you."

"Who told you?"

"A man in Hamburg. Private detective. Gunther Schade."

Rolf nodded. "Yes, Gunther told me you were my size but not my weight. Falkendamn 41? What would that mean to you?"

"Gunther's address."

Rolf nodded, then began clearing and putting away his equipment. "My work here allows me freedom but pays little," he said. "I come and go as I want. I have no hours." The bushy eyebrows elevated. "But I have a weakness for the trotting track at Charlottenlund. My weakness keeps me poor." His laughter was deep in his chest. A merry man.

Cole scanned the room. Everything in it looked musty and ancient.

As Rolf put his dyes away they continued to talk. Rolf's father, Jorgen, had started there in 1920, same shop, back in the days when Denmark had many ships. Taught him the business when he was a boy, he said. He held up his massive hands. "You see these? My father's hands were larger. Yet he could take a needle and put a two-color iris the size of a pin-point in a crab's eye." He laughed again, finishing tidy work, then commanded, "Come, Hickel, we'll have a beer."

225

On the way they passed a ruddy-faced woman pumping a bicycle and Rolf shouted, *"God aften."*

She called back, *"God aften, Rolf, det er vel nok. Fint vejr i aften."*

That catastrophic language again. Danish Morse Code.

"It's a fine afternoon," Rolf translated.

Yes, it was. Sunny and cool.

They went to a hotel coffee shop on St. Annaeplads, Rolf using that waterless gargle to say things to a pretty waitress. Everybody laughed and then Cole felt his teeth jarring as Rolf slapped his back, introducing him. All Cole caught was "A-mer-ika." Rolf seemed to know everybody. Laughter again, and everyone beaming at the tattoo artist. He was home here, obviously well-liked.

"You understand that, eh?"

Cole smiled back. "Like hieroglyphics."

Sitting down, Rolf said, "Terrible. No one knows how it got here. One of our national anthems is *'Der er et yndigt land.'* *Yndigt* land? Who but a drunken Dane could sing that? Written by a man named Oehlenschlager." In English he ordered two beers and two plates of shrimp. "Schade tell you about me?"

Cole shook his head. "Just recommended you."

"That Gunther is one smart man. We have our own little network. Someone here, someone there. Gunther in Hamburg; Sepp, in Frankfurt; me here in Chopenhawn; Erickson in Stockholm and another man in Helsinki, Jonas Moe. We are all retired from our services, though our Danish intelligence is more a branch of the police. So you see . . ."

Cole wanted to do things right this time. No losing guns. Just get to them and catch the next plane home. He had thought about it a lot on the ferry, this new plan. *Listen,* say only what had to be said.

"Now, my friend, what do you need of me?" asked Rolf.

It was too early to talk about another gun. "I need to locate a German who lives here part of the year. Also has a home in Sweden."

The shrimp, looking like tiny pink rosebuds, arrived. The beer was frosty.

Rolf sighed. "I am friendly with Gunther but I just do not like Germans, you see. Haven't liked them since the war. You see, the SS hung my father outside city hall in 1942. They left his body up five days. Twice I saw it hanging there in the cold, turning blue, then black. He was in the resistance, you see. A freedom fighter."

Things were positively looking better.

"A month later I killed my first German, I was only twelve. He wasn't much older than that either..." Rolf's eyes suddenly seemed to go back to '42. "Never will I forget him," said Rolf. "I knocked him off his bicycle with a heavy stick, then pulled him into a ditch, face down. There was plenty of water to drown him."

"Twelve years old?"

"Other boys did it, too, of course. I took the rifle and gave it to the underground, then joined them when I was fourteen, the year before the Germans were chased out, lying about my age."

"Your father would have been proud of you."

"I think so. But young Danes now don't know all that we did in the war. They march with their peace banners around city hall and have no idea what we did to save their skins—"

Cole interrupted to get things onto his track. "The son of a former SS always travels with this German as a bodyguard."

"Former SS, humh?" said Rolf, coming alive, big shoulders moving forward. Rolf's old revenge engine had surely been started. Mere mention of the Schutzstaffel was enough to get it going. "Like father, like son, eh?"

"That's what I hear," said Cole.

Squinting now, under the bushy brows, Rolf asked, "His name?"

"Stefan Noll. His father was Gerhard. A lot of decorations."

Rolf shrugged as if he hadn't heard of the Nolls. "And Stefan is the bodyguard? Father still alive?"

"I don't know."

"I wonder how many of those bloody bastards still live? They have to be in their late sixties."

"Stefan is in his late thirties. When he isn't a nursemaid he heads security for a shipyard in Hamburg."

"And where do you suggest we start to hunt him? And after we find him, what do we do? Beat hell out of him? I'd like that, for old times' sake. Tell him here is one for his *vater*—"

Cole explained that Stefan was not the one he wanted. Klaus Hermann was.

"Oh?" Rolf looked confused.

"Hermann owes me a very large debt and I want to talk to him about collecting. I couldn't very well do it from California..."

Rolf laughed and said he understood about collecting money. Universal problem.

Cole saw no point in elaborating about the nature of the debt. "Rolf, Noll is a dangerous man. Always carries a gun. There's a rumor in Germany that he decapitated a doctor a while ago who threatened the Hermann family." He decided not to mention that Noll had also taken a shot at him. Too much to explain.

The Dane took a long drink of beer, then reached into his pocket for a cigar. The end soon turned fiery and smoke came out in a great whoosh. "Why does this Klaus Hermann need such a body-guard?"

"He's very wealthy. Maybe he's afraid of kidnapping? Maybe he has a lot of enemies?" Keep it vague, Wally had said, and he was right.

"They are both now in Chopenhawn?"

"That's what I was told. Hermann's apartment is at Gunsloggade 12—if that's how you pronounce it?"

"Close enough."

"They are supposed to go sailing Sunday from a place called Tarbake-Strandveg—I looked it up on the map."

Rolf nodded. "Not far from here. North. Strand-*vey*. Your Danish is terrible."

"... then on Monday night Hermann is supposed to play in a chamber music group in a place called Humlebeek..."

"Bake. Bake. Humle-*bake*. An old fisherman's village up the coast. What is this man? A musician? I thought you said he was wealthy." Rolf was frowning now. A little suspicious. This was not shaping up to be the usual referral.

"Amateur musician," said Cole.

———

228

"The worst kind."

"Then he is supposed to go to Sweden on Tuesday. His house is at Karlstrand."

"Never heard of it."

"Near Göthenburg."

"Okay, Göteburg. Now, exactly what do you want me to do?"

"Be a guide for me. Take me to both of those places and then get lost while I take on Mr. Hermann."

Rolf grinned widely. "I do both of those expertly. I get lost in a hurry. A client says 'disappear,' I do."

"And also help me if Stefan Noll interferes."

"It would be a pleasure to do that, especially since his father was SS. Just my luck that the *vater* isn't the bodyguard."

"Sorry."

"You know how Noll looks?"

"Yes, but not Hermann. I've had Hermann described to me but have never seen him."

"He owes you a big debt but you've never seen him?"

"Right."

Rolf shook his head. "You do all your business on the phone?"

"A lot."

Rolf shook his shaggy head again. "All right, we shall do surveillance on that apartment on Gunsloggade tonight, what there is of it. You have come at the wrong time of the year. It is easier to do all this in winter. We have only a few hours of darkness nows. But we can park on the street near 12 and I have binoculars to see this man Noll and the other one. Or do you want to just go up and knock on his door and say, 'Give me my goddamn money'?"

"Let's take a look at them first."

"That is fine."

"But let's talk about a couple of other things. Your fee, for one."

"I am not expensive. Two hundred kroner a day, plus expenses. They will not be much. Gas, oil, food."

"That sounds reasonable," said Cole. He still had about sixteen hundred dollars in his money belt, plus five hundred in Danish money.

"But I would like to be paid the first day in advance. This is Saturday, you know."

As Cole counted out the kroner, he said as casually as he could, "I do need one special favor and will pay more for it, of course. Since Noll carries a gun, Gunther said you could get me one, too."

The Dane's rugged face caved in.

Cole said, "At home you can buy one as easily as you can buy candy."

"Not over here," Rolf declared, drawing back in his chair as Schade had done, as if Cole suddenly had the plague. "There is strict control."

Keeping his eyes steadily on the Dane, Cole pulled up his shirt, opened the green money belt, took out three crisp U.S. hundred dollar bills and placed them on top of the kroner.

"Oh, my," said the *tatover*.

29

"MUTTI, I swear that I've been doing exactly what Dr. Hoger said to do. I swear it. Pills four times a day, exercise in the morning. No drugs. I try to meditate in the afternoon . . . have you ever tried that, Mutti?"

Gerda's voice rose several octaves. "No, and I don't *intend* to."

She had just returned from Spain, phoning Copenhagen within twenty minutes of stepping inside the elegant three-story in Leinpfad. Returning home, old bruises turned black and blue again.

"Mutti, it does you no good to stay angry with me."

"How can I not be angry, Klaus? You have been breaking promises to me over and over." Then mocking, in a falsetto, she said, "'Mutti, Mutti, I will not ever do it again,' and then you do. God rest their souls, your half brothers were never evil. They died as heroes."

"There is no war now," Klaus pointed out.

The old woman sighed. "Sometimes I wish there was."

"We went sailing today, Mutti. The weather was sunny so we decided not to wait until tomorrow. We had a very good sail. The breeze was strong."

Bleakly, Gerda said, "That's nice . . . Now listen to me, Klaus. Play your violin Monday night and then I want you and Stefan to go on to Karlstrand. No visits to the Kakadu. You got in trouble there before. Go straight to Karlstrand and I'll join you. Do you understand, Klaus?"

A look of dismay dropping over his face, Klaus said, "Yes, Mutti." Oh, the Kakadu.

"Now, let me speak to Stefan."

Noll was standing a few feet away, awaiting his turn, and reached for the phone. "Yes, my dear," he said, eyeing the backside of his charge as it plodded into the small kitchen.

"I just told Klaus that I want you two to leave for Karlstrand Monday night just as soon as he finishes that recital. No lingering in Denmark. The sooner you are in Sweden, the better."

"I agree," said Noll. Don't I always? he thought.

"He can paint, watch birds, do whatever he wants except go into Göteburg. He must have some time to think."

"Exactly, my dear," Noll said.

"The more I go over this, the more I shudder. Had he not worked for the embassy he would be in jail in America, I'm sure. My only son, in prison . . ."

"Without doubt," said Noll, "but we may be free of the other threat."

Gerda asked what he meant.

"I mean that the colonel is wanted for killing a whore in Ottensen, for beating her to death. He is posted at every exit. He is on the run, so he cannot be concerned with Klaus." Noll stopped to chuckle in appreciation of himself. "Here he comes to kill Klaus, and instead winds up in our prison. What is the word I'm seeking?"

"Irony," said Gerda. "You mean he actually came to Hamburg?"

"Oh, yes, I saw him. A tall man with a gray and brown beard. I tracked him back to the Brahms where he was staying. And then I read in *Bild* today that an American named Charles Harvey, his pseudonym obviously, was being sought for the murder." Noll began laughing again, was quickly cut off.

"None of this is to be laughed at. I have been embarrassed in the highest circles at Bonn. I doubt they will do me any more favors. I never should have trusted Klaus to leave here."

"My dear, it was just the word, irony, that caused me to laugh. So clever of you."

"Do the police know that 'Harvey' is the father of that girl in California?"

"Not unless he tells them, not unless they catch him."

"I hope they don't. It would crack things open. Can you imagine what *Bild Am Sonntag* would do to me if they got their hands on this? Ruin me! That's what I thought about over and over again in Alicante. Not this colonel but what would happen if the whole story comes out. They have left me alone for years, but I know they are always waiting in the wings."

Noll tried to calm her, wishing she'd stayed in Alicante. He really felt capable of running the whole shipyard, not just security. *Someday* . . . "He is military and probably has friends at Rhein-Main who should be able to find a way to smuggle him out on a military aircraft."

"Let us hope," said Gerda.

"My dear, if I knew where he was I would go after him right now and take care of him forever."

"That could complicate matters just now. But as for those who cause us trouble . . . be very careful, Stefan. Call me just before you leave Copenhagen, and make Klaus behave."

"Trust me," said Noll in his most devoted voice. "You know how I have always felt about you."

"Yes, dear Stefan, I do know, and I'm so lucky . . . Klaus and I are so lucky to have you."

They exchanged a few more endearments and then hung up. Noll went into the kitchen were Klaus was having a four o'clock snack. Crackers and herring and schnapps. He looked at his hairless charge with disgust, not dissimilar from his sentiments about the mother.

30

IT WAS EARLY EVENING when Cole went off to Tatover Jorgen's. They had made a date to do the surveillance on the Gunsloggade apartment after eight. Rolf said he would park his car down the street and they could use the binoculars. Cole had left Rolf laughing and talking at the bar in the Codan, returning to the Broen to nap. He had asked the desk to call him in two hours and woke up feeling fresh.

The door to Jorgen's was cracked open and Cole called several times. No answer. He went on in. No sign of life in the needle parlor section either. He proceeded into the back room. Rolf's cot was as it probably always was, unmade. Whatever, he was not in it.

Cole went back to the tattoo room and sat down, amusing himself looking at the designs, all tame enough to go on a preacher's behind.

Twenty minutes later the Dane showed up and crossed the room as if the floor was slanted. Looking at Cole, he asked suspiciously, "How'd you open the door?"

"Wasn't locked," Cole replied, shaking his head. Wouldn't you know? Drunk.

"Hmh." Rolf looked back, eyes narrowing as if the door had

been playing tricks. Smelling of Scotch all the way across the room, he teetered, then tottered, rocking on his heels, rubbing his jaw, pursing his lips.

Cole said, "Maybe we ought to make some hot coffee, Rolf. We were going over to Gunsloggade tonight. To check out that apartment. Remember?"

Rolf stared at Cole. "What?" and then plopped down heavily on a stool.

Son of a bitch couldn't wait to spend some of those kroner on Johnny Walker. "What we talked about this afternoon," Cole said, fighting his annoyance.

Rolf nodded. "Ah, yes. I see them putting the gun into my mouth. They did that once, you know. At Ringsted. This *Verfügungstruppe* pulled the trigger and laughed and laughed when it wouldn't fire. I was only fourteen." Rolf was silent a moment, staring at the floor, seeing something down there, then added, "I killed him three weeks later, with a knife."

Cole was beginning to smell lies. "Great, Rolf. Now, how about some coffee?"

The tattoo artist raised his head and knotted those heavy brows, letting loose something indescribable in Danish. Then he roared. "You expect me to sit at the Codan for four hours with *drikkevand?*"

"I don't know what that means. All I know is that we were supposed to find Noll and Hermann tonight."

"*Drik-keh-vand* is water, Amer-i-kan. We Danes use it to wash our feet," said Rolf.

Cole went over to the little kerosene stone. "Okay. I see the pot. Where's the coffee?"

"No coffee," shouted Rolf. "Don't need coffee . . ." He got up and lurched into the back room and onto the cot.

"Well, I could do with a cup," said Cole, shaking his head.

Rolf put the back of his hands over his eyes, said with a thick tongue, "I'll sleep a little while and then we'll go to Gunsloggade."

"Yeh, okay," said Cole, standing over the big body and thinking the little while would be several hours.

Hands still over his eyes, Rolf said, "All my life I have wanted to come to Amer-i-ka and raise oranges, pick them when they look like the moon . . ."

"Yeh, Rolf. You bet. Terrific."

The *tatover* went to sleep and Cole went outside, slamming the door, making sure it locked. He had dinner up the street at a seafood place with sawdust on the floor and went back to the Broen.

Saturday evening

Dearest Kot:

Things aren't going so hot. I hired a man today as a guide and six hours later he was snockered. I'm again tempted to call you but can't, won't. I know that if I heard your voice or Jen's or Skeet's, I'd head for the airport. I'd come home and never sleep again.

You know me better than anyone on earth and you know that I always try to give everything my best shot, and that's what I'm doing now. The only thing I ever quit was the Corps and that, of course, has to do with where I am now.

But I feel adrift for the first time in my life. Mostly, I guess I've always been in control. If I didn't like the sound I wouldn't take the machine up. I always knew what I was doing. Here I don't know. I feel vulnerable, like I'm in hands I can't trust.

I hope it will all be over by tomorrow night. We're all going boating. I think of you, and Jennifer and Skeet, and Ellen . . .

All my love,
Cole

He shut out brown-gray twilight at about eleven and sprawled on the bed. The drapes leaked, and Cole closed his eyes to shut out the light.

Ellen on a swing, pumping higher and higher and dissolving to Ellen exploding with laughter when the sled turned over in the snow on that hill in Virginia. Always so pretty in the cold, cheeks flaming. Then when she was valedictorian during the second Cherry Point tour, so anxious to help the world, so proud of the speech she'd written . . .

Late Sunday morning Rolf apologized and then dug around in the back room litter to come up with a gun. It was not one that

237

Cole knew. It felt cold, although the day was warm. He read the engraving: *Ceska-Zbro-Strakonice*.

"No registration on it here," Rolf said. "The former owner, a Yugoslav, is long dead. It could be registered in Dubrovnik, I guess. But we won't worry, eh? You like it?"

"If it shoots straight."

"Podnik .765. A Czech gun, very accurate."

It did feel trim but the silencer was almost as long as the barrel. Rolf loaded it and the Podnik went into the deep right-hand pocket of Cole's new leather jacket.

They got into Rolf's rattling old MG, Cole's head pressed into the canvas top. The broken passenger seat had a slab of wood under it, raising the frame by three inches. The MG was older than Cole's Austin-Healey and sounded like it.

Cole said, "After we get there, and make sure that Hermann and Noll are there, I'll need your help in renting a boat, and then you can leave."

"Whatever you say."

The trip to Tarbaek did not take long and they stayed the rest of the day, seeing nothing of either German, though checking every sailboat in sight with binoculars. Neither was there a record of Hermann or Noll having rented a boat. Finally, after six they returned to town and ate dinner at a hole-in-the-wall, most everything else being closed on Sunday.

They went on to Gunsloggade, where Rolf found a parking place about two hundred feet from No. 12. It was ten o'clock and still light.

A few minutes after eleven, when it was just beginning to get a little dusky over Copenhagen, a blue rental Ford with license plates DN 44 533 pulled up seven or eight cars in front of Rolf's MG and backed into a parking slot.

A moment later Cole saw Klaus Hermann in the flesh for the first time. Just as described by that baby-faced highway patrolman. Grabbing the binoculars, he made certain. Chunky, square-faced. Wig.

Noll walked around the back of the car. Same face as in Wally's sixteen millimeter, same walk. A man from the Alps. "That's them," he said to Rolf.

They went into No. 12.

Cole found himself holding his breath. Finally, *target*.

Now, did he have the brass balls to do it? Think about Ellen on her knees in that nurse's cap . . . just that one scene that Louderholt had thought about. That should be all he'd need. But there was also Teddi Hagner and the fists that had been used on her.

In front of the Broen, Cole asked, "Any place we can get a drink?"

"Plenty, even Sunday night. What did you have in mind, girls?"

"No, someplace where we can talk."

Rolf parked and they walked to 71 Nyhavn, where a warehouse had been converted into a semi-posh hotel.

All day Cole had fought guilt. Teddi's death was still haunting him, and there was a reasonable chance that Rolf Halvorsen might end up the same way. The Dane seemed to be a good man, not so crafty and grasping as Schade.

After they sat down Cole said, "Rolf, I don't want to get you killed."

The Dane laughed. "I share your sentiments," and beckoned for a waiter.

"I haven't told you the truth."

"Most of my clients never do."

"I came here to kill Hermann. That's why I needed the gun."

Even while he was saying it Cole thought it might be another nice-guy mistake. Be honest and end up on your butt. Nice guys finish last. Dead last. Still, he couldn't really allow Rolf to walk into a potential slaughterhouse without knowing where an exit was. In combat you got briefed. You might get killed on the mission but you at least got briefed.

Rolf's eyes did a double-take and he murmured something in Danish, looking to see if the next table's occupants were within hearing distance.

After the waiter took their order and departed he said, "Say that again to me, slowly."

"Let me tell you about my daughter, Ellen," said Cole, beginning at UCI. He left out nothing. Twenty minutes later he was saying, "I like you, and I wanted you to know, all of it. Think about it tonight, Rolf. Tell me to shove it in the morning. But I would like you to drive me up there tomorrow night and just drop me. Forget you ever saw me."

Rolf sat there in silence for a while, just looking around the bar, not once letting his eyes meet Cole's. Finally he said, "I have a daughter in Odense with three little children. If anyone harmed her or those children I'd try to have them dead by sundown."

Cole nodded. "The way I feel . . ."

Rolf said, "I'll let you know in the morning."

"Good enough."

31

AT ABOUT EIGHT MONDAY EVENING, North Sea cloud cover
cutting down the natural kilowatts over Denmark, they went up to
Humlebaek, up the coast from Copenhagen toward Elsinore, up
where Danskland bulges in toward Sweden, twenty minutes away
by ferry. The road traveled close by the solemn waters of the Oresund. Almost as busy as the Santa Ana, Cole thought, tourists
heading back from Elsinore bumper-to-bumper. Rolf's beat-up
dusty MG purred along in the coolness. Good taste in cars, Cole
thought, even if it was a wreck.

Rolf had not said much about his decision to help, just that he
thought no man should get away with kidnapping, sexual abuse
and murder, screw diplomatic immunity. He also said if there was
trouble he was going to be the dumbest Dane in all Denmark . . . he
was hired as a guide, that's all he knew, shocked at what happened . . .

The Podnik was a long, hard lump in Cole's side, a reminder of
every kilometer of what was ahead. Ticketed on SAS 931 to Los
Angeles, he wanted to make as sure as possible that he was on it.
Katta and the kids deserved better than what they'd gotten the past
weeks. Until now, oddly enough, nothing had seemed imminent.
Working out at El Toro, running near Oakwood Terrace, George-

town and Wally, even Hamburg—all of it seemed preliminary. Cole had thought many times the past two months about the role of an assassin but there had been an unreal, almost detached quality to it. He could not picture himself in the role. Now, here it was . . .

It had been a strange day after another tossing, restless night. Maybe three hours of sleep and even that relief again came about from exhaustion. Tempted again to call Katta just after he got out of bed, he pushed temptation away. He was afraid to hear her voice. Though he did not feel sick, he had thrown up after breakfast. Some hitman.

On the way Rolf prattled on, observing that Hamlet's home, big Kronborg Slot, the great three-towered castle, was up ahead. Just past Snekkersten and Helsingor.

"I can't wait to see it," said Cole.

"We won't be going that far tonight, but there was intrigue for you, Hickel. Finely done."

"Uh-hmh."

"But I really don't like Hamlet. And Kronborg has always made me uneasy. Give me comedy."

Cole sighed. Lord help me. "Well, Shakespeare wrote some pretty good comedy, too, as I remember." His nerves were beginning to scream.

"Give me clowns," Rolf said. "Pretty girls. Have you caught the circus? No, of course you haven't. You've been with me all the time."

Cole wanted to tell him to please shut up.

The MG sped along, and Rolf talked about the best circus he had ever seen. Chinese, it was . . .

They soon pulled into quaint Humlebaek and found the auditorium, but Rolf thought they should not go into the parking lot until the blue Ford with the DN 44 533 plates arrived. Then they'd know how Klaus Hermann and Noll would walk back to the car.

Rolf said, "Turn around, look behind the seat."

Cole did. A bundle of fireworks.

Rolf was beaming. "Two days from now is *sankt hans aften,* the shortest night of the year, and we celebrate it with parties and

---

242

bonfires and fireworks. Now, out in the parking lot I can be a drunken Dane celebrating early just as Hermann comes out with Noll. A lot of noise, a lot of smoke. Then you . . . shoot."

The old diversion tactic. Military stuff.

"The light worries me," Cole said, looking around. "I feel naked."

"Come back in November. It's so dark you can't see your shoes."

"If I can't do it here . . ."

Rolf seemed unworried. "So we'll do it on Gunsloggade."

A moment later the blue Ford, with two occupants, rolled in and went around to the side of the old building. Hans Christian Andersen was in knee pants when the brick-layers finished the low box with its hand-hammered wrought-iron shutters. Ivy clung to its arches. Hobnail boots had been scooping out the brick walks for a century. They watched as Noll and Hermann got out, Klaus carrying his violin case. Three other cars were parked close by the side entrance, into which the Germans had disappeared.

Rolf said quietly, "After a while, I'll fix his car. I'm an expert at sabotaging electrical systems." Rolf, Cole suspected, was using this job to wreak vengeance on Noll's father, living or dead, more than to help avenge Ellen. Who could blame him? He said, "Stay in the car."

Cole watched as Rolf went up to the auditorium entrance and talked to a lady who appeared to be passing out programs. He trudged back and inserted himself into the MG. "The program will last almost three hours. We'll come back for the last hour. I'd go crazy listening to that screeching and scratching."

He suggested they go get a drink in the village. A little toast for right against wrong. Cole was all for that.

To the left of the auditorium entrance was a glass-fronted announcement case. Translated from Danish, it read: June 19, The Christianborg Chamber Music Ensemble. Ole Wulff, Oboe. Klaus Hermann, Violin. Borge Jacobsen, Viola de Gamba. Torsten Juhl, Harpsichord.

243

The lines below said: Performing the works of Buxtehude, Telemann, Bach and Ariosti.

A final line said: Sponsored by Hermann Werft, GHBH, Hamburg.

A door to stage-left opened, and the Christianborg Ensemble made their entrance, looking as though they were dumbfounded to see anyone in the auditorium. The third among them, the youngest, was Klaus Hermann.

Light, polite applause went up into the ancient rafters. A chair was scraped, and then another. A man came across the stage with a pitcher of water. A big moth circled around the footlights, banging heads with a bulb. Sheet music was rustled and scales began to be run.

It was not exactly a sell-out even though free. Who but buffs would travel to hear Buxtehude and Telemann? Indeed, the place was only quarter-full, the buffs mostly pushing fifty and beyond. Windows were open in the nearly warm night, and some devotees were out on the grass, enjoying the start of summer.

The ensemble was an informal lot, larking it up while fixing music and stands. Handkerchief tucked under his double chin, Klaus raked his bow soulfully to tune up for Telemann. Wulff tootled his oboe up and down the scale. Jacobsen, the viola de gamba, had white hair and looked like a judge. Tiny Torsten Johl worked at his harpsichord. There were squeaks and bleeps and bloops; plunks and sawing.

Klaus did a quick glissando, nodded to himself, then rested his violin on his knees and began to peer out beyond the soaring moth and footlights.

Now Stefan Noll entered and sat down in the last row, far right, scanning the audience face by face.

Kay Louderholt's call to the Hickels in late afternoon was answered by Skeet, who said, "Just a minute, who's calling?"

"Detective Sergeant Louderholt."

"Oh," said Skeet, impressed, although he'd never heard of a lady dick aside from *Cagney & Lacey*. He shouted up the steps, "Mom."

244

"I'm in the tub, tell them I'll call right back."

Skeet relayed the message, then went halfway up the stairs to shout, "That lady dick from UCI."

Katta winced, hurriedly drew the curtain and turned the shower tap to rinse. Out of the shower, she toweled off quickly, pulled on a robe and went to the bedroom to call Kay Louderholt.

The last time they had talked—the second time they had talked since Cole went away—Kay had said, "Mrs. Hickel, please forgive me for saying it, but you look awful. You should get some rest." It had left an impression. Katta didn't much like looking "awful."

Louderholt later said to Chief McManus that she believed there had been a marital blow-up at the Hickels. The colonel wasn't around. That often happened after a family tragedy. Everything fell apart. Truth was, Katta Hickel was living on pills, sleeping on pills. She had lost eleven pounds in less than two weeks. Cole had called only once. The last few days she'd been thinking he was dead.

Katta now dialed UCI and Kay Louderholt said, "I have to talk to you. Should I come to your house?"

Katta said hesitantly, "I don't think so. Every time someone comes it upsets the children. They don't know what to think. Can we do it now, here on the phone?"

There was a pause. "I honestly think it would be better if we met."

"Can you tell me anything?"

"It's about Ellen . . ."

Katta drew in a breath. What else? Oh, why couldn't it be about Cole? "All right. How about Chantilly over in Woodbridge?"

"I've been there."

"Thirty minutes, okay?"

"Fine," said Louderholt.

Katta got dressed, fixed her face as much as she could, told Skeet she would be back in an hour and to tell Jennifer. Get three frozen dinners out of the fridge. Whatever they wanted. Whatever . . .

Then the station wagon rolled for Woodbridge.

A sonata by Dietrich Buxtehude, who had been born and died not far from Humlebaek, was being performed, but Klaus Hermann was dwelling somewhere else, eyes closed, as he stroked the box and the sound caroomed off the flat surface of the room.

Stefan Noll was bored silly and suffering, his eyes also closed. He liked big band tunes, even liked beer garden tubas, did disco now and then at the Ebony, but what was being played here was deadly and he longed for the intermission. Without doubt, Stefan thought, he was the only member of the audience carrying a gun. The garden variety war-vintage black-gripped Luger, tucked in a shoulder holster, produced a bulge over his heart but chamber music patrons would have been the last to recognize it.

This was only the second time that Stefan had been trapped into enduring a Klaus Hermann concert, and he desperately hoped it would be the last.

Buxtehude soon segued into Ariosti, but Stefan Noll was unaware of the difference.

Kay Louderholt was saying, "Early this morning the Garden Grove police picked up a young suspect in a rape and murder case in which two older boys were involved. By older I mean he was nineteen and they were twenty-four, twenty-five. All of them in deep trouble. But the younger one, scared out of his brains when one of the officers began talking to another one about the death penalty, began to talk. It seems that this wasn't the first time they'd done this. According to the nineteen-year-old, the first time was out near the Edison plant on Coast Highway. They picked up a girl staggering along the roadside. She was wearing a yellow blouse and denim skirt . . ."

"Oh, my God," said Katta.

"All along those tire tracks at Dana Point bothered me, as I told you."

"Oh, my God," Katta repeated, fingers on her right hand absently on her throat. She stared at the detective sergeant, eyes wide, face even paler than the last time they had met.

Louderholt went on. "Everyone has to move carefully, and I

think you would have been notified in a day or two about the *possibility.* But I promised I'd let you know the minute I had any kind of news. Please don't say anything to anyone, let it come officially from the sheriff's office . . ."

"This means the German might not have raped Ellen, might not have killed her . . . ?"

Louderholt nodded. "*Might* not, is right. There's a doubt now in my mind. But there's *no* question that he kidnapped her and forced her to commit certain acts . . . after that we don't know. I have my doubts that he actually raped her. Even if we did get him back here we'd probably have trouble proving murder in any degree, which hardly lets him off the hook. Not in my book." She stopped, caught by the look on Katta's face. "Mrs. Hickel? Are you all right? What is it?"

Katta began shaking her head, as if trying to sweep away concussion. "Cole's over there now."

"Over where? *Where* is he?"

"In Germany, going after Klaus Hermann. Maybe he's found him already, done away with him—I've been going crazy."

"Good God, he's too sensible a man to do that—"

"No, no, he isn't. Especially not after what happened to Ellen." She put both palms alongside her head.

Louderholt said, "I thought maybe you two were split for some other reasons. Are you in touch with him?"

"I'm not sure . . . there's a man in Washington . . ."

Louderholt tried to sound hopeful. "Maybe he's come to his senses? Maybe he's flying home right now, Mrs. Hickel."

"No. Not Cole. When he gets like this no one can stop him. Knock him down and he'll get up and come back again . . . and again . . ."

As a little hand-bell pealed out, summoning the faithful to return, Stefan Noll went back to his seat in the last row after looking around outside and finding nothing suspicious in the gradually fading light. Nonetheless, the events in Hamburg had shaken him, that rider on the white Yamaha spoiling it all . . .

Telemann soon began to waver out from the stage. Such music

should be restricted to cathedrals, Noll thought. But an hour, more or less, and they could return to Copenhagen, thank God. He had booked the early morning SAS to Göteborg, which meant getting out of bed at Gunsloggade at five forty-five.

He stayed in the auditorium another thirty minutes and then, yawning, got up and slipped out for a smoke, going to the last window on the right side. From there he could watch Klaus and most of the auditorium. His rear end was complaining. Two hours on the wooden seat was too much.

Rolf pulled the MG to the edge of the parking lot, facing out onto the street, having doused the lights a block away. He checked his watch. "Good." He was excited, he had admitted back at the tavern, more so than at any time since the war. He had had four drinks when Cole, who had had one, cut him off. Nonetheless he seemed to be in rare form. They had talked for more than two hours, Rolf wanting to know all about "Cal-ee-forniah."

He parked the car headed out to the street so that all they would need to do was go straight ahead for six or seven feet, take a hard left and in four minutes, a right, and they would be on their way back to the city.

Cole said, "Let's go over it once more."

Rolf nodded.

"I go up by the last window on the left side and stay until they start to come out of the stage door. When they get halfway to their car you set off the fireworks, I shoot Hermann, then Noll, and we both run to the MG. Motor will be running, off we go."

"Correct. But before any of that, I fix Noll's car."

"Right." The Podnik in Cole's right-hand jacket pocket felt like it was already heated.

Wally had said just get close, pull the trigger and take off. That's what the pros did. There wasn't any better method.

They strolled slowly toward the auditorium, which was about six hundred feet away, winding through cars haphazardly parked, two music lovers happening by, hearing the ensemble, going over to take a look and listen.

248

There were still a few people along the open windows on the left side; a few in the grass. One couple asleep on a blanket.

Cole looked at his watch. Eleven-fifteen. Getting dark.

They stayed in the shadows by the last window, looking in with a clear view of the Christianborg ensemble performing the last of Bach. Cole edged closer to the window frame, searching the audience for Stefan Noll. He pulled back, whispering, "I can't see him."

"Maybe he's asleep in the dressing room. That's where I'd be, with earplugs," Rolf whispered back.

Ten minutes and Bach was over. A moment of conversation on the stage, then the viola de gamba player, ancient Jacobsen, labored up. Jacobsen said—Rolf translating quietly—"There is a change in the program. Herr Hermann will now play a solo, Rondo Capriccioso, by Saint-Saens, his own favorite for many years. It ends tonight's concert and also ends the spring season here." A bone tossed to Klaus because Gerda put up the house rental.

Klaus lifted violin to chin and began. It was the same musical leaf that Cole had heard in Wally's apartment, Menuhin on the bow, drifting and gliding down a crystal stream. Watching Klaus that close, long simmering rage went to boil. The prayer rug, the doctor's coat, the nurse's hat. Ellen begging. Cole was tempted to gun him down right now while he was still stroking that violin down the stream. Even sixty feet away, a genuine degenerate. Not those red-eyed bewhiskered alkies in old army coats, wretched shoes with toes busting out and no socks. You could feel sorry for them. They just made you want to steer clear. This one, knowing what he did when he wasn't sawing music . . . Elephant Valley days in a different setting.

Rolf touched his shoulder and whispered, "I've got some work to do," and moved off.

Cole stayed by the window, scarcely breathing, putting his hand into the jacket, removing the safety on the Podnik. Soon. Very soon.

* * *

With only a few minutes to go Stefan Noll moved away from the right side of the old building and walked out to the flagpole to take another look around. His eyes swept over the parking lot, then toward the side entrance just in time to see someone lowering the hood on the Ford.

Noll cursed softly, slipped the Luger out of the holster and angled over to follow the man. Even in the brownish semidarkness he could tell that whoever was fooling around the Ford was a big man, and the American colonel certainly fit that description. Moving swiftly but quietly, he reached into his side pocket for the silencer, screwing it on as he went around a final car, seeing the big man open the driver's side of an MG with Danish plates. He was reaching in for something.

Noll covered the ten feet in two long steps, held the Luger no more than a foot from the man's back and pulled the trigger. The man's gasp was almost as loud as the pistol sound. Grasping hair, Noll pulled the head around and immediately saw that it was not bearded Cole Hickel. He dropped the shaggy head back onto the seat.

Applause was coming from the auditorium as Noll ran the six hundred feet, arriving at the entrance just as the audience began to file out. Hand on the Luger resting again in the shoulder holster without the silencer, he began backing down the aisle against the flow. Those departing could not understand this blond muscular man with one hand in his jacket, walking backward.

Cole saw Stefan Noll retreating down the aisle, face taut, eyes searching the entrance and off to the sides. Cole pulled deeper into the shadows. Something was very wrong. He looked back toward the MG, which was not visible from his position. Enough darkness had lidded down to make the cars just shapes out there. He stayed a moment longer near the window, then went quickly toward the top of the lot.

Noll continued backing until he was against the footlights, then said rapidly to Klaus, "Get off the stage, get into the dressing room, if there's a bathroom get inside and lock the door."

"What's wrong?" Klaus asked, startled. He was putting his violin away.

"Just do as I *say*."

Klaus shut up and hurried off the stage.

The phone in Georgetown kept ringing and the machine kept saying: Hello, this is Wallace Stonebridge, I'm not available to answer your call at the moment but if you'll leave your name and number at the sound of the tone . . .

Katta called every thirty minutes for three hours saying, "Katta Hickel calling again." The last time she said, "Wally, please answer my call. The police out here don't believe Klaus Hermann killed our daughter . . ."

There was Rolf, on the driver's side of the car, looking as if he were praying. His knees were in the gravel, the upper part of his body was inside the car. What in hell was he doing? "Rolf?" Getting no answer, he looked closer. The Dane's head was alongside the gearshift. Passed out? "Rolf, for Chrissakes . . ." And then Cole saw that the back of Rolf's jacket had a stain the size of a watermelon, reddish blotch coming through the corduroy. Not believing it for a moment or two, not wanting to accept it, Cole muttered, "Oh, God," shaking the Dane's shoulder. "Rolf . . . *Rolf* . . ."

No movement, no sound.

Cole leaned in and turned the Dane's head, holding his hand in front of Rolf's mouth. There was still warmth. He felt for a pulse and thought there was a slight beat.

Standing a moment longer over the praying form, Cole knew it was decision time. Go back after Noll and Hermann or try to help Rolf. He shook his head and opted for Rolf. After reaching into Rolf's pocket for the car keys he went around to the other side and dragged the heavy body over, Rolf's head rolling around as if attached with rubber bands. It ended up chin on breastbone. The broken seat slid down, and Cole had trouble tucking the legs in. Finally he could slam the door shut.

The old car fired off on the first starter rotation and vaulted out of the lot, turning left toward the water as they had planned. For a moment Cole considered driving to the village police station, which he had spotted on the way in, but thought better of it. There would be a sinkhole of questions. He turned south on the shore road and built the MG to a hundred twenty-five kph. There had been a *hospitalet* sign on the outskirts of Copenhagen less than twenty minutes away.

There was still some traffic going south, even at this hour, nearing midnight. People came up north and spent the evening across from Sweden picnicking or having dinner, then driving back. Time was not an object. Cole knew that the *tatover* was dead, sitting in a pool of his own blood. The merry man was gone.

Rage, grief tore at Cole as he drove, dropping the speed to a hundred. Another innocent victim of Stefan Noll, protecting his boy. Cole wished he had known Grandfather Rolf at another time. Nice man, fun man, full of laughter. Cole's kind of man, and he would have been alive, just like Teddi Hagner, if it weren't for a former Marine and a couple of murdering Germans. He looked over at the slumped corpse beside him. "I'll get him for you. The least I can do."

The little towns were going by. Niva, Skodsborg. Now Tarbaek, where they had wasted yesterday. Charlottenlund, where Rolf had bet on the ponies. Then, near Hellerup, just above where Tuborg brewed its beer, Cole spotted the *hospitalet* sign, taking a sweeping right on Tuborgvej, then going straight to the huge medical facility at Bispebjerg, driving slowly by it until he found a place that was mostly in shadows near a brightly lighted building.

Opening the door on his side, he held Rolf's hand a moment, then took a wooden match from the console tray and broke it off. He jammed the butt into the horn button lip, heard the *aaaaarg* and started running, knowing he would remember that last sight of the *tatover* and the sound of the bleating horn for as long as he lived.

Slowing to a walk about half mile away from Bispebjerg, he found a cab to take him back to the hotel. He felt ninety, and looked some of it when he walked through the Broen's door.

* * *

252

Noll's face, lit by the dashboard, held little expression. They were driving toward Copenhagen. "He was up to some mischief and I just happened to see him. He was putting the hood down and I suspected he had tampered with the wires. That would have given him time. We come out, the car won't start, and *bang . . .*"

"He was going to kill me getting into the car," Klaus said, now thoroughly alarmed.

"Yes, Klaus. That's exactly what he was going to do." And, you freaky shit, I hope you tell your mother that I saved your life once again. In any case I shall tell her.

"It was the American?"

Noll glanced at his hairless charge. "Who else would it be?" Keeping Klaus in a state of fright was not a bad idea.

"How did he ever find us?"

"I think I know, and I will take care of her when we get back to Hamburg."

"Did you shoot the American?"

"No, I just knocked him unconscious."

"So he may try again?"

"Yes, Klaus. He may try again. Listen to me, keep that gun I gave you, the Walther, with you at all times. For protection when I am not around. I showed you at Agerup how to take the safety off, to aim and fire. You're in constant danger."

Klaus nodded, shivering slightly.

Noll was enjoying himself. Let Klaus believe the worst.

32

"KATTA?"

He said it like his hat was in his hands, like he was at the bottom of the steps, like he'd been a bad boy and wanted to come in from the cold.

"Coley? Oh, my Lord, it's you."

"Yeh, me. I'm sorry I didn't call, honey. . ."

"Just to hear your voice, you don't know—"

"I know I had to hear yours this morning."

"Never do this to me again."

"I won't, I promise."

"You're all right, Coley? You're okay? You're not hurt? Oh, my God—"

"I'm okay. I'm fine. Believe me."

"By Friday and no call from you I was beginning to think . . . well, you know. . ."

"I'm okay, really."

"Cole, where are you?" Her voice had settled down some.

"I'm in Denmark . . ."

"Denmark?"

There was a shout down the stairs. "Is that daddy?"

"Yes, Jennifer."

Cole said, "God, Kot, it's good to hear your voice...Skeet okay?"

Jennifer got on the phone upstairs. "Why didn't you call us? We were worried."

She sounded so grown-up. "How you doin', Jen?"

"Better now, daddy. I heard mom say Denmark. What are you doing there? When are you coming home?"

"A few days, Jen. How's Skeeter?"

"He's okay but we were all so worried about you. We weren't even talking to each other the last few days."

"Put Skeet on. Katta, you still there?"

"Yes, I'm here. Cole, give me a flight arrival time, I mean it. We've had enough—"

"Kot, I can't yet...hey, Skeet, how are you, buddy?"

"I'm okay, dad. We've missed you."

"I'm glad, Skeet. And I've missed all of you."

"I wish we had three phones," Skeeter said.

Cole said that he did, too. Talking to them, he felt like he had a fever. His whole body felt hot.

Skeet asked, "When are you coming home?"

Katta answered for Cole. "As soon as he can pack up. Right, Cole?"

Cole hesitated. "Pretty soon."

"Hey, husband, you've got a pee-oohed wife and two pee-oohed kids back here. So don't give us any of this 'pretty soon' stuff."

Cole strained a laugh. "Well..."

Katta said, "Okay, Jen and Skeet, off the phone for a little bit. I'll turn him over to you in a few minutes but there are some things I have to say to your father. Off the phone now..."

Jennifer said a grumpy "okay" and there was a click.

Katta was recovering, he thought...her next words had some bite in them. "Why in hell didn't you call me? Do you know what you've put me through? *Us* through? You promised you'd call every night. We've been going crazy. *I've* been going crazy..."

"I know. Things just didn't work out that way, I'll tell you later, I can't now..."

"Well, did you *do* it? And you know damn well what I'm talking about."

"No, I haven't had the chance—"

"Thank God—"

"What does that mean?"

"Listen to me, Cole—that UCI detective called yesterday to say that the German did not, I repeat *did not,* take Ellen's life . . ."

"What do you mean?"

"He kidnapped her, all right, but three other men did the rest. They're in custody."

"What?"

"You heard me. One of them confessed and implicated the other two. They picked her up on the Coast Highway near the Edison plant after Klaus Hermann shoved her out of the car . . ."

"That's hard to believe—"

"Well, believe it, please, Cole. And come home while I still have a little sanity left."

"But Hermann did kidnap her?" And more . . . the nurse's cap . . . the doctor's coat . . .

"Yes, but he didn't rape her or kill her."

Was she making this up to get him to come home? Katta was so straight, but she was upset enough now . . . Never mind, either way, he knew what he had to do . . .

"You still there?" she asked.

"Yes, I'm here . . ."

"Cole, we can't bring her back. Yes, he kidnapped her and probably did some terrible things to her and should be punished. But the law is going to take care of the men who took her life, we'll have to accept that . . ."

She was afraid for him, for herself, and she had a right to be. But that didn't change some other facts . . . "Katta, remember, *Klaus Hermann* started the whole thing when he took her, forced her into his car, did what he did . . . *Nothing* would have happened to Ellen if it hadn't been for *him.*"

"Yes and I wish God, *not* you, would strike him dead. But—"

"Katta, it's more complicated now . . ." How to tell her about

Teddi Hagner? How to tell her about Rolf Halvorsen? Didn't he owe them, too? And how to pay that debt if Hermann and Noll were free? Good, the law would take care of the killers at home ...but not here. Here it was still up to him...

"Coley, are you there? Look, I don't want to argue with you across an ocean. I just want you *home*. You say it's complicated. So make it simple. You always had a knack for doing that. *Whatever* it is, drop it, Coley."

Cole shook his head, knowing he shouldn't have called home. He couldn't cope with Katta. He had to stop this. "Kot, I don't want to argue either. I wanted to call and say I loved you, all of you... and that I'm safe ..."

"Do you like it there?"

Cole hung up then. He couldn't handle anymore. None of them could.

His eyes stung, head ached. There was Rolf's blood on his trousers, in a pile there on the bathroom floor. Wash those and get rid of them. Another pair was in the flight bag. He could sleep on the train, the ferry. The clerk had already said that a good sightseeing way was to take the train to Elsinore, then cross on the ferry to Sweden. Twenty minutes over the Oresund. Then take a train or bus from Helsingboro to Göteborg. Very nice along the Swedish coast, some of it in view of the Kattegat, the clerk had said. Up past Halmstad and Falkenberg and Asa, the clerk had said. One couldn't see anything from the air, could one? Cole agreed that one couldn't. He also did not want to go through the X-ray security check at Kastrup airport.

He dozed on the short train ride to Elsinore; dozed again on the ferry across the Oresund; went through Swedish customs and immigration as if they didn't exist—the Swissair bag with the Podnik under two shorts was not opened... who wanted to hijack a ferry? ... and fell asleep before the train left the station. He did not wake up until halfway to Göteborg, when the sea was no longer in sight. Now the train glided by neat villages, with forests off to the east, then wound back out again to seaside at a place called Varberg.

Yawning, he gazed out of the window, thinking of the call to Katta, awakening with it on his mind; not to think of Katta, or what she'd said, was the only way to handle it; put Katta and the kids out of mind until it was all over, then call... Whatever the truth about the three men they'd picked up, *Hermann was still responsible. If he had not taken Ellen, Ellen would be alive.* Hold that thought...

The rails clicked on north.

Katta, Art Hoberman, Mike Goody, the highway cop, Red Rough and Ready, they had all faded some. Up front now were Teddi Hagner and Rolf Halvorsen, joining Ellen. All three were right up front *and waiting for him to do something. So do it.*

The car was about half-full in midmorning. Mostly students with books and old people with shopping bags. It was smart not to fly today, aside from avoiding the X-ray machine. Trains gave you a chance to get down to earth, he was discovering. What would Wally do at this point? Not so much Wally personally but what would Wally know how to do? How to track down Hermann in a foreign country without a Schade or a Rolf?

The train came to a whistle stop, five or six people getting off, the same getting on, wheels rolling again in five minutes. The sea, golden this late morning, briefly came into view, then vanished on a curve. What it was now, for damn sure, was that he was strictly on his own, up or down.

A ruddy, white-haired man across the way smiled and asked with a heavy accent, "Tourist?"

Cole smiled back, said he was.

"British?"

"American. On my way to Göthenburg."

"Ah, Göteborg. You will like it. Lilac time. Very beautiful. I say go to Liseberg, the park. Better than Tivoli."

"Sure, thanks."

Lilac time.

Just find him, then... maybe Noll too... do it and get the hell out. Wally's original advice kept repeating itself. Remember Wally had also said that police, anywhere in the world, usually took sev-

eral days just to untangle things. A cushion of time to get away
... After crossing a couple of rivers, the train plunged back into
the woods, skirted more spic-and-span villages, jiggled for another
forty minutes before reaching the outskirts of Göteburg, then
screeched around bends and came to rest at Centralen Station along
Burggrevegatan.

It was 12:40.

The lady at the accommodation desk recommended the Siljan.
"It is inexpensive."

Fine and thank you, said Cole, taking the slip of paper from her
after she had made the reservation.

The Siljan was a small hotel sporting a peppermint awning and
situated on a side street. A place to sleep and take a shower was all
that was needed. Cole signed up for the night and climbed the steps
to his room, pausing only long enough to remove the Podnik from
the flight bag. The silencer was already in his left pants pocket.
The gun itself went back into his jacket. Back down the stairs and
into sunlight. He asked no questions at the desk; just picked up a
street map and located where he was, the Siljan. It appeared to be
central to everything.

Learning, orienting, his confidence was slowly coming back. He
walked to the center of town and not far from a big statue of
Poseidon found a Hertz office.

"No, I just want to ride around and see some of the places by the
sea."

He was smiling at the dark-haired girl behind the desk. She had
Ellen's nose.

"We have much sea. You must tell me which places."

"How can I do that? I don't know them."

"Okay, let me show you," she said, leaning over, drawing on a
map with a red pencil, her perfume and closeness momentarily
unsteadying him.

"Here is Langedrag, very close through the western suburbs.
And Marstrand, of course. And Styro is lovely but a little further
away."

While she was talking he was looking at other places on the map and finally spotted Karlstrand. "May I have this?" he asked, touching the map.

"Surely, sir."

Cole next asked what kind of cars she had for rent.

"Volvos, of course, BMW, Fords . . ."

"Ford compact?"

"Surely, sir."

He judged she was also about Ellen's age.

Though Stefan Noll loathed Spain and everything Spanish except baby eels fried in garlic oil, he enjoyed Sweden and the Swedes, particularly in summer. Off and on, he had been coming to Karlstrand ever since Gerda hired him to service her. He had once spent a week here with a Gulf Air stewardess and had had a most pleasant time.

Klaus, however, did not much like Sweden or the Swedes or the old house that Gerda treasured. He preferred the Kakadu in Copenhagen. But he did like to paint out on the skerries and usually occupied his time at the easel on sunny days.

At two o'clock Klaus came putt-putting up to the Karlstrand boatyard dock, two cylinder Sweboat outboard pushing a skiff that had suffered several decades of abuse. No one ever used it except Klaus and he did so only to go to the outermost skerry, the one with the most wildflowers.

Staring unhappily at the flabby man in the straw hat and paint-spattered trousers, Noll wondered just how long he would have to do this. Gerda was up in her beloved cottage, with her beloved poodles, puttering about after having her hair done. And how long did she plan to stay this time? It was fortunate that she could take only so much of her son. Once her limit had been reached they would all pack up and fly back to Hamburg.

As soon as the engine cut out with a backfire and puff of white smoke, Noll called, "I was beginning to think you would never come back." Not an unpleasant prospect at that.

"Light was good today," Klaus replied, kneeling down on the gunwale to tie up, boat tipping heavily to port.

Noll sat there, not offering to help unload the canvasses, easel, stool and box of paints and some rags. Having no desire to stay out on that rock hour after hour listening to birds quarrel, no interest at all in seeing Klaus daub colors to make bad pictures, Noll had brought a beach chair down from the house, parking it on the rickety dock pier that ran parallel to the small shipway of Karlstrand Skeppsbron. He had faced the chair inland toward the sandy road that came down from a low hill to the boatyard. Underneath his folded sweater, by his feet, was the Luger, just in case the American colonel somehow found them . . .

He was still puzzled by what had happened at Humlebaek. When he had gone back out to the parking lot, after making certain Klaus was secure, the old MG was not to be found; nor was the man he had shot. Yet he was convinced that the Dane was in no shape to drive very far in any direction. There was also no sign of the bearded American. Puzzling.

Klaus was now away from the skiff and holding up the finished seascape. It showed part of the skerry and acres of wildflowers; then the sunny Kattegat out ahead. "Do you like it?"

"It's fine," said Noll, finally getting out of his chair. He had slept some in the midmorning and could feel the heat of a sunburn.

"I think it is very good."

Noll nodded. Passable if you liked seascapes. Which he didn't. "Are you ready to go?"

Klaus collected his painting paraphernalia and they trudged up the pier.

Soon the yellow VW that Gerda had bought years ago for Karlstrand visits was chugging up the sand road, away from the collection of weathered boatyard shacks.

In late afternoon Cole drove slowly around what there was of Karlstrand village, gambling that he would not run into either Noll or Klaus Hermann; gambling that Noll would not know him if he saw him—the beard was gone . . . What he needed was the address of the Hermann cottage, and to get that he would have to stop and ask. He went slowly past the police station, which, ironically, was the logical place to ask. In his case it would, of course, be suicide. Two bicycles and a motor-scooter were parked out front. The village crime rate probably didn't call for more than two bikes. The post office was the next choice, and Cole had just about decided to try there when he spotted a little art gallery in a cluster of gift shops. He promptly made a U-turn and parked in front of the gallery.

An attractive, dark-haired, middle-aged woman—where were all the legendary blondes?—said she spoke a little English, and yes, she knew Klaus Hermann. In fact, she had a few of his paintings up on the wall. Just back there. He paints at Karlstrand, you know. "Comes every summer for a few weeks."

Looking at the oils and watercolors, Cole moved slowly to the back of the gallery.

Pointing, the woman said, "There, those are Hermanns," as if they were Van Goghs.

Cole allowed a proper moment of appraisal before saying, "I . . . think they're good."

"Do you?" said the proprietor. "Do you really?"

"They're local scenes?"

"Oh, yes. Each morning that the weather is clear he goes down to the skeppsbron, gets into his little boat and goes out to the very last skerry, staying most of the day."

Cole stood there, nodding, gazing at the half-dozen Hermanns on the wall. He knew almost nothing about art, just as he knew almost nothing about music, but he knew enough to judge these paintings as awful. "Whenever I buy a painting I always like to photograph the artist. If I buy one of these, do you think he might be willing to pose with it?"

"Oh, I'm sure," said the lady, her eyes betraying the fact that in seven years the only Hermanns that had moved were bought by his mother, who had sworn the gallery owner to secrecy.

Cole chose the blue sea crashing over brown rocks, a white-and-black gull winging through.

"Yes, that is the best," the lady quickly agreed, and Cole bought it for a hundred kronor, unframed.

As he was paying for it she said, "He lives at 29 Vastragatan, all the way to the end of this street, then curve down by the water when this one goes off to the north."

Cole thanked her, started to walk out, turned back. "Oh, in case I miss him at his house, when does he go out to paint?"

"Very early. He says he likes the morning light. Six or six-thirty."

"And he goes out to the very last island? What's out there?"

She laughed. "Only birds. Some of the skerries in close are inhabited, but only crabs and birds live on the ones out in the sea."

"And where did you say the boatyard was?"

"Go back the way you came and just before you get to the village you'll see a sign, Skeppsbron, with an arrow."

Cole thanked her again, took the painting, got back into the car and found the sandy road that led to the boatyard. He took a long look at the weathered shacks, the little shipway and the rickety pier with small boats tied along either side.

Then he went back into Göteburg to buy a cheap camera. He planned to have dinner and get some sleep. It was 7:20. He wanted to be up by first pale dawn. Which would be about one-thirty.

"Mrs. Hickel, I can't be of any further help."

Wally, in his Georgetown apartment, used the "Mrs." to distance himself from her, from Cole, from all of it. "Believe me, I've used every resource in Denmark that I have during the last twelve hours. No trace of him."

"Do you think he's still there?" Her voice was a weak monotone.

"I have no idea. I'm sorry."

It seemed the trail of blood behind Cole had lengthened. Asking an agency man in Copenhagen if there had been any mayhem in the city during the past forty-eight hours, Wally was told about the bizarre discovery of Rolf Halvorsen's body outside Bispebjerg hospital. Halvorsen was a minor league operator, he was told. Wally guessed he was in that flimsy network with Schade. So, two dead. Was Cole next?

"Is there *anything* I can do?"

Wally knew he was listening to a woman on the raw edge. And that frightened him. Who knew what she might say to almost anyone . . . "Well," he replied, "you might try to find someone in Copenhagen to call all the hotels. Find out if he's still registered. Maybe an embassy wife would do that for you. Try using his right name."

Katta said in the same tired flat voice, "You know, he hung up on us."

"Mrs. Hickel . . ."

"Katta."

"Katta, I wish to God I could help you. I can't, aside from getting the phone number of the embassy in Copenhagen. I'll find that and call you back. But I'd appreciate you not telling them of my advice. In fact, please don't mention me at all."

He mixed himself a double Manhattan with two cherries, downed it, then went to his at-home book for the Copenhagen number.

33

IT WAS JUNE 21, the day before Midsummer Day, shortest night of the year. Cole had overslept, which he seldom did. He had always had that kind of mental alarm clock where you said to yourself, Wake up at 2:30, and you did it. Even in Vietnam he could do that. He never needed a wake-up call in the hootch. Now his watch said 5:19, and when he pulled the drapes a soft golden light entered the Siljan room. Good painting light for Klaus.

Dressing hurriedly, putting his shirt on wrong-side out, he knew he could never make the shipyard by six. It had taken more than forty minutes yesterday. Not all that easy to drive and look at the road map in new country, to go along without making wrong turns.

He stumbled around trying to find his shoes. Same terrible sleepless problem over here in Sweden. Thinking about everything, he had turned the bed into a torture rack by midnight, finally saying over and over what he had said as a small boy and a couple of times as a bigger one: "Now I lay me down . . ." Sometime in early morning, maybe around three, it had worked.

In the bathroom he looked at his face long enough to see somebody he didn't know very well, thank God. Cheeks gray and hollow; longish hair tangled. White pellets at the eye corners, below them crescents of darkness. No question, the admiral's son was a mess. He threw water on the ravaged face and didn't look at it again. He vaguely remembered a dream...Rolf was loading a shotgun with tiny pieces of scrap iron, saying that was the right load to use on Hermann. Cole was telling Rolf he had never heard of loading a shotgun with scrap iron. Even in Nam they didn't do that. Then Katta was there and damned if Rolf didn't turn the barrels on her. Cole woke up screaming, and whoever was in the next room was pounding on the wall.

He lifted the mattress, pulled out the Podnik, screwed the suppressor in, stuffed the gun into his pocket and ran down the stairs and out to the compact.

The Ford zipped away from the peppermint awnings. Five-thirty-one the watch said.

The Danish operator on the embassy switchboard did not know what to do with the call of this distraught woman from California. She knew, though, that the woman would not have called all that way unless it was important, so the operator did what she usually did with calls that had no category—switched them to an information specialist.

"This is the very height of the tourist season in Denmark and the hotels are loaded with Americans. There could be two thousand here today, three thousand, four. And you don't know where he's staying?"

"No, I don't, *I don't.*" The lady sounded pitiful, anguished. Death in the family?

"All right, I'll make a half-dozen calls for you to likely hotels. I'm really not supposed to do this kind of thing but I will. If I find him I'll tell him it is urgent to call you. If he's not there I'll leave a message. Now, that last name is H-i-c-k-e-l. Not l-e."

"No, not l-e. Oh, thank you, I can't tell you how much..."

Now and then, these odd things happened at the embassy. Usually an elderly tourist dropping dead in Tivoli or on the Kongens Nytorv. Next of kin to be notified.

* * *

There had been little traffic in central Göteburg, almost none in the suburbs. Cole had concentrated as much on Ellen, Teddi and Rolf as he had on his driving, creating images of them—Ellen laughing, Teddi sitting in Ottensen talking about her son, Rolf, with his orange grove and hatred of the S.S. He badly needed them now to go forward, do what had to be done, what no legal process in any country would do.

He arrived at 6:10.

The village was still asleep. Only the dogs were out, sniffing about, baptizing trees and bushes. The few cottages on the south end had shown no signs of life. No smoke from chimneys. He parked parallel and looked down at the boatyard. No one seemed to be around. A yellow bug was parked down there but no other cars. He had not, he thought, seen that VW around the night before.

The air was still cool but the day was already bright, the sky a north country chalky blue. Cole went slowly down the sandy hill, reaching to take the Podnik off safety. He had in mind making himself scarce by one of the weather-silvered sheds, getting among them, waiting there for the Germans to show up. Take Hermann first, if possible. Then Noll. Hope they'd live long enough for him to say a few things. Words needed to be said. He walked closer to the VW, then stopped, seeing a head, hat perched on it, on the driver's side.

Cole moved around to the back of the car, looked in again, then came alongside it. When he bent down, hand on the Podnik, he saw the hard, handsome features of Stefan Noll in gentle slumber. Which meant Klaus had already gone out to the the skerry to paint. Cole pulled back and unwound the camera from his neck, pushing it under the car, then bent forward again.

The security man was even snoring a little, mouth ajar, African game hat brim cocked down over his eyes, shielding them from light. A perky blue-and-red feather extended from the hat brim. A sleeping beauty. On the passenger seat was a gun, barely visible under the morning paper.

Cole straightened up, wondering if the car door was locked on the driver's side. If not he could open it, slap the gun off the seat and jerk Noll out in the same motion. He studied the handle a moment. *Push the button with the left hand, pull the inner lever and jerk with the right hand. Then reach in.*

Looking up the hill, still no one in sight.

Except for those two "Marines" in the Reeperbahn, Cole had not used his fists on anyone since that jerk captain in the O Club at Marble Mountain; hadn't boxed since the club at Annapolis. But it seemed right to use his hands now, to *feel* Noll. To activate that good left hook. He slid the Podnik about a foot under the VW where he could get it if he needed it. Then he counted. *One-two-three . . .*

Pushed the button.

Pulled the lever.

Jerked the door, took both hands to ram the hat down over Noll's eyes, slapped the Luger to the floor, grabbed the German with both hands by the collar and heaved back, hearing Noll's startled curse.

They landed in the sand, Cole on his back, Noll pulling the hat up from his eyes and rolling.

Cole scrambled to his feet and kicked the twisting body in the ribs as Noll finally got the hat loose and jumped up, avoiding another kick aimed at his head.

They stood, panting, eyeing each other. Saying nothing. Cole's reflexes were not sharp anymore, but there were still leftovers from those days in the ring, automatic responses and moves.

Stefan broke to the left, grabbed up a piece of two-by-four from a scrap pile and swung it.

Cole jumped back, ducking, hearing the wood whistle over his head.

Noll swung again, back the other way.

Cole dove for his legs, dropping him, two-by-four falling to the side.

Rolling free, Cole got up on his knees, connecting with a right cross that did not have a lot of steam in it but hit Noll on the side of the neck, momentarily stunning him, dropping him again.

This time on his feet, Cole's kick landed solidly, just behind the right ear. The German was shaking his head like a bull that suddenly realized it was in mortal battle with a matador.

Cole reached down and laid in a left hook, feeling something crack in his hands, pain burning all the way up to his armpit.

Eyes wide now, still on his hands and knees, Stefan tried to struggle up. Cole kicked him again. Blood was coming out of Stefan's mouth and nose. "Pleeze no, no . . ." he said, falling backward.

Cole moved around to another angle, aiming at the temple. The shoe hit solidly, Stefan's head snapped into the sand. Cole went to the other side. "This is for all of them," and kicked one last time at the back of the skull, feeling it collapse, at the same instant feeling another explosion of pain in his foot. He knew he had sprained it and sat down in the sand alongside Noll's inert body.

For a moment he felt nauseous, killing a man in this terribly personal way, but the longer he looked at Noll the better he felt, sitting there, rocking, holding his right foot. Noll's cheeks were encrusted with sand that was slowly staining from the blood around his mouth and coming out of his nostrils. He was not pretty anymore; was not ski-slope healthy anymore. His eyes were open, staring into a clabber sky. Cole was wishing Teddi and Rolf would know what had happened out here, how Noll had paid.

Finally he got up and dragged the German along the pier, right foot sending off signals. Pretty dumb, Wally would say, when you had a gun to use. Yep, you're right, Wally. You're always right . . . Except this was the way he had to do it.

At the deep end, after pressing down on Noll's stomach to push air out . . . actually he had read that in a Travis McGee novel long ago . . . he rolled the body into the water, hoping it would be at least forty-eight fish-nibbled hours before the security man would greet another day. Bubbles came up as the corpse sank.

Cole limped back to the VW, picked up the Podnik, on second thought got the Luger off the floorboard, lifting it up by the barrel. Someone might want to examine it later to connect with Rolf's death. He put the gun back into the glove compartment, then limped over to the boatyard office, Podnik back in his jacket.

After brushing sand off his clothes he sat down to nurse the left hand, which had now begun to swell. The sprained right foot was also asking for sympathy. Just before seven an old man in scruffy work clothes—stained veterans of red lead and oily oakum and white putty—trudged down the sandy lane carrying a small tin pail.

Cole got up and said hello.

"Morn, morn," the old man said, obviously surprised to find a stranger, a foreigner, at the boatyard so early. "No *farja,* no *farja,*" the old man said.

Cole said he did not understand.

"No ferry," the old man said and began pointing. The ferry dock was to the north. This was a skeppsbron, not a ferry dock.

"I don't want a ferry," said Cole. "Charter. Charter a boat. Pay money."

It was the old man's turn not to understand, and he motioned Cole into a shack, offering to share his pail of hot milk.

Cole thanked his host just the same, sitting down to wait for someone who could speak English.

About 7:15 a young man, no more than twenty, he figured, trooped in. He spoke passable English but scratched his head when the visitor said he wanted to go out to the skerries. "Nothing out there except birds and moss and wildflowers."

"I want to photograph the wildflowers," said the tall stranger, dangling the cheap camera from his neck.

Looks were exchanged between the young man and the old man. This American did not seem the type to take pictures of wildflowers. He looked too rugged, and he also seemed to be injured, standing on one foot like a heron.

"Did you hurt yourself?"

"Sprained my ankle a little."

"Sorry," said the young man, dialing the phone. "Do you need a doctor?"

The American said he did not.

The captain shook his head. "Flowers?" Well, it was the American's money, after all, but to go look for flowers . . . They were always difficult to figure out, these Americans, spending their dollars for senseless things.

———

"Would you like some coffee while you wait? It will take ten or fifteen minutes."

The American said he would like that.

Twenty minutes later a boat came into the little bay and tied up at the end of the pier, almost over Stefan Noll's temporary grave. The name roughly painted on the stern was *3 Falke*.

34

COLE STOOD by the small wheelhouse of the *3 Falke* as they put Karlstrand village in their wake. Bearing weight on his left foot, shivering, he didn't know whether it was a delayed reaction to what he had done or just his body telling him it was near the edge. There was a cool wind blowing in off the sea and the chill of it cut at him. He had always thought he was fairly resistant where heat and cold were concerned, yet his teeth were chattering.

He looked seaward, to the west. If Klaus Hermann wasn't out there somewhere, if he couldn't find him, then he'd come back, drive that Ford into town and call it quits. Tell Katta he'd given up. His body was just about out of fuel. Mental tiredness that had begun to settle in even before he left Tustin, the weight of what had happened, were now sapping him. And they'd all have to understand, everyone, good old Mike Goody and Art Hoberman and General Joe Ferguson and Major Farrar of the Red Dragons who'd said, "Cut his balls off, Colonel," and meant it . . . every one of them would have to understand. Would they understand? To hell with them . . . would *he?*

He opened the door to the wheelhouse and limped in to get out of the wind, the gaunt man at the wheel motioning for him to take a seat. There was another high stool and Cole got on it, glad to feel some warmth.

The *3 Falke* looked to be about thirty-five feet long, wide-bellied and heavy-timbered, built for rough work rather than yachting. It pounded slowly out of the bay at about eight o'clock, laying a frothy track behind.

Ahead, the innermost skerries were rocky brown mounds, uneven teats of stone eroded and smoothed by thousands of years of punishing wind off the Kattegat. To Cole they looked like some of the nubs off the New England coast. A few were inhabited. Little gingerbread houses in red and white squatted there in the morning sun. Very cheerful.

Other skerries appeared barren except for small clumps of grass that squirted unexpectedly out of crevices. The gaunt thin-wristed man at the wheel, long face as salt and wind-worn as the skepps-bron shacks, guided the *3 Falke* in total silence, his eyes ranging over the channel side-to-side and forward.

Fifteen minutes out he motioned to Cole to look at a chart of the channel and the waters westward. The lady at the art gallery had said the outermost skerry was where Klaus painted, and there it was, larger than all the others. Cole tapped it and the skipper nodded.

Ellen was now *the* person to think about. He *needed* her, thoughts of her above all else. It was the little Ellen that had always claimed him. What was that song about little girls? Maurice Chevalier sang it . . . think of that prayer rug, the nurse's cap . . . all right, enough, get *on* with it . . .

The inhabited rock islands began to grow scarce as the *3 Falke* went away from land and Cole could now see blue water, whitecaps folding over, on the horizon. Breeze sharpened and the boat began to pitch a little. Cole looked toward the stern. A few fishing boats and work skiffs were following. A trawler passed them to starboard, husky steel ship throwing up a white V.

Some twenty minutes later the skipper pointed. Over the port bow, isolated from the other skerries by a wide distance, was a large rock island, maybe fifty acres, maybe more. Even at this far distance there was a yellowish tinge to the surface. Cole picked up the binoculars. The yellow cast moved with the wind. Wildflowers. The skerry was at least five miles away, a front barricade to the Kattegat.

Looking at the chart, the yellow movement was about four miles inland of the shipping channel carrying traffic to Norway and Russia; south to the Baltic, Denmark and Germany. Cole studied the yellowed rock. No sign of Klaus Hermann.

Beginning to pitch heavily, the boat tasted open water at the end of the bay channel, dropping her bow into waves, climbing again for another drop. Spray shot into the air, falling back over the wheelhouse.

Cole began to feel the ticking deep in his gut; pulse rate increasing, he knew. He reached down to make sure the Podnik was still nestled safely. He wanted to touch it again. He wanted no personal contact with Klaus Hermann, didn't want to touch him. The man was a disease, worse than Noll. He just wanted to wipe the world, his world, clean of him with a clean shot from the Podnik.

Still watching through the binoculars, Cole finally made out a small boat pulled up on a shelf on the lee side of the skerry. He turned to the skipper, pointed.

"There."

The gaunt man nodded, cut the engine and walked out to the bow to judge his distance and check the bottom depth. He observed the wave action against the north side of the rock, then returned to the wheelhouse and spun the helm and yanked down on the gear lever. The *3 Falke,* with a spit of exhaust and reverse thrust, began to drift slowly alongside the shelf, where the battered skiff was already sitting.

Standing by the port rail, Cole saw that the flowers were black-eyed daisies, washed this way and that by the strong wind. No sign of Klaus and his easel. The big rock humped in the center. If he was on it he was to windward, beyond the lump of the skerry, out where it met the sea.

Beginning to shallow sharply now, the water below the hull was clear, looked icy cold. Ropes of seaweed waved on the bottom through stairsteps of filtered sun. Swarming schools of gudgeons climbed the wavering steps. Starfish down there, too. All so icy cold.

With the side of the *3 Falke* only twenty or thirty feet off the shelf, drawing closer, the skipper nudged Cole, pointing to his watch with a question. Cole tapped noontime and the gaunt man nodded.

In a few seconds the boat was within a leap of the shelf, but the skipper held up a hand to wait. Cole's left hand held the camera; right hand on the Podnik. Then the wave washed in, lifting the *3 Falke,* and Cole heard, "Jooomp."

He landed on the rock, yelling silently as the injured foot hit, going to his knees.

"Pick me up in three hours," he managed to get out.

The pilot nodded, the diesel roared and the boat slowly backed off, then circled out to return to Karlstrand Skeppsbron.

Cole stayed down for several moments, eyes shut tight, waiting for the pain to subside. Momentarily he became aware of another sound lapping over the diminishing pound of the engine . . . seaward across the rock's crest there seemed to be millions of birds, a malevolent white cloud of them. Between the caw-caw-caw of the birds and the surf roaring on the windward side, Hermann might well not have heard the *3 Falke* approaching. On the other hand, he might be up on the crest waiting for a head to stick out.

Cole crawled over to the skiff and looked in. Lifejackets, oars, a bailing scoop, a spare can of gas. Just the usual, but on the middle thwart was a ladies' manicure kit. Good God . . . Klaus doing his nails on the way out? A little grapnel anchor wedged in a rock crevice on a short length of rope tethered the boat, and he thought about setting it adrift to make sure Klaus couldn't escape. But if Klaus should even make it back to the boat, it would likely mean that Col. C.L. Hickel, USMC (Ret.), ex-gunshipman, was dead. So it wouldn't matter, would it?

The birds were coming closer, skidding down and circling; div-

278

ing—threatening with strafing runs at Cole's head. Gull-sized with orangish beaks and cold, ferocious eyes, they were, Cole guessed, complaining about intrusion, about eggs to be guarded in this short Scandinavian summer.

Tipping the safety off the Podnik, he tried to ignore the beaks and wings, edging now across the rocky surface, dragging the injured foot, bending low, deciding to move around the south side and to go up to the crest from about midpoint of the island. No matter where Hermann was, Cole would either see him plainly from up there or come on him head-to-head. Not too much difference, either way. If Hermann had a gun and knew how to use it, it wouldn't matter where the hell they met out here on this rock. Chances were he didn't have one, Cole thought. Coming to a skerry with a gun in his paint box? Of course, this was the same kinky clown who had carried a toy gun once upon a time in Orange County...

Daisies were even thicker in beds on the crest above the salt line. Fed by rain water and guano, their yellows were bold enough to have come out of a pot. Their black eyes winked coolly at him as the wind played with them. On gaining the crest he figured he would crawl through them for cover if they were also on the windward side—they stood up almost two feet. Down low on the lee side where he was inching along the going was mushy, and secreted in the cracks of the rock face were clumps of wet moss and long-stemmed grass that had razor edges.

It took him some ten minutes to reach the crest, going slowly, foot and left hand shooting pain, the last thirty yards traveling like a crab, face pushing through the winking daisies. At the crest, raising his head out of the flowers, he could not believe what came into view—right out of Looneytunes.

With the Kattegat in the background, blue and sparkling, there was Klaus Hermann about twenty feet from the edge of the lapping sea in front of his easel, his big rear end in baggy pants settled on a cross-legged canvas stool, a wide-brimmed straw hat on his head, busily painting away like some Gauguin by the seaside. Some eight feet away and facing him was an old woman seated in a small overstuffed blue chair. Her face was to the light, to the golden morning sun, which was over Klaus' shoulder, and even from a distance it was clear she had had her share of plastic surgery, likely, Cole thought, from the late decapitated Dr. Rensch of Lubeck. The glorious sunlight was doing her a very dirty trick, showing just how much yellow she was using to hide her white hair.

Gerda Hermann, herself, in the flesh, in living color, just the way Schade had described her, trying to pose for her son Klaus, trying not to squint while he moved his brush to immortalize *Mutti* on canvas.

Take care of the son of a bitch right in front of his dear mother. Kill the rancid fruit of her womb three yards from her chin. Why not?

Gerda was wearing a long red velvet gown with a little white collar that must have been a problem as she stepped over daisies and wet moss to get down to seaside to pose for Klaus. A pair of muddy boots were three or four feet away, alongside a picnic hamper her glasses rested on. Glasses, after all, would ruin the effect. Her feet were encased in dainty red slippers. Like a grotesque duchess to be hung in the castle.

One weird setting to paint your dear mother in, Klaus . . . Cole dropped his head back into the daisies to think, to decide what to do. There was no reason to shoot Gerda, and he also had that ingrained all-American boy's belief that mothers, even Klaus's, were special. But as for the son . . . he was running into overtime. "Okay," he murmured to himself, eased over onto his back and took a sitting position, elbows on his knees, aiming the Podnik seaward, sighting on Klaus' straw hatbrim at ear level.

He, engrossed in his painting, she in posing, Klaus and Gerda still had not seen him. He decided to make them turn around, see who was up there on the crest, give them a moment to think why he had traveled so far, why he was here . . . remind Klaus of a spring night when he took a student named Ellen Hickel out for a ride in a splendid white Mercedes . . .

Cole moved the Czech gun slightly to the left so as to miss Klaus by only a few feet, called out *"Guten morgen,"* and fired.

The birds with the vicious orange beaks went wild at the sharp explosion, screaming at the noise. Klaus fell off his stool, turning and looking uphill, mouth open, eyes filling with terror as he saw the colonel sitting in the daisies, pointing a gun. Quite a picture in itself, Cole thought—*Man in flowers with gun.* The easel had been toppled over, spilling the half-done portrait of Mother Gerda into green moss.

She sat there motionless, staring in disbelief at the muddy stranger in the Greek fisherman's hat. She looked defiant, even with the gun aimed her way. She got up quickly, moving on those dainty red slippers, taking two or three steps, and it appeared to Cole that she was going to shield Klaus, still down on his hands and knees, cover him with that red-velveted body the way she had, in a way, always done.

Was he going to have to go down and shoot the son of bitch with his mother on top of him . . .?

Cole saw her reach down as if to help Klaus, then quickly turn and come up with what was, unmistakably, a gun. A gun that fired. Cole thought he heard the bullet whiz by, then pitched sideways and rolled, knowing what he had to do as more rounds came his way. Thank God she was a lousy shot or wasn't wearing her glasses. He rolled back the other way, came up on his elbows and got off a shot, hitting her in the temple. Without making a sound, she tumbled across Klaus and onto her back, still clutching the gun.

"Don't touch it," Cole called out to Klaus, but Klaus was already up and scrambling away, splashing in puddles, not once looking back at the red clump that had been his mother. He fell on the wet, slick moss, glancing back at Cole; got up to run again onto the south end of the skerry, where there was no place to go except the sea. His straw hat had been lost.

He fell again, scampered, crawled, got up and ran for the other side, and as he did the wig finally came completely off and, at last, Cole saw the real Klaus Hermann . . . a shock, revulsion, and then a bizarre thought in between that the man who was responsible for his daughter's abasement and violent death looked for all the world like an old picture he'd seen of the strutting Italian dictator Benito Mussolini. Klaus's mouth was moving, mouthing something, but the bird-shrieks were drowning him out.

Watching him, shifting the Podnik's aim to follow him, Cole was abruptly struck by the vulnerability of the man, a stick figure running and stumbling and waving his arms like one of the frenzied, screeching birds flying about, dive-bombing him, making him duck to avoid them, crazed witnesses to this confrontation of noisy invaders.

Recovering in the wake of their attacks, it seemed to Cole that now Klaus was supplicating, on his knees . . . was he praying or begging or both . . . ? Whichever, his determination to finish him off with a clean shot, and enjoy the process with a few choice words delivered before the coup de grace, was no longer so strong. God, was he going to back off, to blow this after all he'd gone through . . . ?

And then the birds were coming again and he had no time to think, only to try to roll away from them, and still keep Klaus in sight.

On his knees, playacting as he had so often done so many times in so many ways . . . with *Mutti* for her sympathy . . . with Stefan to keep him faithful by playing the inept fool . . . with the girls who had to understand he really never meant them harm, only *needed* them to help him . . . most of all with himself, convincing himself that a victim, which he was, had his rights too . . . now on his knees and seeming to beg, he knew it had to be his best performance. The enemy, that absurd American that Stefan had warned him about, had somehow found him. So do what he had done before, divert, confuse and deceive, and meanwhile get over to *Mutti,* pry the Walther from her hand . . . Stefan had taught him to shoot this gun, had insisted he bring it with him. Hold it straight out in front of him with both hands. Take the larger target, the body, and that was where he was now pointing the Walther, at the rolling, flailing body twenty feet away. It was difficult to follow, but he did his best to keep it in the gunsight, and pulled the trigger . . .

282

* * *

Batting at the birds crossing his vision in white blurs, rolling to get away from them, Cole nonetheless caught a glimpse of Klaus Hermann reaching for the gun in his mother's hand, heard the shot moments later, then the sound of a bullet carooming off a rock behind him. He rolled several more feet, realized the birds had apparently stopped their attack, twisted around and got to his knees, leveling his gun at Klaus, who no longer was a pitiful stick figure so vulnerable that his resolve had nearly weakened. The son of a bitch had nearly convinced him, buying time to get a shot off to kill him.

Silently he thanked Klaus for that shot, for bringing him back to his mission. Who would fire first, he wondered? Never mind, they were squared off, each with a gun, and somehow that was fitting.

Except that Klaus Hermann was no honorable character out of the Old West. This was no gentlemen's duel, pistols at twenty paces. Why hadn't Klaus fired? And then he realized the gun was out of bullets, that Gerda had fired all but one. Did he mind the odds shifting to him? This was not time for playing Boy Scout. This was the time for getting done what he had come to do.

"Drop the gun, *tropfen*." The cassette stuff was coming back.

Klaus did, and it clattered to the rocks.

"Back up."

Klaus's feet did not move. They seemed glued to skerry rock.

"Back up, into the water." He could not remember the word for "back," but Klaus understood, and now slowly moved, eyes on Cole. Back, back into the sea, knee-deep, holding up one hand to ward off what he was sure was coming.

Cole stood up, free of pity, and limped down the slope, angling past Gerda's body, going to the water's edge, watching Klaus, the Podnik now down by his side. "Swim," and the German understood that too.

"*Nein, nein.*" Klaus tried once more, only this time there was no playacting.

Cole lifted the Podnik and directed a bullet into the water not a yard from him. "Swim." He said it matter-of-factly, hardly loud

283

enough for Klaus to hear. A second bullet raised a spurt on the other side of the German.

"*Bitte, bitte . . .*" The peach skin, make-up washed off, was showing large patches of white.

Cole fired again.

Klaus looked past Cole to his *"Mutti,"* as if she might arise, kiss and make it all well one more time. Then, turning toward the open sea, he began to stroke slowly out, until some fifty yards from the shore he stopped swimming, appeared to tread water for a moment, and then disappeared.

Cole watched the sparkling surface, then turned away after first heaving the Podnik out as far as he could, followed by the Walther.

For a moment he considered leaving Gerda where she was, in her white-collared red velvet dress, half-finished duchy portrait, then decided it was wiser to have her join Klaus. He managed that, feeling numb as she sank in the drop-off.

Also into the Kattegat went the easel, paint box and lunch hamper, and muddied canvas, all to be distributed by the tides. Only the little blue chair, looking very lonely, was left. It seemed too innocent to disturb.

The birds seemed sated too, raising less of a din as Cole limped back through the crest daisies, beginning to let go at last, and with the letting-go feeling was exhaustion he had never known, not even in Nam, as he went on down to the shelf and sat down on the bow of the skiff to wait for the *3 Falke*.

———————————— EPILOGUE

COLE, FORMERLY "HARVEY," now once more Hickel sat in the living room of his home, thankfully alone, Katta and the children having gone to her mother's in Wisconsin for a few days. Considering the strain that had followed his homecoming, it had seemed a good idea for them all. The initial reunion was a joyous thing, but the long silences, the burden of the unspoken and unexplained that had soon after built a wall between him and them . . . it was better that they all have some time to handle it alone.

Reviewing it now, as he had started to do so many times since he had been home and had cut himself off, not wanting to relive it, not wanting or able to acknowledge it as more than a nightmarish episode, he was amazed that he had even been able to get back. He allowed himself to see once again the *3 Falke* come into sight as he waited for it, to remember getting in, being returned to Karlstrand, saying only that the wildflowers had been interesting, getting into his Ford, driving in a daze to Göteborg and the airport, starting to make the call home, deciding not to, that he couldn't talk to them, not then, parking the car, and as Harvey getting through the SAS international entry gate and onto the plane. Strangely he remembered how his mind had fastened like a terrier on his shoes that still bore the skerry mud stains, overlooked in his hasty attempts to clean up. At the time they had seemed sure to bring officials who would arrest him, accuse him of being at least implicated in the strange disappearance of Klaus Hermann and Gerda Hermann, not to mention the death of Stefan Noll.

But it had not happened. Nor had there been inquiries or any sign of suspicion during the difficult two weeks he had been home. It would come, though, he was certain of it . . . The Göteborg police would have to wonder about the disappearance of the Hermanns, mother and son, and would sooner or later wonder about the mysterious American who had said he took pictures of flowers and had chartered the *3 Falke* . . .

But would they be able to trace him, to connect him with the deaths? Perhaps not, stranger things had happened. And even if they did, how would they prove their suspicions? They had no idea who he really was. They knew nothing of Ellen. He had gone to take pictures of wildflowers. He had come back. The Hermanns had not. Gerda's body had a bullet in it, Klaus's did not. He had never been touched. Who was to say there had not been a fatal falling out between the mother and son—they were known to have been at odds for years, he with a peculiar reputation, she supporting him. They had argued, he had shot her and then committed suicide by drowning . . . What about Stefan Noll? If John D. McDonald's Travis McGee was right about pushing the air out of a body to make it sink, maybe he'd never surface, just be permanently missing. And if he were to be found and identified, would he not likely be considered another victim of his former charge, the erratic, some would say crazy, Klaus Hermann?

Cole shrugged, liking the scenario but not altogether believing in it. Who knew? He would have to try to get on with his life, help Kot and the kids do the same, someday maybe even risk telling her what had happened.

He had done what he had felt he had to do. No medals, this time. No commendation and promotion. The future was the challenge, to face it and take it. Well, challenges were something he had always been pretty good at.

He got up, went to the phone and put through a call to Kot.

"Come home," he told her when she came on the line.

Two words . . . all she needed, or wanted, to hear.

———

286